Dusting Angels

J. D. Smith

DUSTING ANGELS

Cactus Moon Publications: Info@cactusmoonpublishing.com; http://www.cactusmoonpublishing.com

Book cover design: Melissa Carrigee

ISBN 978-0-9988932-8-0

This book is dedicated to my Mother, a woman who loved me as much as humanly possible. May you rest in peace knowing that your son has taken a huge step toward accomplishing his dream.

And to my Father, my hero, who continually shows me what it means to be a man and a father.

I love you both and thank you for never giving up on me.

The Morning Sun

It was early in the morning. The birds were awake and perched on thin branches singing, before soaring free through the light sky. I sat motionless on a hard, wooden chair; my elbows resting on the matching desk. My fingers pressed into my temples, I listened to the hum of the street commotion. It grew louder by the minute. Soon it would be an irritation taunting my frazzled nerves. My eyes filled with contempt as the rays of light crept through the small crevices of a defective blind. The darkness that surrounded me was dissolving and I shuddered at the thought of another day beginning.

The disruptive brightness that was filtering in warmed the room. My body moistened with perspiration. It collected along my hairline, above my brow, and eventually, would drip slowly down my face against the sun's gradual rise. I was a prisoner in this little box, tired, but wide-awake for my torture.

"What the fuck are you doing up there? Stop staring out of that window and come down here and help me," Nikki demanded.

I spun around in my chair, knowing what I was going to find. Nikki, on her hands and knees, frantically spreading apart the fibers of the carpet searching for drugs. She stopped and stared up at me as I turned. There was a crazed determination in her wide-eyed glance. I shook my head and frowned at her foolishness. This angered her; she scowled and then resumed her examination of the floor.

"Please help me Jay. I know there is some down here somewhere," she begged, as her shaky hand held up a small piece of rock for me to examine.

"Is this?" she asked desperately.

"Baby it's a rock; a gray rock."

"Is it a good gray rock?"

"It's a bad rock; a street pebble, baby. Please don't try to snort it. It'll just make you bleed, I promise."

My face tightened, as I struggled to conceal my repulsion. I closed my eyes. I took several deep breaths, swallowed my disgust and got off of the chair. I kneeled down next to her and lifted her chin. I refocused her attention on my face and forced a smile. I hoped this would relax her. It didn't; she immediately shook free of my grasp and resumed crawling the floor like a desperate animal seeking dinner scraps.

"Would you please stop and get off the floor baby?" I asked, as I reached out my hand and gently grabbed her arm.

"What are we going to do?" She asked, glaring at me.

"There's still some time left, why are you panicking?"

"I don't want to come down Jay; but if I have to, I need a pill or something, I can't just crash. We don't even have anything, we need something." She whined.

"Baby please, stop. Just try to relax. We will figure it out."

"I can't relax, I can't." She told me as she again shook free from my restraint.

I remained on the floor watching her. Nikki crawled in small circles desperately collecting pieces of rock and dirt. She would accumulate and then evaluate each piece. Regardless of color, shape, or texture, she held onto each finding with a tightly closed fist. I would interject, but if I weren't convincing, the jagged particulars (which didn't resemble the desired drug) would eventually become trapped in her nasal passage.

"Baby please, you need to stop. You are going to hurt yourself if you don't." I begged, as I again moved towards her. "You need to trust me. We are both thinking the same thing. I'm just choosing to do it quietly."

"If we are both thinking the same thing, then why aren't you helping me? Why the fuck were you just sitting there, staring out of the window?" She asked, glaring at me with suspicion.

"I'm trying to enjoy the end of my high."

"Since when do you enjoy the end of the high? Why are you calm? Are you holding something back?" Nikki asked, and stood up beginning to hysterically examine the desk area.

"Are you serious?"

She ignored me ripping the drawers out and dumping their contents. The pens, pencils, and markers bounced and rolled onto the floor; papers scattered while the stapler, scissors and a compass clanked against the wooden desktop. When she was done rummaging through the mess, she tipped the desk backwards, banging it loudly against the wall. She checked underneath and between the crevices. Once she was satisfied she turned her attention back to me.

"Take your shoes off." She ordered. "What? No."

"Take your shoes off now. I know that's where you like to hide your shit."

"Really?" I asked as I stared at her. She continued to stare back, but she didn't respond. "You've lost it." I told her as I took off each shoe and handed it to her.

The willingness to grant the inspection of my shoes convinced her I wasn't holding out. She stared at them for a moment, shook her head in disappointment and then tossed them to the side. She then refocused on me. The sorrowful look in her eyes expressed her shame. I bit my tongue and decided not to scold her or take offense to her allegations. I understood her desperation and couldn't fault her for it.

"Baby please, you need to relax."

Nikki's voice rose to a fever pitch. "I can't relax. I wish you would stop telling me to relax and start telling me what we are going to do to fix this. You tell me that and I'll fucking relax."

"Can you two please shut up? Your relentless jabbering isn't helping matters," Lenny interrupted.

Lenny had crawled into bed and pulled the covers over his head three hours ago and we hadn't heard from him since. He had emerged from his cocoon only a few times to change the music and get some water. A short smile and a small nod had been his form of communication, and this only happened when he had felt our curious eyes on him. Nikki's obnoxious rant had just disturbed his peaceful state of nonexistence.

"You're driving me crazy with all your yapping," Lenny continued, as he moved toward the end of the bed. He slowly repositioned himself Indian- style at the edge. "Counterproductive whining that's all you're accomplishing."

Nikki snapped her head in his direction and immediately responded.

"Nobody asked you Lenny, go back to sleep,"

"I wasn't asleep."

"Go back to being quiet then."

"What the hell happened over there?" Lenny asked pointing at the desk.

"We had a little situation, but it's over now." I answered.

Lenny continued to stare at his desk shaking his head. He then turned his attention to me. He looked me over trying to gauge my mood. "I don't feel very well," he finally announced while rubbing his arms. "My skin is crawling and it's hot in here. We need to seriously start considering our options. Naively pretending that there is an abundance of time remaining on this high would be a grave mistake in my opinion."

"Talk about yapping and jabbering, could you use more words to basically say nothing Lenny?" Nikki quickly added.

"It's an opinion."

"Is that your opinion?" I sarcastically asked. "I think we are all aware of the situation. We don't need you exercising the entire extent of your vocabulary to remind us."

"That was hardly the entire extent." He retorted.

"Lenny, please, it's annoying and you know it."

"I'm just saying. You don't need to get angry with me."

"I'm not angry…frustrated."

Nikki had grown bored with the conversation and had decided to skirt her way over to me. She wrapped her arms around one of my legs and was staring up at me like an eager child. It wasn't her intention to aggravate, but that's what she had accomplished. Her desperation amplified my sense of urgency. I had the impulse to kick her to the side, like she was a small dog trying to take advantage of me.

"I don't want to crash, I really don't. I want to go back up. Can we find a way back up? I want to feel good; don't you want to feel good again?" She pleaded.

I stared down at her, wishing that there was a viable solution to our problem, but there wasn't one. Drug dealers don't wake up before noon. Everyone else that we knew that might be holding was either sleeping, or indulging. If they were indulging they weren't going to be sharing what they were holding, not while everyone else was busy dreaming. We were fucked and I knew it. They realized it as well, but their relentless stares told me that they were willing to disregard the reality of our situation and hold me accountable.

"I'm still a little high," Nikki admitted, as she stared upward. "You know what I think we should do?"

"No, baby I don't, and I can already tell I don't want to."

"I think the three of us should get naked. Lenny was right, it's hot in here and you are frustrated. Maybe, if we all got naked and had some fun that might be good for us. We could steal some vodka from Lenny's mom and see what happens." She suggested as she began to caress my leg.

I continued to stare down at her. I assumed that she was kidding, maybe even trying to torture me. The thought of disrobing, and pressing my hot sweaty body against hers, or Lenny's for that matter, forced an involuntary shutter that shook my entire body and I closed my eyes for a moment.

"What do you think?" she asked eagerly.

"I think…why don't you get started and I'll join you in a minute."

"Really?"

"No, not really."

"Why?"

"It's a terrible idea."

"But it's not."

Nikki's desperate plea and the steadily increasing temperature of the room had put me into a full sweat. A repugnant chemical-laced stench was being omitted from my body, which my clothing was failing to adequately conceal. The thought of two damp bodies thrusting against each other was nauseating. She couldn't be serious about this proposition. Nikki and I barely had sex, only on the rare occasion when all the drugs were gone and we found ourselves drunk and bored. Granted, all the drugs were gone now, but there was no way that sex would enhance our experience.

"I think this is a passive threat to be honest. A 'find-me-drugs or fuck- me' situation."

"Find me drugs and fuck me. How about that? How is having sex with your girlfriend a fucking threat?" Nikki asked, giving me that fake pouty look.

"I know what you are doing." I responded, while shaking my head at her.

"I thought it sounded fun."

"No you didn't, you didn't, and I know you didn't."

"What if I did? You are hurting my feelings."

"I'm not. And now I'm sure of it."

"'Cause I don't have feelings?"

"And why are you throwing Lenny into the mix? It's already a terrible idea, but that makes it so much worse."

Nikki sighed, while recalculating her request. "Nobody said you have to have sex with Lenny."

"Oh, well in that case, maybe I could just watch you kiss him while I'm still high. You know how I love it when you do that. What do you think?"

"Can you stop please? I will figure something out."

"Jay, for me? We can all kiss, like we do when we feel good. Just try it."

Her relentless pout made me squirm in my chair and I diverted my attention. Lenny had retreated from the conversation and was now sprawled out on his back. He had removed the mirror from the nightstand, and was holding it an inch above his face. His long tongue was extended, and he was licking the smooth glass, cleaning it of residue. I had been trying to ignore this display, but with each lap of his tongue my revulsion was mounting. The sound of saliva spread across the mirror and then being sucked up was echoing and I was about to snap.

"Look at Lenny, look at him and tell me you really think us getting naked would be a good idea." I instructed as I pointed.

Nikki took a look over. She tried to suppress her disgust, but her tight face and wrinkled nose told me all I needed. She turned her attention back to me and covered her ears like a small child. I smiled. I hoped that this would end the conversation.

"Lenny, please, enough with that, seriously. It's disgusting and futile. If there was anything worthwhile on that mirror, I promise, Nikki would have licked it off an hour ago."

"I did." Nikki informed us, while smiling up at me.

"See, Lenny, put the mirror down, please."

It was a rare occasion when a person would consider Lenny disgusting. Usually, he was a beautiful sight. His piercing blue eyes, a shade of blue that could only be discovered in places where man didn't exist; places like the sky or the ocean, places of beauty. Olive skin, dark brown curly hair, and magnificent eyes contradicted each other in such a way that they created perfect harmony. The features of his face were sharp and distinct, like those of a Greek God. His strong chin and jawline, the shape of his perfectly oval eyes and his straight narrow nose would have created the most breathtaking statue. He looked like an angel and when we were high, I would tell him so.

However, I wasn't high enough right now. I was sick. We had reached the desperation point of the journey, the place where speed turns the most beautiful and free creatures into caged animals. Lenny's long tongue lathering the bare mirror was repugnant and it reminded me of the reality which was closing in on us. Soon I would be reduced to the likes of a feral animal, desperately seeking. I would be on my hands and knees just like Nikki. I would turn that imaginary piece of rock into a solution.

"Please, Jay, just one kiss, it's so beautiful when you kiss, I love watching you kiss," Nikki cooed.

"I'm definitely coming down." Lenny whimpered from his back. "Which, consequently means that I find the thought of Jay sticking his tongue in my mouth utterly and positively repulsive; sorry Nikki, I'm not a circus animal and I don't feel like performing for your amusement."

Lenny then tossed the mirror to his side and slowly rose, retaking his previous position at the end of the bed. A strand of his curly brown hair dropped down the middle of his face. It hung there barely touching the tip of his nose. He stared at me, eyes cold and glassy. His lips trembled as he silently begged me: do something, anything.

"All this talking is becoming detrimental; I'm definitely coming down," he repeated, but this time he was staring at his lap and shaking his head.

"Maybe if Jay kissed you, you'd feel better; let him kiss you."

"Nikki, please, enough," I begged. "Enough with the kissing talk, nobody is kissing."

"But."

"No, seriously no, stop."

She was a tenacious little bitch when she wanted something She once confessed that her highest climax was during a night of cocaine-induced passion, where she had snuck away and pleased herself while observing us. We were not only slightly embarrassed to find out that we had been participating in a threesome without our third, but we also took offense to her statement, considering that we had both engaged sexually with her in the conventional way.

"What's our plan here Jay? Do you have any thoughts I can search for optimism in? We aren't surrendering to the crash and burn are we?" Lenny asked.

I thought hard. The options were limited at best. Manhattan was always an easy place to score, but we would crash long before reaching Grand Central. I could waste time on the phone, but I feared that this would only foolishly raise our hopes. A drive to South Norwalk, the neighboring ghetto, would assuredly produce the same result. It would be at least three hours before the streets produced a product that would be of any benefit.

"What about Marshall? Didn't he score in the city last weekend? Maybe he's still holding," I blurted out. This announcement caught their attention. They immediately straightened and stared. A slight flash of optimism flickered. It was only an inkling of hope, but it permeated throughout room.

"You're right; we haven't seen that snake-fuck in days," Nikki said, fueling the escalating enthusiasm. "He must be holding something, right? We would have seen him by now." She waited a moment for a response, which I wouldn't offer for fear of increasing the already disproportionate sense of hope.

"Right?" She asked again.

This time she wouldn't wait for a response. Instead, she sprung to her feet, and in one swift, precise motion, she managed to straddle me, pick up the phone and begin punching numbers. This fluid movement was a rarity for Nikki. The girl was seldom graceful. In fact, she was only graceful when it came to scoring speed, or any other drug for that matter. Then, and only then, was Nikki capable of a miraculous transformation. From boxer to ballerina, she could tiptoe then slip and slide with precision and refinement. However, on your average day, she trounced and clunked. There was no way around it. Her only pair of shoes weren't shoes at all; they were big, bulky, oversized, black combat boots. That's all she would wear, and she hadn't learned to be graceful in them either.

Nikki's boots weren't her only oversized and unattractive article of clothing. She wore large ratty sweaters and baggy cargo pants. Her tattered, unflattering dress concealed her beautiful slender body. It was a suit of armor and that protected her from a world of savages who lusted to be inside her. She wouldn't admit this, and if you asked her why she dressed the way she did, she would simply say: "My body is a present; you don't know how beautiful it is until you unwrap it." She was right; it was beautiful, and so was she.

Nikki resembled a porcelain doll draped in a homeless person's clothing. She had flawless, silky, pale skin, accentuated by her straight, light brown hair, which she neatly tucked behind her ears. Her long, dark lashes turned her soft olive-green eyes vibrant. Her lips appeared luscious and pouty, but when placed upon you, there was a tenderness that could make you forget everything. Her devilish smile brightened her entire face. It was alluring, and I would make a number of suspect decisions just trying to keep those cheeks pushed high.

"He's not fucking home. Weasel, pick up the fucking phone, damn it!" she screamed, as she slammed down the receiver.

"He's not fucking home," she said, staring at me, as if I could change the result of her inquiry. "Well then," Lenny interrupted, but then paused.

I watched as he reached up and grabbed a little strand of hair from the top of his head. He began twisting it. This is how Lenny debated with God. We always knew that Lenny was pondering an immoral solution to our problems when he twisted that hair. I swore it was the same piece every time. He was twisting slowly on this occasion, which was always a good sign, the slower the better. If you watched closely, you could see him arguing with his Catholic conscience. He never listened, even though he truly believed that with every sinful action we took, he was moving us further and further away from Jesus. It was a dilemma that Nikki and I couldn't comprehend. To us, Jesus was, well, Jesus really didn't exist, and God was only called upon when our heads were in the toilet; or when we were squinting down the highway, paranoid that there was a cop following close behind itching to flip his lights. No, God rarely existed in our world, but for Lenny the story was a little different.

Lenny was once a good Catholic altar boy. Years were spent dressed in his Sunday's best accompanying his mother to church. He didn't even argue about it, he actually enjoyed it. Then one night his father left. He left without a good-bye. There was no cliché statement like, I'll see you next weekend champ, and we will get some ice cream and watch a game. He had gone out and was never heard from again. At least that's how Lenny told it. Nikki and I weren't certain. We assumed that Lenny's father had been murdered and probably by someone he owed a lot of money to. He liked to drink and he liked to gamble. He made money, but not enough to support a family and both habits. Lenny wouldn't entertain the thought. Deep down he still had hope that someday he would see his father again.

As each fatherless year passed, Lenny would step further and further away from God and the church. Eventually, we would find each other, and I would show him a different world, a world without judgment. There was no Supreme Being sitting on a cloud watching us. Lenny enjoyed the freedom, but there were times when it was obvious that our decisions didn't sit right deep within him. He was in the middle of one of those decisions right now.

"Well what, Lenny, what?" Nikki asked.

"Just because Marshall isn't home doesn't necessarily mean that his speed isn't," Lenny announced. He was purposely avoiding being specific, in fear that God would clearly hear his intentions.

I watched as Nikki's eyes widened. She smiled brightly, "I like the sound of this."

"Break in?" I asked, but Lenny didn't answer he just shrugged his shoulders. "In the middle of the day? Actually the middle of the morning?"

"I suppose waiting for all the suits to leave and head to their cages might make sense."

"We don't have time. The time is now, before it's too late and we are too low." Nikki interjected as she hopped over to Lenny's dresser.

Nikki was a junky for anything, and that included excitement. She was going to try to rush this decision. She didn't want to allow us the time to ponder the pros and cons. This endeavor had no downside in her eyes. Breaking into a house and stealing speed, this was her favorite way to obtain her drugs. Before we could blink, she already had the equipment out: the gloves, wool hats, sunglasses and the crowbar were on the bed. This wasn't a hi-tech operation. We weren't scaling walls or breaking security codes; it was almost always smash and grab.

"Let's do this. Are we doing this?" Nikki asked, as she snapped her head back and forth at us, dropping her devilish smile in the process.

"I like the idea, but we are talking about Marshall here. Do you really want to fuck him like that?"

I knew what her response would be, and I was only posing the question to myself. Timothy Marshall and I were technically friends. I knew him as Tim or Timmy and during a different period of life he had been my closest friend. We had spent our childhood running wild, playing capture the flag and kick the can. We had endured the tortures of puberty together. We had basked in our successful interactions with the opposite sex. We had slammed phones, punched walls and offered inadequate forms of distraction after failing miserably in our female endeavors. We had been inseparable until eighth grade. That is when our roads parted.

I dropped acid, so chasing imaginary butterflies and rainbows became a full-time hobby. I happily quit football, baseball, and basketball soon after. I entrenched myself within a tightly knit group of social misfits. We dressed in black and mourned the tragic living deaths we were leading in the sprawling suburbs of Connecticut. Timmy and I were suddenly on two different sides of what used to be a double-headed quarter. With my bleached blonde hair, unshaven face and facial piercings, I was forced to relinquish my jock status. I slid down the ladder into the abyss of social outcasts, mocked and eventually forgotten by most. Timmy on the other hand, continued to swim and thrive in the testosterone-polluted waters of jock-hood. He started going by his last name, Marshall, and publicly shed any childhood acquaintances that knew him well enough to refer to him as Tim.

"Jay, you know that little weasel would fuck us if he could. If it came down to him crashing or staying high, he would totally fuck us. I have no problem with this, none whatsoever," Nikki answered, as I predicted she would, and she was probably right.

"What do you think, Lenny? You loving this idea?" I asked.

"Look at him, he is sick. Of course he doesn't love this idea. No one is loving it, but it's the only idea we have," Nikki lied. She absolutely loved the idea. "Besides, he brought it up in the first place, he wouldn't have mentioned it if he didn't somewhat think it would work."

Lenny looked up at me. He was clutching his stomach with desperation. He was sick, and getting sicker by the moment. Speed takes away your desire for food. Eventually your body has no choice; it begins searching for nourishment within its own muscles. You begin to eat yourself from the inside out. It's a painful process. It feels as if there's a very small creature inside you, and it is frantically trying to claw its way out.

Nikki witnessed the tortured glance Lenny delivered. She sat down next to him and began slowly rubbing his back. She stared into his eyes with concern. This was Nikki at her best. She was a tough little girl from an abusive home. She had built walls around herself from most people, but at moments like these, I was able to see inside her. It made me realize that even though she hated herself, there was a caring side to her; a human side that she bestowed on a select few.

"Mommy is going to make it all better," she said in a quiet and reassuring voice.

At times she liked to refer to herself as "Mommy". It was ironic because she hated kids. She had no desire to ever have any, but she did like to think on occasion she was able to take care of us. Lenny and I found it humorous. We would joke about her being our mother and how it was the only plausible excuse we had for our abundant maladjustments. We would elaborate on the scenario and paint a picture of Nikki dropping acid and sniffing cocaine while we were in the womb. The best times of our lives were spent in her belly. The liquor was flowing and there was an abundance of drugs. The best part was that we never had to get dressed to go buy our dope. How we yearned for the days when we had a cocaine-filled umbilical cord feeding us our medicine.

"The baby is sick. We need to get him help, Daddy."

Lenny was always the baby. She liked to call herself "Mommy" and me "Daddy". I think this was her idealistic way of viewing this bizarre arrangement. I guess when you broke it down and assigned percentage of ownership, I was ninety percent Nikki's, and she was ninety percent mine. The three of us may have shared each other from time to time, but at the end of the day, if I wasn't staying, neither was Nikki. In some twisted reality, I could see how Nikki could believe that we were the parents, and Lenny the baby.

The truth of the matter was, that on any given day, or on any given drug, each of us was susceptible to being reduced to the likes of an ill- equipped toddler, unable to deal with his or her surroundings. But it was unusual for me to find myself in this predicament. I was fairly aware of what my body and mind could handle. I liked to rise as high as the stars, and beyond if I could, but I always made sure to leave a trail behind me so I wouldn't get lost. Nikki, on the other hand, was the worst. Her favorite saying was, "If I'm still alive, then I can do more." She truly believed that experiencing death and living to tell about it was the highest high achievable.

"Daddy, the baby is sick," she said again, still rubbing his back.

She was now staring at me as if I was refusing to accept the grim reality. I could see Lenny's pain, and I knew what had to be done. Fuck Marshall and the years of adolescent triumphs and tragedies. The reality was that if one of Marshall's jock buddies needed him to fuck me over, he would do it without thinking twice. Lenny needed me right now, and my baby would need me soon enough.

"Seriously, Jay, we need to do something, or I am going to have to ask the two of you to leave and let me die in peace," Lenny whimpered.

Nikki shot to her feet. The second vote was in and it was clearly in her favor. It was on. She grabbed all the supplies and headed to the door. She spun around one last time and said, "To the Bat Mobile." She always said "to the Bat Mobile" before a caper. She claimed it helped her get into character to think of herself as Cat Woman, me as Batman, and Lenny as Robin. It was an ironic twist to a childhood favorite, considering we were creating crime instead of fighting it.

"Nik, wait up a second."

"Fuck, what now?" She barked, angered by my lack of motivation.

"Just hold up. I like the plan, but it's too early. We need to give it a minute, let everyone get out of the house."

"Jay man, how long is this minute? 'Cause I'm definitely feeling some time constraints; anything longer than a short minute, is more time than I have," Lenny told me.

I understood what he was asking, but I didn't answer. Instead I spun around in my chair and opened the desk drawer. I had been hiding a quarter piece of speed from them. I had taped it flush to the ceiling of the first compartment. I knew that if Nikki knew about it she would have forced its consumption before it was absolutely necessary. The other part of the scenario was, I hadn't actually decided whether I was going to share the piece with them at all. Nikki had guessed right, she knew me well and I had been calm for this reason alone. It was a sufficient amount of drug for one person, but split three ways it would barely buy us enough time to get into Marshall's house and do what we needed to do.

"You're fucking kidding me? I fucking knew it, you ass-hole." Nikki screamed.

"How long were you going to wait before you remembered that that little baggy was conveniently hidden in the desk?" Lenny asked. He was understandably annoyed, but I knew his only option was to get over it.

"That's bullshit, Jay." Nikki continued.

"Relax both of you. I was keeping it in case we couldn't come up with a plan, and we needed to soften the crash. I didn't want to do it too early," I told them, as I tossed the piece to Nikki.

"It feels dishonest." Lenny told me.

"It was dishonest, but we both know, Nikki would have forced us to take this way before it was necessary. I did us a favor."

"Fuck Jay, you know I hate that fucking theory. It's such a fucking waste." Nikki told me, as she quickly moved over to the nightstand, and emptied the package onto the glass mirror.

Nikki was usually in charge of the division of our drugs. This was only because she loved the ritual of chopping and cutting, not because she was the most accurate, and definitely not because she was the most trustworthy. She was, however, the most efficient. Some of the pharmaceuticals we snorted were large and difficult to break down. Nikki would pulverize these pills until they were mere dust, and she would do so without losing a single grain. Lenny and I didn't have the patience for this. If it were left up to us, we would just break them up and swallow them. It was a less effective method, but it still got the job done.

"It's not only the theory that bothers me, it's the situation. It just feels a bit sneaky, like, if we hadn't put a plan in place, would I know about this package?" she continued, piggybacking Lenny's sentiment.

"Don't ask me questions that you've already silently answered. You know I hate that," I told her, delivering a cold glare in the process. "Whether you choose to believe me or not, I know it was the right decision to keep that stash from you. Your junky ass would have had us snorting it three hours ago, and then where would we be?"

"I still don't like it," she told me, as she slowly made her way over to the desk, glass mirror in hand.

"You may not like it, but you know I'm right."

I didn't wait for a response. I quickly placed the mirror on the desk and snorted what I considered to be the largest line. Nikki continued to stare at me, but eventually she decided that prolonging this argument would be a waste of time. She snorted her line and then resumed her position on the floor. Lenny also said nothing as he made his way over to the desk. I was sure that he had come to the same conclusion as Nikki. He eagerly ingested his line. Then he grabbed the mirror off the desk and ran his tongue over it tauntingly, while looking directly at me.

Three Black Kids

Fairfield County Connecticut was a place like no other. People usually meant the statement as a compliment. I didn't. I hadn't seen much of the world. My family wasn't wealthy so our vacations rarely extended past the Jersey shoreline or above the mountains of Vermont. We were close to Manhattan, which many considered the center of the universe. People from all over flocked to the city, to gaze up in wonder of the tall, magnificent buildings. Broadway was full of talented dancers and singers, who amazed their audiences each night. History's greatest artworks were displayed at the museums, the world's best chefs prepared vibrant dishes nightly, and there was an abundance of less sophisticated attractions for simple amusement. I wasn't interested in any of this.

The corner of 2nd Avenue and Saint Mark's Place offered me more relative insight. The avenue was inhabited by conniving street hustlers with long tables of falsely-labeled merchandise; desperate junkies haggled with dealers over the price of a bag; and thieves slipped their hands in and out of pockets with such finesse, it was like watching a magician with a disappearing rabbit. There were gutter bums, with pints of rum hidden in boxes, searching for oblivion, and under-dressed whores in ill-fitting tight clothing. They littered the street and were anything but shy. They screamed and hollered, scratched and clawed over perspective clients like starving rats fighting over an insignificant crumb. They didn't teach me much but they were fun to watch, especially when they were angry and yelling at some poor john who had received services he couldn't pay for.

These elements didn't exist in our small corner of Fairfield County, Connecticut. There was no ethnic diversity. There was no culture to be witnessed, no talent to be watched. Old men with gray hair, dressed in dark suits had pounded their closed fists on a large oak table years ago; while pigheadedly arguing for a singular purposed, close-minded, agreed-upon-ideology for the town. This included a distinct set of religious beliefs and intolerance for any objective points of view. The generation that followed had fallen in line like cattle following the one ahead to the slaughter. They asked no questions and accepted the notions that the absence of contrary thought kept the town unified. The lack of racial diversity kept the neighborhoods safe and clean. Spanish people and African Americans were a problem the big cities could deal with.

"Let them blacks and Puerto Ricans kill each other if they want, as long as they do it away from us." That's what my father would say.

There were only two types of neighborhoods African Americans lived in, *according to my father*, the ghetto and the projects. It didn't matter to him if it was a community of honest, hard-working, decent middle-class people; if they were black then it was the ghetto and if you added a few tall buildings, it became the projects. It was an ignorant view, but my father was very clear about one thing, "White people don't go there, and not for nothing."

So naturally I had never visited such places.until a few years ago. I was shaky. My stomach had folded and twisted into a tight knot. I had knocked on doors and rang bells only to receive a shrug of the shoulders or shake of the head. My skin was crawling and I was desperate. My wallet was thin and my options were restricted to a stone's throw.

I crept slowly south, down the interstate, staring at each exit as they passed, second-guessing my decision. My final destination was an area of the neighboring city, which my father declared unfit for white people to enter. I remembered him sitting in his chair, beer in one hand and the local newspaper in the other. He was engaged in his nightly quest for oblivion, which included laughing and mocking the misfortunates reported about in the paper. Overwhelmed with excitement, he would yell to my mother who was busy in kitchen, "Lil, Lil, did you see this bullshit? A house got robbed on Keillor's Ridge. Goddamn Niggers are coming up from South Norwalk and robbing us. If this bullshit keeps up, we're going to have to keep the kids inside."

I was driving through South Norwalk that night, searching for someone on a corner with a heavy pocket. Wild dogs, paper-thin, scampered across the street in front of me with little regard. Homeless men picked through cans of waste searching for value. The decaying, boarded up buildings appeared as if a heavy sneeze would cause them to crumble. They offered little evidence that life existed between the walls; occasionally, frightened eyes would peer out from behind rotten wood to investigate my arrival. Frustrated and sick, I wiped the sweat from my forehead, tightened my grasp on the wheel, and cut it hard to the left. I headed further south down Martin Luther King Blvd. My hands were shaking and my heart was pounding as I entered the area known as Father Panic Village. My father called this area, 'The heart of the jungle'.

As I approached, I imagined white, suburban junkies scattered about the streets and sidewalks, lying face down on the ground, dead or beaten, unable to finish the task I had just assumed. Large black men, unfazed by the death around them, licking their lips in anticipation of my arrival. Another lamb to the slaughter, "I hope his wallet is worth my bullet," they would mumble to themselves. Blacks would be beating Puerto Ricans and Puerto Ricans would be stabbing blacks. Young women in ripped clothing would be stumbling aimlessly, crying and hollering, searching for their innocence. There would be violence and blood on every corner.

But none of these preconceived notions were accurate. The area resembled your local swap meet, with an abundance of homeless people wandering purposelessly around. Young men stood on various corners selling everything from women to car stereos. Junkies in dirty tattered clothing did line the street, but none of them white and none of them beaten or dead. There was an excess of under-dressed children playing unsupervised and unaware of the vagrants roaming among them. I found this disturbing, but it was none of my concern.

I was there to buy what I needed and get out alive. This proved to be a lot easier than I thought it would be. I stopped my car at the first corner and rolled down my window. I was recognized as a customer and was approached by a young man. He asked what I needed, I responded, he turned and made a hand gesture. Another man walked over, took my money, handed me the product and walked away. As I left Father Panic Village, I felt like I was pulling out of a parking lot after ordering a cheeseburger and fries at the local drive-thru.

I stopped at the first gas station I could find, hit the bathroom and snorted. My eyes barely widened, the hairs on the back of my neck stood up for a second then fell back asleep almost immediately. The taste of the drug was peculiar; it had been cut more times than a Jewish infant at a Bris. Still, the ease and convenience of the situation helped to make up for what the drug lacked in potency. My stomach had unknotted, my skin wasn't crawling and I realized that father had been wrong. White people *could* go to the ghetto, as long as they were consumers. Acts of violence would be economically irresponsible.

My ride home was a victory parade. I was a warrior. I had driven straight into the 'jungle' and come out triumphant. I was now confident that I would return and conquer again. My father's angry rants were unfounded, but I knew he wasn't the only one reading the paper at night and pointing his finger. "The Goddamn Niggers are coming up from South Norwalk and robbing us." There had been no evidence to support his claim. It was just the easiest explanation to accept, but more importantly, it meant that white suburban junkies had a license to steal with impunity and the blame would be placed on the blacks in the ghetto.

I thought about that trip every time I sat in the front seat of Lenny's red Cutlass with my sunglasses on, black wool hat pulled tight, and crowbar in hand. My eyes scanned the landscape as we canvassed the Marshall residence. Three white suburban junkies, high on speed, willing to break glass, smash doors, and destroy this home to find what we needed. And if the Marshalls reported the crime, the newspaper would undoubtedly list us as black males, early twenties, average height and weight. Everyone that read the report would shrug their shoulders, nod and accept it.

"Why the fuck is there a car in the driveway?" Nikki asked from the backseat as she ripped her gloves off and threw them at the window.

Lenny had become that beautiful Greek statue, still and staring at the shiny automobile in the driveway. It might as well have been a vicious guard dog growling and foaming at the mouth. It was mid-afternoon and no one was supposed to be home. Nikki had called Marshall several times but gotten no response. Marshall's parents should have been strapped to a desk in a Park Avenue high rise stealing their next million from a group of ignorant investors.

"Why is it there?" Nikki asked again.

The crack in her whiny voice explained her disappointment. She was slumped in her seat and pouting. Lenny's vacant stare expressed his skepticism. I kept hoping that he would reach for the top of his head and start twisting that strand of hair slowly.

"I don't understand; it's the middle of the day." Lenny added as he turned and looked at me. He then removed his hat and shook out his hair. Again I waited for him to grab and twist, but he didn't." Jay, I'm not confident. An occupied house is a gamble. It might be best if we retreat . . . go home."

"It's one person, not the entire family and I know that house." I told them, as I removed my sunglasses so I could get a good look into their eyes. "We can still make this work. Seriously, I can make this work."

Mrs. Marshall complicated what was supposed to be a simple smash and grab. I was never fond of entering an occupied home, but the Marshall house was ideal for this sort of job. The front doors would certainly be unlocked. They opened up into an entranceway. On the left there was a set of stairs that I would be heading up. Mrs. Marshall would most likely be to the right in the living room or the kitchen. If we could confirm this, I was confident that I could slip in, up, and then back out without being detected.

"What are you thinking? You still want to go in there? I can't go in there, not like this. I'd like to pretend I could, but I can't do it, not with her in there, I'd freak out, I know I would." Nikki babbled.

She was a wreck. She was sweating profusely in the air-conditioned car. She was fidgety, nervous and unable to maintain eye contact for more than a brief moment. Normally, this was an adrenaline rush she would crave, her apprehension worried me almost as much as her appearance. She couldn't be relied on.

"I agree with Nikki. I don't think I can go in there."

Lenny was also in terrible shape, maybe even worse than Nikki. His forehead was pressing hard into the steering wheel

His eyes were closed tight, and he was clutching his stomach with both hands. His posture did little to inspire confidence, so I was somewhat glad he wasn't enthusiastic about the scheme.

"Three people would take too long and make too much noise. I know this house. This one is on me," I told them.

"Are you sure?" Lenny questioned without moving.

"It's a one-person job. That's the only way it will work."

The plan was simple. Lenny would park the car down the road, while Nikki camouflaged herself in the woods to the left of the house. There was a large bay window in the kitchen. Through this window you could see the majority of the living room. Hopefully Mrs. Marshall wouldn't wander around, if she did, some intuitive assessment from Nikki would be required. This worried me, but the risk seemed limited to the entering and leaving of the house. It was unlikely that Mrs. Marshall would venture upstairs and even if she did, Nikki would most likely regain sight of her before she hit the stairs.

Lenny's job was less complicated. He was to sit in the car and watch Nikki. If for some reason Mrs. Marshall went upstairs, or if Nikki lost sight her, Nikki would signal to Lenny. Lenny would then signal to me with two short beeps and I would quickly find a place to hide. I would remain hidden until Lenny gave me one long beep.

"Have you got it Lenny? If Nikki signals you, I need two short beeps. One long beep is good, two short beeps is bad. Do you understand?" I asked. Lenny barely moved his head, but I could tell he was nodding. "Lenny, you've got to do better than that. I'm not going in with you like this."

"I got it," he told me, and then with all the strength he could muster, he threw himself backwards into his seat and glanced over at me. "One long is good, two short beeps means you need to find a place to hide. It's not that complicated."

"No, it's not complicated, but it *is* hard to do when you are resting your eyes for a minute. Don't rest your eyes, Lenny. Stay focused on Nikki. I'm depending on you."

"I've got this, but please get it done fast."

I reached out and placed my hand on the top of Lenny's head. I did so not only to calm him but also to halt the slight tremor he had developed. "Trust me, I'll get it done, just don't go fucking up those beeps. I need those beeps. Keep your eye on Nikki okay?" These words brightened his eyes. He dropped a small smile on me. I could tell that he believed in me, although I wasn't convinced that I believed in myself.

The loud creak of the passenger door drew both Lenny's and my attention. Nikki heard my words and was motivated. The door slammed shut and we watched her sprint towards the woods, hop over a small bush and duck behind a tree. She reappeared moments later and began motioning for me to join her. I smiled, then turned my attention back to Lenny. He put his hat back on and tightened his grasp on the steering wheel.

"Well, I guess she is ready, are you?"

"Two beeps is bad one is good."

I got out of the car and ran to the woods, encouraged by Nikki's enthusiasm and Lenny's comprehension of the beep system. We stood in the camouflage of the bush and shrubbery. We watched as Lenny repositioned the car across the street. A three-point turn took him six points, and he accidentally hit the horn, and bumped the neighbor's mailbox in the process. The confidence I was feeling drained from my body and was replaced by pessimism.

"Well, that didn't make me feel good at all."

"Maybe we should just go down to the market and rip off some vodka. We could try to get drunk and ride this one out," Nikki suggested.

This worsened my pessimism. Nikki's declaration was an admission. She not only had serious doubts about Lenny, but she was also questioning her own abilities. She wasn't the one taking the risk; and if things went south, she could simply jump into the car and ride off. She wanted to make sure I was sure and that I knew all the facts, that way no blame could be assigned to her later.

"Just tell me that you can see her from here. Can you see through the window into the living room?"

"You're sure about this?"

"I'm sure and I understand."

Nikki's face relaxed. She gently grabbed my hips with both hands and pulled me forward. She placed her lips softly against mine for a moment, then moved back and smiled. She had tried to stop me, and I refused her. She could now skirt responsibility if the plan failed. I nodded, knowing what she was thinking.

"Can you see her from here?" I asked again.

Nikki dipped her head up and down. She swayed back and forth; with each movement my confidence in her decreased. This was a kamikaze mission, a total crapshoot, and I was willing to shake the dice and roll. I knew that regardless of her vantage point, a cricket's chirp could break Nikki's concentration. It didn't matter if she could see in the window. It didn't matter if Lenny could see her. Their presence here served no real purpose at all.

"Nikki stop moving around, you are making me nauseous."

"I'm trying to find the right angle."

"Just tell me if you can see her or not."

"I just told you I couldn't. I think I saw her for a second, but it's a bad angle. I have to move to the middle of the yard. That's the only way I can see in the house, and remain visible for Lenny. I have to go to the middle," she told me.

"You don't need to move," I told her.

"I do. I can only see a small portion of the living room. Don't argue with me. I know what I can and can't see, and I can't see enough."

"Alright, baby, if that's the way it's got to be, then do what you have to do."

Although I thought it was completely unnecessary, I still had to respect her wishes. Nikki was always meticulous. Lenny and I appreciated this. We had a tendency to be careless. I was ready to go storming into the house blind, but Nikki wasn't having that.

"Right there," Nikki told me as she pointed. "That's the spot. That's where I am going."

I looked to the middle of the lawn. There was a large oak, and a medium pine, and both were surrounded by shrubbery. It was a good choice. The trees and bush would serve as cover. She

could see easily into the house, but she would be hidden sufficiently from the cars on the road.

"If it'll make you feel more confident, then go."

"It's the best possible spot," she said, looking at the trees.

I grabbed her face with both hands and slowly turned her attention back to me. I stared deep into her eyes. She nodded
slightly in my grasp, while we smiled at one another. I gently
kissed her lips and she closed her eyes. This was a pre-emptive
apology, a final good-bye…just in case, and was the closest that
Nikki and I ever came to admitting the love we felt for one
another.

"Okay," she whispered, opening her eyes and ending the
moment.

"Okay, baby."

Then she was gone. I watched Nikki glide like a cheetah
stalking her prey. Within the snap of two fingers she was across
the yard. She dove over the thick shrubberies and disappeared
from sight. I laughed at her unnecessary effort. Then her head
popped up from behind the large bush like a gopher from a hole,
searching for her shadow. It was a good spot. I knew she was
there, but it was difficult to see her.

I took a glance over at Lenny. His eyes were wide. He was
laughing and smiling like a proud father willing to take credit for
his child's achievement. Lenny could feel my stare. He turned
and looked at me, our eyes connected; he gave me a small nod
and a smirk. It was supposed to elicit my appreciation for Lenny
having chosen Nikki. We would routinely debate her discovery
while drunk and sentimental, but if we were being honest, we

knew that it was Nikki who had chosen us. I didn't have time to engage in this dispute, it was time for me to go.

I moved steadily through the bushes and trees. I carefully ducked and dodged the branches and vines that attempted to slow me. I wasn't quite the cheetah Nikki was and I knew it. A little voice in the back of my head screamed, the girl is watching. If I couldn't be slick like a cheetah, I had to at least be strong like a lion and roar my way through. 'I am a lion.' This is what I told myself as thorny stems from the thick vines grabbed my flesh, tearing the skin from my arm. I wanted to squeal like a little pig, but I was the lion and lions don't squeal. Instead, I bullied my way through the remainder of the forest.

I paused at the edge of the woods to make sure that Nikki and Lenny were prepared. Nikki's eyes were transfixed on me. She shot a little wink in my direction for good luck. Lenny was still staring at Nikki and smiling.

The lack of recognition for what I had just accomplished annoyed me; however I found it reassuring that he was at least focused.

I quickly slid from the camouflage of the forest and up to the front door. I slowly turned the handle, and, as expected, the door was unlocked. I pushed it open. A vision of Mrs. Marshall standing in the middle of the foyer, mouth open, and eyes filled with disgust as she pounded on her phone; angrily explaining my trespass to the authorities.

I shook off the premonition and continued. I entered the house and disappeared from sight. I disappeared—leaving behind the small reservoir of morals that I still possessed. I disappeared—forgetting my mother's dreams and the life she had envisioned for me. Every time I disappeared, I moved a little further away from society, and what a young man should be and what a young man should do.

The Little Panther

I could hear Mrs. Marshall on the phone gossiping like a teenage girl the day before prom. Her words echoed from room to room, helping me track her movements. I took my first step. The old wooden stair let out a loud creak. The second step was softer, but again, the agony of my weight was voiced so I stopped. Mrs. Marshall had paused to listen to the giddy schoolgirl on the other end of the line. An enthusiastic screech suddenly funneled its way down the hall. The hairs on the back of my neck stood up and I quickened my pace.

My eagerness caused a misjudgment halfway up. My front foot landed on the edge of the step and slipped. I stumbled forward and extended my arms to brace myself, but my hands smacked hard against the wood. The sound bounced off step and hit the wall. Mrs. Marshall's conversation stopped and I was paralyzed by the absence of her voice. I took a look at the front door and considered it, and then I looked up the stairs. My feet were firmly planted in the middle.

The chatter resumed and I was able to move carefully, making sure that each step was treated like an eggshell that was ready to crack. I stared at my feet and ignored the fear that was coursing through my body. My slow pace was preferable to moving faster and falling. With each minimal squeal of the wood I gained confidence. I began to relax and pick up my speed just slightly.

I reached the top of the stairs and found carpet. I moved with ease down the hallway where I was out of sight. I kneeled and took a minute to breathe and regain my composure. I wiped the sweat from my forehead and then dried my hands on my pants. I practically skipped down the hallway, rejoicing in the freedom afforded by the carpet.

Marshall's room had a suspicious museum feel to it. The bed wasn't just neatly made, it was perfectly tucked tight. The floor was bare. The books on his desk stood straight between bookends and were in order according to height. The walls were a light gray and blank, except for two framed posters. The first was a black and white photograph of New York University. It was placed above his desk for motivation. The second and more disturbing poster was of Manhattan at dusk. It hung directly over his bed. This was an illustration of his destiny. Monday through Friday, nine to five, he would sit at a desk and this is what he would see. He hadn't been afforded an opportunity to voice his opinion.

I moved over to the window to check on my reinforcements. Lenny was still awake and staring at Nikki or at least that's what I wanted to believe. I could only really determine that he was still sitting upright. Either way I counted this a positive sign. Nikki noticed me in the window. Our eyes met and she attempted to fake a smile, but she was tight faced and hunched back. I jabbed my finger in the direction she was supposed to be looking, and she redirected her attention.

I spun around Marshall's room checking the dresser and desk drawers first. I was hoping for a simple solution. I slid open the closet door, and checked underneath the soles of his shoes and cleats. This spot was a personal favorite. When my father's eyes grew suspicious and I knew a search was inevitable, I would moisten the inside of whichever sneaker was holding my stash. If he stuck his hand in the slime, it would send him on a trip to the sink for soap. I slid my hand under the mattress making sure not cause a wrinkle. There was nothing there and I was now out of easy options. I scratched my head as I looked around the room. I was headed for the poster on the wall when the sound came, one long beep, this was followed by two short beeps. I stopped to think. I wasn't sure what this meant. I took a step towards the window, changed my mind and headed for the closet. Three more long beeps followed, ending indecision and rendering me incapacitated. I stood still and began to panic. Three long beeps wasn't even part of the fucking plan. I didn't know what this meant. Maybe she was coming, maybe she wasn't. Or maybe Lenny had pressed on the horn, passed out, and his head had bounced. Anything was possible.

The sound of footsteps interrupted my debate. They echoed and were apparently coming from the stairs, or at least the wooden floor of the entranceway. Mrs. Marshall wasn't a small woman and her steps were heavy, which made it hard to pinpoint her exact location. I wanted to believe she was just pacing around the entranceway, but the light shake of the walls indicated otherwise. Not wanting to take too much time or make too much noise, I got on my belly and wiggled my way underneath the bed, but I wasn't alone.

Bright yellow eyes and a hiss greeted me. I watched as a small animal inched away. It pushed itself up against the wall and let out a second and louder hiss. The cat had been patiently hiding from me and it wasn't pleased. Its fearful retreat was just a temporary solution. I was expected to leave.

"Shhhhh, kitty, kitty," I whispered. "I'm nice."

The animal disagreed. There was a third short hiss, a final warning. I couldn't move. The cat lunged, like a panther protecting its youth from a hungry predator. Its paw extended and its claws landed on the bridge of my nose. A small amount of skin was torn clean from my face. I jolted upward, banging my head against the crossbar of the bed. My chin then hit the floor. The little creature struck again. This time, its claw dug into the flesh of my cheek.

"Fuck you," I whispered.

I made a fist and thought about retaliation, but the impulse was replaced by fear, as the door to the bedroom swung open. My heart began pounding, I worried it might bounce off the floor and draw attention. I took a deep but quiet breath and tried to calm myself. Luckily, the arrival of Mrs. Marshall had distracted the little panther. For the moment we were both hypnotized by her feet, which were making their way around the room to the closet. She slid the glass door open, and then shut it. She may have just been putting away laundry, but I was convinced that she was searching. Soon, she would check under the bed, and I would be discovered.

This caused me to react. I jammed my finger into the side of the cat. It zigzagged its way out from under the bed like it had been lit on fire. It collided with Mrs. Marshall's feet, spun in a full circle, stopped and regrouped for a split second before darting into the hallway. I had just given Mrs. Marshall an explanation for any noise. I just had to hope she accepted it.

"Muffin, what's wrong with you?" She said.

That cat was no 'Muffin', I thought as I watched Mrs. Marshall's legs hesitate. Eventually she walked out of the room closing the door behind her. I exhaled. I was safe, but not in the clear.

Her steps indicated that she wasn't headed for the stairs, instead, she moved to the next room over.

I lay there baffled not knowing whether I should get up and run, get up and search, or stay here and sleep. Blood was drying in the place of the missing skin on my face and nose. The stress had caused my brain to throb and I was a loud sneeze away from being discovered. I was a hot, sweaty, ball of anxiety radiating a stench so pungent that even I was nauseated by the smell.

I twisted my body so I was lying on my back. I might as well get comfortable while considering my options. I could jump out of the window, but plummeting through the sky towards the hard ground empty handed seemed like needless pain. The sun had started to depart and there would be a buzz of activity occurring downstairs in the immediate future. Exiting through the front door was something that needed to happen before the footsteps multiplied. I could stay right here, close my eyes, and drift away. In the middle of night I could sneak out while everyone was in bed.

I wondered if I could still count on assistance from Nikki and Lenny. It was possible that Lenny had abandoned me, spooked by the sound of his own horn, he might have driven away like a mad man leaving Nikki in the woods. Nikki would wait for a while by the tree hoping I would appear in the window. Her sickness would eventually overwhelm her and she would give up and begin walking, probably back to Lenny's. She would scold him for his betrayal. He would try to convince her that he was sorry and that there wasn't any other option. She wouldn't argue, but she would silently disagree. They were probably drunk and listening to music at this very moment.

Playing dead under the bed wasn't an option. The stench alone would surely draw curious eyes. As I began to wiggle my way out from under the bed, I noticed a hole at the top of the box spring. I had created a spot just like this in grade school. I stored a small box in it, which held little bottles of whiskey and rum, small bags of weed, and sheets of acid tabs. The thought raised my cheeks and I eagerly skirted myself up to investigate. This hole was no accident. It was neatly constructed storage unit. My little friend Timmy waited for the house to empty and then turned the bed on its edge. With a blade he had created a nearly perfect symmetrical square. He had lightly singed each of the sides to assure that it wouldn't fray and command any unwanted attention. It was quite impressive, if only his jock buddies could see it, some jaws would definitely drop.

I jammed both hands into the hole and discovered a thick stack of cash. I pulled it out and shoved it into my pocket without counting it. I searched the area above my head, but it was bare. I swept the sides, but found the same result. I pinched my forehead while shaking my head angrily. My teeth clenched as I struggled, but failed to contain my disappointment. Overwhelmed, I grabbed a hold of the material covering the box spring and ripped it violently downward. A large portion of fabric busted free from its stapled restraints. It not only slightly relieved me, but it gave me a clear view of the wooden skeleton supporting the bed. There it was, a vial of pills neatly taped to a wooden rib just out of my reach. I scooted myself down and ripped it free. The pills were tightly packed into the bottle and made almost no noise when shaken. I cringed, because I knew I would soon be leaping out of the window and spiraling downward towards an unforgiving earth. My pockets were heavy; all my pains would be washed away by what was weighing them down. Even if I had to hobble my broken body to the street and limp to Lenny's, at least all the blood and missing flesh wouldn't be in vain.

I shook the bottle a second time just to confirm its contents. It was full. Rejuvenated, I wiggled my way out from under the bed and stood up. I examined the vial. Dexedrine, this was my favorite form of pharmaceutical speed. I popped the top and dumped four capsules out, threw them into my mouth and swallowed them with a dry gulp. Then I checked the name on the bottle…Elaine Gould.

She had told me about this bottle a couple weeks back. I was high on acid and feeling good. The stars were exploding in the sky. Their neon fragments fizzled like sparklers in mid-air until a whistling, vibrant, purple wind swept the dust away and painted the trees with it. The surrounding forest was a glowing Christmas display. Our Chocolate Lab named Dingo had suggested that we go for a walk at the park, despite the neighbor's Australian Shepard's lecture about driving while high. That Shepard was always a stickler when I dropped acid. I would sometimes sit in a tree just to avoid his yapping. Dingo and I hadn't planned on staying long, but we ran into some white trash losers with a free cage who delayed our departure.

Elaine arrived late in the evening. She pulled up in a sparkly new car, which drew jealous stares from the people standing around the keg. I took little notice. Most of the kids at our high school were given overpriced sweet-sixteen presents. Her drunken parking job did, however, catch my attention. She skidded to a stop, scraping her front bumper on the curb. The door opened, and one by one, the girls poured out and into the parking lot. They stumbled around looking up at trees like they were a new invention. Elaine's eyes landed on me and she weaved her way over to the fence where I was sitting. The herd followed and surrounded us. Dingo was less than impressed. He got up and left to go find his own keg cup I assumed. I had been stingy with mine and he wasn't drunk enough to deal with this fiasco. Elaine wrapped her little arms around my neck and slobbered on my cheek, without even a hello.

"Do you have any weed?" She asked, foregoing the usual cordialities.

"I don't smoke weed."

"But I bet you could find some."

She was now stroking my arm, and laying what was supposed to be a seductive glance on me, but she looked sick. I stood up, not wanting to be puked on. I scanned the crowd. There were several people that were probably holding a bag, but I had no interest in wasting a favor. I squinted and shook my head in an attempt to appear accommodating and disappointed.

"I have a bottle of Dexedrine I can trade for it, or sell to you for cheap to thank you."

"Is that right?"

"It's not here but I have it and I don't need it."

My father had told me, "Never trust a Jew. If they can get paid double for something they will."

He was right. She cleaned my pockets out for a down payment for the bottle, and demanded that I go into favor-debt for her weed. The old hippie I was forced to do business with had a disproportionate appraisal of the courtesy he was doing me, and I knew I'd be handing over my first born on a later date. Of course, the girls had neglected to bring paraphernalia, so not wanting to owe any more favors; I constructed a smoking device out of a soda can. After they were done, I introduced them around so they could drink from the keg comfortably. I then cornered Elaine and attempted to woo her. The combination of acid, beer, and the possibility of speed, had me spouting sweet, but incoherent declarations.

"Lainey, why do you waste your time surrounded by mediocrity? You're not average, but you are drowning in it around you. You are a dove, beautiful, but shackled. Nobody gets to witness your beauty cause it's hidden, concealed by an ugly flock. You are shackled by dumb bitches."

I sort of knew what I was going for. I wasn't positive that doves traveled in flocks. Elaine was more of a pelican than a dove anyway. She resembled every other little Jewish girl in our school. Her nose was slightly too big for her face. Her skin was a little too pale in contrast to her dark frizzy hair and her attitude was way too aggressive for her looks. She was hardly the best looking of the girls that night, but she had the vial of Dexedrine.

This charade culminated all the way into the woods, where she placed her hands on top of my head and pushed me downwards, insisting that I perform oral sex. I hesitated, but obliged with tightly closed eyes. After my face was wet and she was satisfied, I asked her to return the favor. She declined, claiming that my performance was the conclusion of negotiations for the drugs. I thought it was cruel, but I accepted her terms without much resistance. I had little interest in her mouth. Elaine slipped away later that night, and after several phone calls the following week, I decided to write the encounter off as a bad investment.

I shook off the memory and stepped over to the window. Nikki was still by the trees, but she was hunched over and clutching her stomach. Lenny's car was on the street, but he wasn't to be found. He had most likely curled up in the fetal position and was fast asleep. I unlocked the window and attempted to slide it open. The house wasn't old, but it had seen its fair share of New England winters, and the wood was warped. I pushed again, this time with force.

The window slid slowly upward, producing a loud screeching sound. Nikki heard me and looked up in shock. I waved slightly. She did the best she could to force a smile. A bright light suddenly hit the side of the house. Our heads spun, our eyes widened as we helplessly watched Marshall's car roar down the drive. The vehicle traveled at high speed, and came to a sliding stop inches away from the garage. His immediate exit and charge toward the house sent a chill up my spine. Marshall intuitively knew I was about to leap from his window with his stash in my pocket.

"Now!" she screamed.

"Fuck me," I whispered.

The front door open, then slammed shut, shaking the walls. I climbed up onto the window ledge. I squatted there and stared down at the ground. Heavy, determined footsteps echoed up the staircase. A conversation ensued in the hallway. I leaned forward and looked again. I took a final glance at Nikki, clenched my jaw, and lunged out of the window. I had envisioned myself landing on my feet, and then summersaulting across the lawn. Unfortunately, the adrenaline coursing through my body had caused me to leap with enthusiasm and instead of my feet weren't leading the way I was now executing a perfectly formed belly flop with no water underneath. I forced my eyes shut. My arms straightened towards the earth and my muscles flexed. My hands hit the ground, and my elbows collapsed on impact. My chest and stomach followed, colliding harshly into the earth. I coughed out the oxygen in my lungs. My chin hit next. My brain rattled like dice in a tin cup. The impact pushed my teeth upward and into my lip, and blood filled my mouth. The adrenaline that had forced my ill-advised belly flop was now compelling me to stand. I slowly rose. My back cracked. Sharp pains exploded in every direction like a firecracker had been set off inside my body. I took my first steps, but my knee buckled and I collapsed back to the ground. I pushed myself up. I paused for a moment, reached down and patted my pocket. The pills and money were there. I limped my way towards the bush Nikki was hiding behind. I needed her shoulders they would be my crutch to safety.

Nikki had seen me spiral to the ground. My hard landing was inevitable, but she should have been there to collect humpty dumpty's pieces. She wasn't. She was on the ground laughing hysterically. She was clutching her stomach with one arm and pointing at me with the other. My eyes bulged. I grabbed her hand and tried to yank her to her feet. She was too heavy. I stumbled and almost ended up on the ground next to her.

"Why would you jump like that? You looked so crazy. Were you trying to fly? Did you think you could fly?" she asked me, as she flapped her arms like a bird.

"Nikki, stop fucking around. This isn't funny; I'm in a lot of pain."

"You thought you could fly. Why didn't you just fly to Lenny's car?" She screamed in between cackling and pointing.

She was rolling around on the ground and laughing uncontrollably. Marshall was probably in his room flipping his bed. The open window explained everything that he needed to know. The clock was ticking, and Nikki was going to flap and laugh us all the way into a locked cell. I bent down and scooped her up like a disobedient child. I threw her over my shoulder and began trudging up the lawn.

"You're a crazy bitch, making me carry your ass like this," I told her, as I struggled towards the car.

"Fly me back to the car, fly, fly me back to the car." She screamed.

"Jesus fucking Christ, Nikki, I swear."

I opened the door and shoved her into the car, banging her head against the roof. Technically, this was an accident, although I was furious and any attempt to be gentle was of little concern.

I ran round the car and jumped into the front passenger seat. I looked over at Lenny. His head was pressed against the steering wheel. His eyes were closed tight and a small stream of drool was visible. I smacked him across the face with the back of my hand. Like a jack in the box he sprung to attention. He was about to say something until he saw my bloody face.

"Fucking drive."

"Yes." That's all he could say as he turned the key and hit the gas. I glanced back at the Marshall house. A large silhouette was in the window, staring out over the landscape watching us retreat. I felt a heavy door slam shut on a piece of my past that I once cherished.

Buddhist Meditation

Not a word was uttered as we drove away. I waited patiently, focusing on neither, but expecting some attention from both of them. A simple inquiry about my bruises and blood would suffice. Lenny sat like a Buddhist monk engaged in monastic silence. His focused stare failed to mask his obvious embarrassment. He refused to even turn and acknowledge me. I agreed with his shame, but acting like a deaf mute wasn't diminishing my urge to smack him again. Nikki was sitting quietly, but not still. She rocked back and forth like a psych-ward patient waiting for her meds, debating whether or not to engage me.

"I got it," I told them, aggravated that I had to be the one to end the silence.

My news had failed to elicit the slightest form of acknowledgement from Lenny. His grasp remained tight on the wheel. His focus steady on the yellow line straight ahead. Nikki stopped rocking and inched slightly forward. Her wide eyes swayed back forth like a pendulum counting the seconds on a grandfather clock. She waited, but realized her silent plea couldn't break Lenny's resolve.

Hesitant, she leaned into the front of the car, and turned her attention solely on me.

"What did you get?" She asked, while faking a smile that barely lifted her cheeks.

I didn't answer immediately. I just sat there with a smug look on my face, ignoring her and allowing the tension to mount. "Something good."

"How good is good?"

"Real good."

"What does that mean exactly?"

I was still aggravated by their lack of concern, and I was being vague on purpose. The tightness in her face and the stiffness of Lenny's posture helped ease the hostility I was feeling. It was a cruel form of manipulation, but it was a deserved punishment for their selfish disregard of my needs. Lenny finally began to squirm in his seat. He wanted to turn and look, he made a small motion in my direction, but he couldn't muster the courage to fully commit. He realized that he had failed me, so he decided to quietly accept his torture. Nikki was less reasonable. Half of her body was now resting in between Lenny's seat and mine. Her glare demanded answers that she felt she deserved. I wasn't ready to disregard the previous fiasco, even though I was safe in the car with heavy pockets. She had callously mocked me in my time of need and I couldn't proceed as if nothing had happened, not yet at least.

"Seriously Jay, what did you get?" Nikki asked again. "Stop fucking around and tell us, so we can get excited too."

She had a scowl on her face. My prodding had become more than a petty annoyance. The ice beneath me was thin. Still, I held firm and continued to skate around the question, allowing another ten seconds of silence to tick by. I smirked at no one in particular, but it was taken personally.

The ice broke and Nikki slapped me in the chest trying to wipe the look from my face, but her hand skipped upwards and smacked me in the jaw, rattling my teeth instead.

"Tell me," she shouted.

"Are you fucking kidding me?" I screamed. My voice pushed her backwards. "Are you really this fucking selfish? How can you keep acting like you didn't see me fall? Maybe you should fucking fly away." I told her, while imitating her imitation of the fall that she had found so hysterical. I then turned my focus to Lenny.

"Three fucking beeps, what is that? When did that become a part of the plan?"

"I'm sorry Jay," Lenny replied, without turning.

"Now that you're awake, and Nikki is done laughing, do you think someone might want to ask me if I'm okay?! I mean, instead of 'what did you get?' You are both fucking vultures and you don't even care if the body is mine."

I stopped my rant and took a long, deep breath. My grievances had been aired and I felt slightly relieved.

"Just for the record, I never asked, 'what did you get?' So technically, I'm just a witness to the vulture picking at your decaying carcass in the middle of the road. I mean, if you want to paint an accurate picture," Lenny explained. He continued to stare straight ahead hoping that I would laugh, or at least smile, which I almost did.

"Fuck you Lenny. You're just a scared little bitch that's why you didn't ask," Nikki exclaimed, halting what was potentially a healing moment. She wasn't done either. She turned her anger toward me.

"And you are being a baby. I'm sorry you fell out of a window, but shit happens in these situations we all know that. I'm even sorrier that it was fucking funny, but it was. You're right, I should have been there to help you and I wasn't. But for fuck sake get over it, stop being immature and tell us what you got."

"Really? So that's still the question," I asked.

"It is still the question, but now there are two. What the fuck did you get and how long do you plan on being a dick for? (the for at the end of this sentence is not necessary) Can we look forward to this shit all night?"

"You want to know what I got?" I asked, as I reached into my pocket and pulled out the vial.

"This is what I got." I told her as I threw it at her.

The bottle hit her directly in the middle of her chest, bounced and then landed in her lap. She remained perfectly still. After all the nagging she didn't even bother to look down. The vial rolled off her lap and landed on the floor. She still didn't move. Her eyes went cold and her gaze unfocused. Regret overwhelmed me as I watched her turn to stone.

Lenny watched us and turned towards me, "I understand that you are pissed, and I agree it's justifiable, but you need to fix that, and do it quick."

I had pressed a button on Nikki that Lenny and I strenuously attempted to avoid. My frustration catapulted her into a dark cave full of vicious memories, which haunted her. Her father's repeated and multi-faceted abuse had removed her ability to differentiate between degrees of violence. Even an aggressive restraint could at times cause a dissociative reaction, which would take Lenny and me hours to rectify. My pain and my desire to be comforted had clouded my judgment. With extreme caution, I began to move into the backseat. Lenny slowed the car, and kept it steady. We both realized that under these conditions, any accidental contact would be misinterpreted and a wild animal may spring to life in her and claw me to death.

"Fuck me," I whispered to myself, baffled by the turn of events and my new status as the villain.

This should have been my moment of glory. I moved deliberately. I positioned myself next to her, and lightly pressed my body against hers. Her breaths were shallow. Her body was damp with perspiration. A slight vibration started and stopped in waves. I wrapped my arms around her and held her tightly, but the tighter I held, the more violently she quivered. I could see Lenny watching me in the rearview mirror. A look of disgust spread across his face, as he shook his head in disappointment.

"Baby?" I whispered quietly in her ear. I kissed her cheek, caressed her head, combing her soft hair with my fingers. I gazed into her eyes trying to steal her attention. I then slid my hand down from her hair and paused at her cheek, before I gently turned her head so she was facing me. I delivered a sorrowful glance, hoping it would convey my regret and bring her attention back to the car.

"Baby, you know that I'm sorry, really sorry. I'm in a lot of pain and I wasn't thinking." I explained, as I lightly touched my lips to hers. I held her in that position until her eyes closed. Her psyche finally reset, and I could finally exhale.

It took only a brief moment for Nikki to open her eyes, but when she did, she wasted no time. Without an acknowledgement of forgiveness, she reached down and snatched the vial off the car floor. Before I could blink, Nikki had the prescription at eye level. The sense of excitement that followed was difficult for her to mask. Her front teeth clamped down on her bottom lip as she fought to contain a nonverbal admission of my triumph.

"That's not even everything." I told her.

I unthinkingly pulled out the bundle of cash. I hadn't planned on telling them about the money. It was designated as personal compensation for my pain, but I had gotten caught up in the moment and the possibility of forgiveness. Nikki unenthusiastically looked at the money. She shrugged her shoulders and then turned her attention back to the vial.

"You're a dick," she said, without looking at me.

"I know baby, I'm sorry."

"Can someone please tell me how excited I should be?" Lenny asked anxiously.

"It's time to get excited, Angel." Nikki answered, stealing a small piece of glory from me.

"Yes, but how excited should I be getting, darling?"

"Does Dexedrine excite you?"

Lenny's eyes brightened like a young child walking into an ice cream parlor. His wide smile ricocheted off the review mirror and Nikki eagerly snatched it out of the air before I had a chance. I didn't care for this at all. She then returned the gesture, furthering the notion that I was being robbed of due acknowledgement. This bothered me, but I choked down my pride with a dry gulp.

"Jay, would you consider taking the wheel for a moment, so Nikki and I can get straightened out too?"

Lenny started to slow the car down. His tone had been polite, but I resented the assumption that I had already taken my fix. The four pills I had swallowed in Marshall's room were going to be the only form of compensation I would receive after my foolish disclosure of the money. The cash would be placed in the community pot and used equally, even though it wasn't deservedly so. They could pick my pockets all they wanted, but they weren't charging me for pills they couldn't prove I had taken.

"Does my face look right to you? Do you think I feel right?" I asked him. "Just find a good place so we can all get right."

I watched Lenny, as he shot a backwards glance at Nikki; yet another incident of nonverbal communication that I didn't appreciate, especially since the subject matter was my lie. They held their stare for a moment, and then came to a silent consensus that they weren't going to object.

Their lack of gratitude again infuriated me. My body stiffened and my face tightened as I considered turning this night into a party for one.

"Are you two fucking done yet?" I asked. It was a rhetorical question, intended only to interrupt their silent accusations. "'Cause if you need some time alone I'll happily get out and walk."

"Relax Jay, nobody is getting out and walking. Lenny is going to find us a great spot, aren't you Lenny?"

Lenny refocused on the road ahead without responding to Nikki's question. We drove in silence for another mile before turning onto a poorly lit secluded narrow road. It was a private drive that had a cul-de-sac at the end. This area had concealed past endeavors on a few occasions, but never this early in the evening. The light that remained in the sky made us visible, and if noticed, the residents of the street would surely question what an old Cutlass was doing parked outside their million dollar homes.

"What do you think? This works, right?" Lenny asked.

"It's a little early, but it will have to do, I suppose."

Lenny nodded and then parked the car in the corner of the cul-de-sac next to some thick brush and towering pine trees. This was the best possible position. We were completely out of view from all but one of the houses. There was a slight chance that a resident returning home from work could discover us. This made me uncomfortable, but I deemed it unlikely, considering that the length of our stay would be minimal.

"Is this good?" Lenny unnecessarily asked.

My anger had made him nervous, and now he was going to be overly accommodating. It was slightly annoying, but I appreciated the effort. "It's great, let's just be fast," I told them. Now that we were actually parked, and moments away from bliss, I just wanted to forget and proceed with our evening. My need to punish them had subsided and a sense of forgiveness washed over me. This was due to the pills I swallowed. They were finally taking effect and negative emotions seemed counterintuitive.

"Can I do it?" Nikki asked. She was smiling brightly, overwhelmed with anticipation. Lenny had turned and was also staring intensely. I nodded.

"Count them out," I told her.

Nikki emptied the vial. It was a thirty-day prescription, twenty-five milligrams twice a day. There were ten missing, four of which were in my stomach. The other six were unaccounted for. Even after the deduction, we were left with over a thousand milligrams.

"This is fucking sweet, Jay," Nikki exclaimed, as she divided the pills and handed them out.

After the division there were two extra pills. I would hold onto these. They would be reserved for the end of the night, and designated to be emptied, crushed, split equally and then snorted; that is, if Lenny and Nikki didn't get too high and forget. It was unlikely that Nikki would forget, but it was quite possible that Nikki and I would be consuming these pills in a dark corner when Lenny wasn't watching.

"How many to start?" I asked.

"Two is sufficient," Lenny replied.

"Two? I think three should hit us just right," I responded, even though four was the actual number I was thinking.

Nikki frowned and rolled her eyes. Lenny and I watched her, trying not to smirk. Her disagreement was foreseeable. This whole ordeal was nothing more than a charade. Nikki would make the final decision, which would be predictably higher than my suggestion. We had kept our initial quotes ridiculously low, because we were aware of the procedure.

"You both are crazy. I was thinking more like eight."

"No, absolutely not," Lenny responded. "That's totally ridiculous, even for you."

Nikki's counter-offer raised our eyebrows, but for different reasons. Eight pills, that was definitely excessive, but considering the low Nikki was riding, it wasn't totally ridiculous like Lenny had suggested. I had gotten off that ride in Marshall's room. I felt good, my body was warm, my back was relaxed and I seemed to be melting into my seat. It was possible to feel better, but I feared eight more pills might have me feeling dead. Lenny, on the other hand was just being cautious, eight was a big number.

"I think four will do the trick, at least until we find a better spot," I told her.

"Split the difference; six," Nikki countered.

"Nikki, this is a terrible spot," Lenny argued, even though it wasn't totally true. "We are just trying to straighten out. Once we accomplish that, we can reassess the situation and devise a better solution. Four pills, that's it, end of the story."

"Five. Any less than five is just stupid," Nikki argued.

Lenny thought about it for a moment. He opened his mouth and was about to argue, but then decided against it. This was the smallest acceptable dosage in Nikki's mind. Lenny realized this. His submission concluded when he reached over and opened the glove box. He removed two Ziploc bags and handed one to Nikki. We counted out five pills and they bagged the remainder. I would keep the vial and use that. At the end of this night it would be an empty souvenir.

"So five, we all agree?" I asked. This was one more pill than I wanted to consume, but I had come to the same conclusion as Lenny.

"We are going to do this right, aren't we?" Nikki replied.

The beauty of this drug, besides the high, was the multicolored balls in the capsule. They didn't require any preparation before ingestion unlike typical pills, which needed to be crushed, chopped, and divided. Twist off and snorted, that's all that needed to be done. Under optimal conditions, we would complicate the matter just slightly. To ensure efficiency, we would flip upside down when we sniffed. Gravity would then take over ensuring zero waste.

Lenny and I looked at each other. His grimace suggested he was opposed to the time investment required to reposition. He was slightly nervous about the light in the sky and the hour of the day and he didn't want to be here any longer than we had to. I agreed. I didn't care for the idea that we would be hanging upside down oblivious to our surroundings, but I also didn't want to waste any of the drugs that I had bled for.

"Let's be fast about it," I told her.

Nikki didn't hesitate. She spun around in her seat and was hanging upside down in a matter of seconds. This forced Lenny and me to smile. Before we were able to finish the sentiment, Nikki had snorted the first pill and was pinching her nose. The sound motivated Lenny to move into the passenger seat.

"Shall we?" He asked.

"See you in a bit."

Lenny and I were taller and wider than Nikki, so the process of flipping upside down within the confines of the car was awkward. I could hear Lenny muttering to himself as he accidentally kicked the passenger side window. I understood his frustration. I was slightly larger than Lenny and I was in the backseat, which made the task even more challenging. Lenny's only real difficulty was the length of his legs. Once he had managed to get them up and over the seat, they dangled comfortably. He could then relax and allow his body to slant its way down to the floor of the car. I didn't have this luxury. I had to jam my feet into the rear window. My head pressed tightly against the floor and the driver's seat. My body bent at each indicated point. It was an uncomfortable fit, but it was worth it.

"Ahhhhhhhh," Lenny sighed loudly, after he had finished ingesting the first pill.

The exaggerated sigh of relief echoed loudly throughout the car. Nikki began to giggle which induced laughter from Lenny and me. Normally, we would have basked in the mutual sense of relief, but our slight paranoia wasn't going to accommodate this. We would have to revisit this moment at a later time.

Methodically, we twisted the top off each pill and carefully placed it at the opening of our nasal passages. We then inhaled deeply and pinched tightly. I could feel the drug passing through my nasal tissue and into my blood stream. What a miraculous sensation. It had been a necessary decision to swallow the pills in Marshall's room, but I couldn't help but feel a sense of remorse after ingesting the drug the correct way.

"Two more for good luck?" Nikki asked, after the final pill had been snorted.

"Nikki, for the final time, no, we have all night," Lenny yelled from the floor of the front seat.

I was grateful for Lenny's response. Only a few moments had passed since we snorted the first pill, and the drug was already rushing through my veins. My heart was pounding, almost to the point of concern. My body temperature was rising, increasing the warmth that engulfed me. My inner monologue had become nothing more than wild chatter with no singular focus. A normal person would have sprinted to his car and driven to the hospital, but in our world, this was simply a good sign. I was about to sprout wings and fly.

"Fuck that's good," I whispered to myself.

I closed my eyes tightly and burst into the sky. A flock of eagles flying nearby stopped their travel just to marvel at my speed. The wind whistled in my ears as I cut through the clouds and cruised past God, who was quietly observing. I caught a quick smile from my baby brother who never had the opportunity to experience this pleasure. My grandfather was holding my brother's hand, while waving at me with the other. He had died while attempting this flight and he understood why I traveled. Eventually, heaven was beneath me in all its glory. I had rocketed into a different hemisphere where gravity didn't exist.

I continued to float for what seemed like hours but was probably only a few minutes. When there are no requirements to fulfill and no expectations to meet, time becomes nothing more than an irrelevant measurement of nothingness. I had achieved the exact state of being I had been striving for: an isolated existence divorced from society's relentless attempt to shackle me with the monotonous pursuit of contentment.

A hard knock hit the car window rattling the glass. The sound yanked me back to reality. I opened my eyes and I stared upward, searching for the cause. A dark figure loomed outside. The shadow staring in suggested that it was a man of considerable size. I watched in fear as his hand rose into the air and landed on the car again. My body tightened, as the man angrily and continuously hit the car.

"Why is that happening?" Nikki whispered, as she turned her head and looked at me.

"There's somebody outside our window." Lenny unnecessarily told us, as he repositioned himself in his seat.

Nikki and I attempted to do the same, but the process was awkward. Nikki rolled to the right. I fell to the left. Our legs met in the middle and intertwined. This tangle would have been easily rectified, but our interlocking joints baffled us. We seemed to be continually moving in opposing directions. Eventually, we submitted to the enigma. We halted our struggle and accepted our fate.

"What the fuck?" Lenny asked, as he stared down at us. "Get up, you retards, get up."

"It's too hard," Nikki answered.

The man's next attempt to gain our attention shattered Lenny's nerves. He convulsed slightly, causing him to jerk his head. Nikki and I found his involuntary movement humorous. We snickered tauntingly, which frustrated and embarrassed him. He snapped his head in our direction and shot us a devilish glare. He had intended on silencing us, but it had the reverse effect.

Our unified giggle mutated into a laugh.

"Shut the fuck up, it's a cop outside," Lenny told us, as he rolled down the window.

"What are you kids doing in there? You smoking dope?" a rugged voice inquired.

"No sir, we don't smoke dope, never cared for it much," Lenny answered.

The man paused to consider Lenny's response. It was a good answer, it was an admission and a denial wrapped into a simple statement. There was also a level of respect in his words. Lenny had basically told the man, 'I'm not going to insult your intelligence. It's obvious that we are druggies and it is possible that we might be smoking dope in here, but no, you didn't catch us this time.'

"Why are they sitting upside down like that then?" the man asked, as he pushed his way partially through the window.

Lenny turned and looked at our feet and, without a pause, he answered, "It's a form of Buddhist meditation. You have to let the blood rush to your head. We learned about it in World Religion class."

What followed was a long period of silence. This time I wasn't confident in the response. It was a blatant lie with an origin that seemed unlikely. I, myself, was baffled as I continued to consider the explanation.

Lenny was high and had panicked. I couldn't really fault him for this.

"They teach World Religion in High school?" the man finally asked.

"Yes sir, they sure do, as an elective, of course. They teach philosophy and psychology if you prefer."

"What happened to good old social studies?"

"Social studies?" Lenny asked. He was honestly confused by the question, as was I.

"Yes, social studies."

"You mean sociology?"

"What is the world coming to?" the man asked, as he shook his head.

Lenny didn't bother to respond. He had satisfied the man's curiosity and he was now walking away, baffled and disgusted. The pressure was alleviated. Nikki and I now found our repositioning surprisingly easy, which Lenny didn't appreciate. The shock had been somewhat sobering. This feeling was emphasized when I realized that the man who had been leaning into our car was actually dressed in a business suit. He was nothing more than a resident retrieving his nightly paper after a hard day of work. Lenny had manipulated the situation for our benefit, and I found myself in appreciative awe.

Jesus-Freaks

We drove peacefully and silently into the night, admiring the sun as it completed its departure. All that was left of the day was an illuminating glow of desperate, but magnificent, colors that stubbornly fought to remain in the sky. My eyes clung to the horizon, stunned by this inexplicable beauty. I could feel the colors enter me. The orange and yellow tints warmed me, and this warmth surrounded me as I began to sink into my seat, engulfed by the sensation.

"It's amazing, isn't it?" I asked, but neither Lenny nor Nikki offered a response.

I was hypnotized by the creeping darkness that was slowly infecting each bright color like a hungry parasite feeding with a singular purpose. We were being forced to exchange the sun's warming heat for the invisibility of night. This was an exchange that I usually looked forward to, but for some reason, and at this moment, the trade saddened me. The dark, cold sky seemed haunting. A chill ran down my spine as I watched the destruction.

"I'm glad it's finally dark, I feel like I can breathe a little easier," Lenny stated, interrupting my trance.

I wouldn't respond. I sat still in the darkness. The night sky had brought with it an angry wind violently attempting to remove the remaining color from the thin trees that lined the road. I watched as desperate leaves stubbornly clung to barren branches, eventually submitting and spiraling downward, landing where they helplessly waited to be demolished.

"It feels eerie out tonight, don't you think?" I asked Lenny.

"There's nothing eerie about how I'm feeling right now. And thank you for that. It feels good to feel good again."

"This is good, really good; it's much better when it's dark. I feel like a ghost, like I can move and no one can see me," Nikki added from the back seat. I smiled, pleased that everyone was happy and I was finally receiving a small amount of acknowledgement.

"I wouldn't necessarily say I feel like a ghost, but I definitely feel more relaxed now that it's dark," Lenny added. They were right; the lack of sun was calming. I reached over and tapped the small silver button that controlled my window. I thought the cool, night air would be refreshing, but I was wrong. A vicious wind immediately attacked the small crevice and slapped me in the face. It wasn't the invigorating sensation I had imagined, but there was something about the cold landing on my hot wounded face that I found soothing.

"Seriously?" Lenny asked, as he turned and stared at me. "Please tell me that you're kidding with that."

"What? It feels good and the air smells good."

"Actually no, no it doesn't," Lenny responded as he reached over and turned on the heat.

"Honestly, it feels especially cold."

I nodded, but ultimately chose to ignore Lenny. I was paralyzed by the symbolically potent aroma of autumn. The unique fragrances evoked an onslaught of memories that overwhelmed me. I allowed them to engulf me, even though I realized that succumbing could result in guilt and remorse. I closed my eyes and began to drift.

I found myself standing in a large field of freshly cut grass, which accommodated the needs of dirt-covered children. A smile pushed my cheeks high. I was in the middle of a pack of neighborhood kids. I was waiting, focused on a brown leather football that at any moment would be hurled through the air. Then I was chasing, running with determination. This was a special time.

It was a period of life when there were no expectations or requirements. I was a child. The word disappointment had not yet been mentioned; it couldn't be spelled, so it remained unrealized.

Like an avalanche, my memories engulfed me. I was now sitting beside my father in his old pickup truck. He silently chained-smoked, driving through the Bronx on our way to the ballpark. Out of the corner of his eye he would catch me studying him, and slap me in the chest.

"You excited?" he'd ask.

I'd shake my head 'no'. He would chuckle at my contradictory smile and wide eyes. Yankee Stadium in the middle of October was our most cherished tradition. We were miles away and I anticipated crossing the bridge that led to the ballpark. My father's large hand would land on the back of my head, engulfing it, as he guided me toward the entrance gate. I was lost in jubilation, unaware of the sacrifices my father had made to grant me this memory; a day's pay, plus the price of the tickets, hot dogs, popcorn and soda. Money was never a consideration of mine and he didn't expect it to be. I swam away from this memory only to run into my mother baking a pumpkin pie weeks before Thanksgiving. She was standing in front of the oven with mitts covering her hands and a smile plastered across her face. She had no reason to be cooking pie, no reason other than the anxious child tap dancing a few feet behind her. She was a terrible cook and she hated doing it but I was her little prince, and for me she would spread pumpkin paste and she would spread it early.

In the oversized recliner in the living room, my grandfather was deep into a whiskey-induced slumber. His bottle was still in hand and a cloud of cigar smoke hovered above. I would creep over to his chair and tug on his arm. He would squint at me but I would ignore his scorn and raise my arms into the air. He would laugh at my nerve. His brown bear eyes would open wide and he would reach down and wrap his strong paws around me. I would spend the night nestled in his bear stomach, safe and secure.

"Hey Eskimo boy, can you give me a break over there with that window?" Lenny asked, as he glared at me.

"What?" I snapped, annoyed by the interruption, but more annoyed that I had allowed sentiment to infiltrate my high.

"The window, please, can you close that damn thing? Seriously, it's like an ice chest in here."

I tightened my eyes and angrily shook my head, jolting myself free from my debilitated state. These memories, now incapacitating me, were nothing more than speed-induced inaccurate portrayals of my youth. There were simple truths that discounted the loving nature of these memories. My grandfather had long since died and a void remained in his wake. For every Yankee game, there was a multitude of nights consisting of drunken belligerence, or even worse, complete absence. My mother's pumpkin pies could hardly balance a scale overwhelmed by years filled with emotional instability.

"What are you saying to me?" I asked, as I turned and looked at Lenny.

He had forgotten about his request and was intensely studying the road, anticipating each miniscule twist and turn. His ability to accurately maneuver our vehicle produced a sense of contentment within Lenny. I found it somewhat ridiculous, but who was I to judge.

"You having fun over there, speed racer?"

This question was meant as a joke, but instead Lenny took it as criticism. He pressed hard on the brake, causing the car to come to a complete stop. Our bodies jerked forward and I was annoyed by his overreaction. We had been driving slow; so slow, that if we had been observed, it probably would have been our lack of speed that would have raised suspicion.

"Was I speeding?" Lenny asked as he turned and stared at me.

"Fuck Lenny, it was a joke. You're good, more than good; relax."

"So, you were being sarcastic because I'm driving slowly?" he asked, as he resumed his focus on the street ahead and pressed on the gas.

"I don't know Lenny, I just said it. I wasn't trying to be any-thing. It was more about your level of concentration."

"You should spend your time figuring out where I'm driving to, instead of making ill-timed comments that cause sudden reactions, which almost get us killed."

"At fifteen miles an hour it would be pretty hard for you to kill us; I think you might need a bridge."

"Do you have any idea where we are going, anyway?"

I sighed and thought about the question for a moment. I didn't have an answer so I decided to ignore Lenny for the time being. I turned around and checked on Nikki. I wasn't really concerned with her, but the tension created from our slow motion car crash needed some time to dissipate.

Nikki was doing just fine. She was sprawled out and staring at the roof of the car. One arm was raised straight into the air as if she was trying to grab onto something, while her other hand ambitiously twisted a small strand of hair. It was obvious that she was content, but for some reason, I felt a need to continue my investigation.

"How you doing back there, baby?" I asked as I reached over, and lightly touched her leg.

Nikki pushed my hand away. She then smiled without turning her head. She had no need for me at the moment. She also had no interest in being a pawn in my diversionary tactic. She was being blissfully engulfed by her manufactured reality and didn't want that tainted. I understood, but I had needs as well.

"Can you stop staring at me? It's creeping me out." Nikki asked, clearly annoyed with being interrupted.

"Really? It's creeping you out?" I asked, annoyed by the insinuation that I was a creep.

"Fine, you are annoying me. Is that better?"

"It's probably more accurate, but I don't know if it's any better."

She groaned and shook her head in frustration. I was interfering with her high, and she wanted me to go away. I decided it was probably in my best interest to turn my attention back to Lenny. "Did you ask me something earlier?"

"No, I can't recall asking you anything. Did I? Did I ask you something?" He asked, but he was questioning both himself and me. He then puckered his lips and shook his head no, relieving me of the stress of devising a plan. "If I did I have no idea."

His face tightened as he attempted to recall his previous request. I couldn't help but find irony in this situation. We overindulged on medication designed to treat attention deficit disorder, and here Lenny was, unable to remember a question that had been posed only moments ago. This paradox made me smile.

Out of the corner of his eye he recognized my amusement, which helped him relax.

"Did I ask if you have a plan for this night? Do we have a plan?"

"Shit, not really, but I can tell you one thing, this is the most comfortable I have ever been in this car. It's unbelievable; you could keep driving all night for all I care," I told him, as I again relaxed into my seat.

"Yeah, that's really more of a statement than a plan."

"The plan was to keep driving," I told him, as I motioned for him to refocus on the road ahead.

"Driving around aimlessly is hardly a plan. We should stop some place and clean you up; that face is barely presentable."

"Presentable? Where the fuck do you think we are going tonight?"

"See, if I knew the answer to that, then we wouldn't be having this conversation, would we?"

"You're a dick. And my face is fine," I told him, as I leaned forward and reached for the rearview mirror. I tilted it and I tried to examine my wounds, but the car was too dark. I thought about turning on the dome light, but I knew this wouldn't evoke a positive response.

"That face of yours begs questions, and knowing how much you enjoy conversations with complete strangers, I was thinking, maybe you'd want to do something to avoid that."

"Well then, there's your plan," I sarcastically responded, as I returned the mirror to its original position.

"Again, driving aimlessly, and fixing your face isn't really a plan. I mean the face-business; that should definitely be taken care of. The driving part; that's got to go and I'm hoping you have other ideas."

"You can be so condescending when you're high."

"Condescending? I'm just being honest. These aren't sustainable plans."

"That's not condescending? 'Sustainable', what is that? How about you shove your condescension up your ass, smart guy? How do you like that for sustainable?"

"Now you're just being silly; we both know what happens when things get shoved into people's asses and sustainable would be the last word that comes to mind," Lenny responded with complete sincerity.

"You're an idiot," I told him, trying not to laugh at his response or his demeanor. "I hope you realize that."

"This is your game. I can't help it if you insist on setting me up to win." When it came to vernacular, I was no match for Lenny and I knew it. He had once been an honor roll student. A scholarly future was in his destiny; that is before he met us. Now he was just an underachiever saddled with unrealized potential.

"Since you're always so fucking smart when you're high, why don't you be responsible for the plans tonight?"

"See, that's not my function in this relationship. I drive the car, that's what I do. You make the plan, that's what you do. I may offer suggestions or criticism, but ultimately, the responsibility rests solely on your shoulders, captain," Lenny calmly explained.

"Is that so?"

"It is and I know you are aware of it."

"What do I do?" Nikki interrupted from the back seat.

Lenny and I took a quick look backward and smiled. "You don't do shit. You're just cute; that's why we keep you around," I answered.

"Fuck you," she responded, with a small smile. She then turned her attention to Lenny.

"What do I do, Lenny?"

"I hate to admit it, but I think Jay nailed it."

"Seriously?" she asked; a little disturbed to learn about her uselessness.

"No, not seriously, you actually do a lot. I think your primary responsibility is to be a motivating factor. There have been plenty of times when Jay and I would have given up, but you never let us," Lenny explained, and I had to agree with him.

"I like it," Nikki responded, smiling brightly.

"I call bullshit on that one," I jokingly responded.

"You shut up and just make the plans. Do your job. It better be a good plan too 'cause you're not as cute or motivating as me."

I didn't have a plan. On most nights, this wasn't a question asked. Usually we would retreat to the comfortable sanctity of Lenny's room where we could turn down the lights and turn up the music. We would pull the covers up over our heads and hide if we desired, and we usually did.

"You are aware that it's Friday, right?" Lenny asked.

"Yes, Lenny, and that's exactly why I don't have a plan."

Most people spent all week anticipating this day. It represented the beginning of temporary parole from rigorous monotony, but for us Fridays were a hassle. We routinely found ourselves homeless; our sanctuary infected by the middle-aged, Jesus-freaks Lenny's mother would drag home with her after mass. They would play multiple games of Charades and Pictionary and laughter would fill Lenny's home until the late hours. It was an unbearable portrayal of pure happiness that we had to schedule our high around on a weekly basis.

"It's Jesus-freak night isn't it?" Nikki exclaimed loudly. "I hate those people, they make too much noise; happy noise. How is anyone supposed to enjoy a high with all that noise?" Nikki needlessly added from the back seat as she repositioned herself upright.

"I can't deal with that situation, it will totally ruin the way I feel right now."

"We know, Nikki," I told her.

"I don't even like being there when she is there. No offense Lenny, I just feel like she knows...like she can read it in my eyes and she hates me for it."

Nikki was right. Lenny's mother did know. She would stare at us like we were diseased rats crawling out from a dumpster every time she witnessed us leave Lenny's little cave. There was sadness in her face because she knew that there wasn't an exterminator equipped to deal with her infestation. Nikki and I had a hard time looking her in the eye, and we made a concerted effort to limit accidental meetings. Occasionally we would bump into her on our way out. Nothing would be said but she would deliver a fake, unconvincing smile, while silently begging us to stop contaminating her home. We were systematically removing her son's moral fiber and she was helpless. This devastating reality was a byproduct of circumstance. Her constant absence generated a form of anarchy, where our addiction thrived. Her powerlessness sent her running back to the church where she would search for solace in the warm smiles and comforting embraces of the Jesus-loving and God-fearing.

"Jay, seriously I can't, I really can't. You have to find a different place for us."

"Nikki, I know. Lenny and I feel the same way." I told her. I was slightly annoyed by her rambling but more concerned that if she continued, she might say something offensive.

"Fucking Friday night; why does it have to be Friday night?" Nikki exclaimed as she fell backwards in her seat.

"Well, she's definitely left by now." Lenny told us as he checked the clock. "It will be a little while before they are back. We could stop by, get a little higher, and fix that horrendous face of yours. It's not a plan with longevity but temporarily serves a purpose."

"The embryo of a plan."

"Please stop. You're just embarrassing yourself, and we don't have time for it." Lenny joked.

There was a small window of opportunity for us to go to Lenny's house, get me cleaned up, and figure out a solution. After mass, Lenny's mother and her friends would take their renewed faith and Jesus inspired smiles down to the local diner. They would remain there for just under an hour; basking in the love of their gracious Father, sip low-grade brown stimulants and enjoy the sugar buzz they got from the fried desserts. Once sufficiently high on sugar, caffeine, and the love of the Lord, they would depart the diner only to reconvene at Lenny's house.

"I don't even want to risk it all. Just seeing those freaks brings me down." Nikki admitted.

"What do you suggest Nikki?" I asked, irritated that she could complain about possible plans without offering any input.

"I don't know but there's got to be better place we can go."

78

Nikki's objection left us with few options. We could venture into the dysfunctional halls of her home. There was no real love or happiness in that house; in fact, there was rarely even eye contact. Most of time, we were treated like strangers passing through the lobby of a cheap hotel in the middle of nowhere; that's if you bumped into anyone at all.

Nikki's mother was terrorized by the notion of house guests. Regardless of age or significance, she would routinely isolate herself in the kitchen pretending to wash the same dish over and over until her hands resembled large prunes. Her strenuous attempt to avoid human contact was the result of a family history riddled with abuse; verbal, physical and sexual. Her failure to accomplish the most basic parental requirement had produced a constant state of shame and guilt. This made interacting with people an unbearable charade where her primary focus was the deciphering of nonverbal communication. This would help her assess the quantity of information the stranger was privy to. A simple clearing of the throat or wiping of the brow could send her running from the room convinced that the extent of her failures was known. She was a tortured, neurotic mess, but in my opinion, she deserved every second she lived in this psychological hell.

Whatever you thought of J Nikki's mother, you had to think less of her father. He was a predator, a piranha swimming through the waters of his children's adolescence; feeding off their weakness in the most depraved and gluttonous ways imaginable. Once his children had grown out of physical vulnerability, he had resorted to mental abuse for his own sick amusement. His torment was not only random, it was unwarranted and dispensed equally throughout the house; the only requirement was proximity. He had no shame about it either. On a few occasions, we had run into him while he was drunk, half-clothed and belligerent on the couch. He had mocked Lenny and my intentions with his daughter in such a vulgar obscene way that Lenny and Nikki had to restrain me and force me up the stairs.

If you believed that the Lord resided in Lenny's house then it was safe to say that Nikki's home housed the devil. I didn't care for God, but I personally had no issue with the devil. I figured if the devil was present then he was probably smacking his hands together in approval. Lenny disagreed with my attitude and had confided his distress. It wasn't just that he despised Nikki's family like I did, he hated the actual house. He could hear the skeletons in the closet, scratching and clawing on the doors; pushing and shoving in an attempt to be freed. Black figments roamed through the hallways, cackling loudly at him as he walked to the bathroom. He truly believed that there was a dark presence trapped inside and was afraid it would latch onto us because we were highly susceptible candidates for such an occurrence. My face would struggle to stay straight when he talked like this and he would become frustrated with me when I dismissed the idea as insane. It was the only explanation for the level of perversion that had occurred. I tried to understand his opinion, and I agreed with very minute pieces of it, but it didn't matter anyway. Nikki was uncomfortable in the situation, so we almost always bypassed this option.

Then there was my house, which was always a possibility; however, you couldn't say that it was devoid of dysfunction. My father was an ex-drunk, a lush that had decided to sober up prematurely as far as I was concerned. I didn't understand the decision. For most of my childhood my father had been a pleasant, functional alcoholic. He wouldn't always ask you how your day was and, occasionally, a dish might soar through the air and crash near you; but this was just to get your attention or emphasize a point. He very rarely aimed to kill, and unlike Nikki's dad, he had never raised a fist to my mother or me.

He was, however, very capable when it came to convincing other men to raise their fists against him. He had a big mouth, and sexual appetite, that seemed to focus on other people's meals??. It wasn't unusual to catch my father stumbling through the house at two thirty in the morning, nose busted up and bleeding, shirt covered in blood. There were times when he wouldn't make it home at all, leaving my mother to worry. On rare occasions, he wouldn't be alone when he arrived. These evenings could spiral out of control, but any violence would be between my mother and whatever poor drunken soul my father had manipulated. His involvement never exceeded peaceful interference and at this endeavor, he usually failed miserably. More often than not, my father and I would just watch in silent amusement as my mother ushered the unsuspecting woman from our home. Sadly, these were some of my favorite childhood memories. The scene always made for a good laugh between the two of us; although my mother never appreciated the pleasure we took in her aggravation.

"You see what you are teaching this kid?" She would scream at him.

"He's going to grow up to be an animal just like you are, I swear."

My father would stand and try to wrap his arms around her. "I'm sorry baby, I was drunk."

That was always his excuse and it never worked. He would end up sleeping on the couch, but in the morning she would be up cooking his breakfast and making his lunch. I loved my father, but I never understood why she put up with him. However, after watching Lenny's mom struggle, I realized there are always two sides to the coin, and it seemed that both of them usually sucked in some way or another.

My father had given up the booze a few years back. Like Lenny's mother, he had committed himself to a religious group. His new affiliation wasn't to an established religion with a recognized God. The organization didn't even have a designated meeting place; they assembled at rotating destinations. On Tuesday nights, his group would get together at the local Catholic Church. On Wednesday, they met at a synagogue in the neighboring town. On Friday nights, they congregated at the Masonic Temple. I only knew this because once a year, in March, I was forced to go there for his 'Birthday', even though he was born in October. The whole situation seemed suspect, and I doubted the legitimacy of my father's new way of life. The only place my father and his gang of pseudo-religious nomads congregated regularly was in our living room. Almost every night around ten, they'd arrive at my house. They would smoke cigarettes, drink coffee, and play cards. It was a strange crowd. There was little consistency among them. The only common thread I could find was that they were all ex-drunks; although, some of these quitters had done a lot more than consume whiskey and drink beer like my father. These men had lived. They had lived exciting lives and they loved to sit around playing cards reminiscing about a time when they had something to live for.

I had to admit, I did have admiration for these men and the way they had lived, especially the heroin addicts. They had the most intense stories. One man, in a desperate attempt to obtain a prescription for opiates, actually shot himself in the foot. I was amazed by this level of dedication, as well as extremely entertained when listening to the man as he relived the event from the couch in my living room. There was an abundance of stories like this one, none quite as good, but they all provided sufficient amusement on the nights when I found myself high and alone with nothing better to do than eavesdrop.

"Do you want to go to my house?" I asked, as I checked the clock.

It was still early and I knew my father might not be home yet. This would allow us time to sneak up to my room unnoticed. If we stayed quiet, there was a possibility that we could remain undetected. It wouldn't be a lot of fun, but at least my room could provide safe shelter.

"Really? You are proposing that we go get high at the sober clubhouse? Your father and his friends will love the entertainment, I'm sure. Maybe we can stop by the church first. See my mother and blow a few lines in the bathroom before heading over," Lenny responded with unappreciated sarcasm.

"I'm way too high to see your father and his friends. I wouldn't make it past the living room," Nikki added.

"They might not be there just yet."

"Yeah, it's possible that they may not be, but they most definitely will be. I can't endure the taunting and ridicule that is almost certain. Especially considering how obscenely hypocritical it is coming is coming from them," Lenny said, emphasizing his objection. "What's the next proposal, party planner?"

"Shit, Lenny, I don't know, your house and then the park?"

"I don't want to go to the park. It's too cold," Nikki said.

"The beach?"

"Seriously, Jay? If you are suggesting the beach right after I just told you that the park is too cold; I'm about to fire you," Nikki threatened.

"Jesus, Nikki, we are running out of options here."

"Someplace warm; that's all I'm asking."

"Fucking A&M then."

Lenny shook his head, "I don't want to go to A&M."

"Yeah, well, doesn't that just fucking figure," I exclaimed, and I wasn't joking. I was becoming frustrated by the ordeal.

"Damn my mother and those Jesus-freaks," Lenny added, shaking his head in disgust.

Java and Mushrooms

A&M Java was a melting pot filled to the brim and boiling over every Friday and Saturday night. This small coffee shop consisted of ten tables and twenty chairs, but couldn't contain the degenerates that frequented it on weekend nights. By nine o'clock, all the seats would be occupied, and people would begin sitting on the floor. By midnight, the store would be past capacity and resemble an overcrowded, underfunded, homeless shelter overrun by drunks. The store was an enigma, the only truly neutral oasis in our small town. No particular faction of teenage society held claim to the spot and all major social groups coexisted on a regular basis; yet they did so with minimal conflict. The rest of the town was split into several exclusive nooks and everyone knew what lines they could or couldn't cross.

Cranberry Park was our designated spot during the summer, fall, and spring. The park was conveniently located just across the city line, but far enough away from the judgment we found inside the borders of our town. The area was basically a parking lot and a large open field where ex-hippies and metal heads congregated to drink beer, smoke weed, and reminisce. The only interesting aspect was an enormous weeping-willow tree that sat in the middle of the lawn. It was a mystical looking tree. Its long branches stretched down to the earth, concealing a plethora of indiscretions. Stoners would sit motionless for hours in the green camouflage admiring the beauty of nature. Fake second-generation hippies, loaded on acid, climbed up and down the branches like confused little monkeys searching for a banana. Drunks lay face down, passed out on the dirt floor, sometimes next to their own vomit. We liked to perch high in the tree and look down on everyone, literally and figuratively. These seats also allowed us to poke our heads out of the top, check the parking lot and appease the waves of paranoia.

As the nights grew longer and the sun's influence on the day diminished, we were forced to abandon the park. The bitter cold left us only one real option, the strangely all-inclusive confines of the donut shop. If we remained quiet we could sit unnoticed in the corner of the store enjoying our highs until a better option presented itself.

"I can't believe this is our only option," Lenny muttered to himself, as he slowly maneuvered the car through the maze of people that were assembled in the parking lot. Lenny parked the car further away from the shop than necessary in an attempt to prolong the inevitable. After three agonizing groans and a brief moment of contemplation, we achieved a large enough measure of acceptance to unenthusiastically exit the car. We quickly weaved our way past the collections of cliques that were scattered about. As expected, nobody stopped us to say 'hello'. We found a few smiles, a nod here and there, but for the most part, our presence elicited no response.

As we entered the shop, I accidentally made eye contact with a stoner named Chase. He was sitting at the end of a long row of tables next to the bathroom. His face brightened with cheer, which ironically, forced the exact opposite reaction from me.

Over the years, his response to my arrival had become an annoying reoccurrence. His enthusiasm was partially based on the systematic removal of brain cells. I didn't care for Chase and I was blatant in this regard. Unfortunately, almost all of Chase's short-term memories floated away in clouds of pot smoke on a daily basis, and usually at someone else's expense. The kid was a leech, relentlessly sucking the blood out of past and present friendships.

"Fuck me, not even two minutes and there is already a situation to deal with," I exclaimed to no one in particular.

"Idiocy is always a possibility in this place. You lost the right to complain when you condemned us," Lenny whispered to me, as we watched Chase stand and take his first steps in our direction.

Chase's immediate reaction, and the half-eaten egg sandwich on the table, indicated that he was at the end of his high. Still, he wasn't sober enough to successfully maneuver his way past a young girl who was walking down the slim aisle to the bathroom. With a decent amount of force he barreled into the woman, then ricocheted off her and into the counter where he bumped into a row of neatly stacked paper cups. They tipped, fell, and hit the floor exploding; drawing the eyes of everyone around. Lenny and I immediately looked in the other direction, embarrassed to be part of this situation, but everyone else including Nikki, stared in judgment. Chase took no notice of this. He remained still for a moment to regain his composure, a process that didn't include an apology to the woman or to the employees that were now forced to clean up his mess. He dusted himself off, pulled his shirt tight, and then attempted to style his tangled curly hair. This was all in preparation for the hard sell that he was going to entice us with.

"Fuck this bullshit; I'm not dealing with that train wreck, have fun." Nikki told us, as she turned in the opposite direction and surveyed the room. Nikki would have been embarrassed to associate with Chase on a deserted island, with no ships for miles. Her plan was to kill three birds with one stone. By walking away now, she could procure her usual seat next to the large glass window, escape what she considered a mortifying public acknowledgement of Chase's existence, and avoid the absurdity of his imminent pitch. Lenny and I recognized her intent and nodded as if she had just asked for our blessing. Nikki in return smirked, letting us know she wasn't looking for an opinion. She then made her way to the front corner of the store, turned her back to the glass, and sat. This was her preferred spot. It allowed her to remain invisible to the primarily male assembly outside.

"I realize that you and this fool have a special relationship, but let's not get caught up in the nostalgia of a misspent youth," Lenny mocked me, as he stared at Chase.

"I'll do my best, Lenny."

Lenny disliked Chase almost as much as Nikki did. However, Lenny was never one to miss a chance to feel intellectually superior. Chase would undoubtedly offer an opportunity for this. His confident grin and smug look reminded me of a shifty car salesman with high hopes to unload some old clunker for far more than retail. I had been through his sales routine multiple times and I never drove away in that piece of crap, but he continued to push it on me.

"Sorry, Chase, I don't have any money or any weed for you. I'm broke and dry, so thank you, but no."

I told him before he actually reached us.

"That's fucked up," Chase responded as he took his final steps. "What's with the immediate beratlement? Can't an old friend just be excited to see an old friend?"

"That's not a word, Chase. Beratlement; it's not a word," Lenny enthusiastically added, as he shook his head. The smile on Lenny's face was in mocking appreciation for Chase's stupidity and because he wasn't going to have to wait to be argumentative.

"What?" Chase asked, as he squinted at Lenny. His face tightened as he thought about the comment. "I think you are wrong; it sounds like a word to me."

"I'm sure it does, but still, that doesn't change the fact that it is not a word or that you used your phony word incorrectly."

"You understood what I meant, didn't you?"

"Yes, and a grunt conveys a certain sentiment, but that doesn't make it a word."

"Why are you engaging in this?" I asked Lenny, even though I already knew the answer.

"Boredom, and a sense of intellectual superiority."

"Really? This is necessary? Would you like me to go find you an obese twelve-year-old girl to race across the parking lot for when you are finished?"

"Okay then, tell me, in your opinion, what defines a word?" Chase asked.

"In my opinion? I don't have an opinion, Chase; the diction-ary determines what qualifies as a word."

"Is that right?"

"Actually, Chase, it is."

"What about slang?"

"Slang is exactly that, slang, but there's an urban dictionary for it.

There is no dictionary for beratlement, none whatsoever."

"I don't think a word needs to be in the dictionary to be considered a word."

"Lenny, please," I begged, knowing that this could go on for minutes.

"You were right, and I've had my fill. I won't bother responding to that even though I really want to," Lenny told me as he turned and walked away.

"Jesus Christ, what did I do to him?"

"Don't worry about it Chase. Just understand that my pockets are light; I have nothing for you."

"I want to believe you, I really do, but something tells me that there might be a little bit of change in those pockets for something interesting?"

"Not even enough change for a chocolate frosted donut."

"I'm not talking donuts, but this will make you see sprinkles."

"Fucking stoners." I exclaimed while I rubbed my face in the hope that a genie would pop out and grant me a wish I could use to make him disappear.

"Just give me two minutes of a completely open mind, two minutes."

"Fine, two fucking minutes, but let's talk over there, I'm tired of standing."

I didn't wait for Chase to agree; instead, I made my way carefully down the aisle to Chase's table. Unfortunately, there was a young boy occupying it. In an attempt to prompt his departure I silently hovered over him and stared. He remained still for a moment in the hope that if he didn't acknowledge me I would give up, turn around, and leave.

"What the fuck?" He finally asked. I admired his childish bravery. He wasn't going to be bullied. He stiffened and remained focused, but he was overcompensating. My acute senses had detected a slight tremble in his voice. He maintained his stare, but he couldn't hide the fear in his eyes. He was a freshman right off the bus. He was new to the scene, on his first extended curfew and desperate to make an impression.

"You don't want to do this." I told him.

"Do what?"

"Just get the fuck out of my seat and we can pretend that this didn't just happen."

The boy hesitated for a moment. He glanced around the shop to make sure no one was going to witness his submission. He then took a final look upward to see if I was serious. I was. He realized this and decided to stand, but he made sure while doing so, that he didn't break eye contact. This angered me and I jerked towards him as if I wanted the situation to escalate.

"Do you have something else you need to say freshman?" I asked, forcing him to walk away with his head down.

I rarely played the role of the bully; my hundred and sixty-pound frame didn't afford me the opportunity. I had been in my share of altercations, but I couldn't call them fights. These scuffles almost always occurred when I was drunk and belligerent. I would verbalize an opinion about the roundness of an ass, and make a vulgar suggestion for the future. A boyfriend would then emerge and air his grievance. I would shrug off the complaint and continue. Ultimately, I would get punched in the face and, sometimes, more than once. The severity usually depended on the vividness of the details included in my intentions for future endeavors. On a few occasions, I had gotten a swing or two in, but I always ended up bloody and on my back, so it was hard to classify these encounters as legitimate fights.

"You've really become quite the dick," Chase told me, as he made his way to his seat.

"I saved some for you, be careful."

Chase smiled as he took his seat. He immediately leaned back in his chair like we were two old buddies that were about to be reacquainted. I didn't appreciate this. His decision to quietly relax was indicative of the blatant psychological game he was about to employ. His intention was to force me to initiate the conversation; assuming that I would inadvertently deceive myself and forget that I really had no interest in this discussion.

He was wrong, and I found his ruse insulting.

"Your two minutes started thirty seconds ago, so I'd stop fucking around if I were you."

"Alright, alright, relax. Jesus Christ, man." Chase replied as he put his seat down and inched towards me. "Here is the deal. I got this guy," he whispered. "He's meeting me 'round back.

He's got a bundle of mushrooms he wants to unload. I thought that might be something that you would be interested in."

I shook my head at Chase's proposition, not because I wasn't intrigued, because I was, but I knew it meant investing more time into this situation. These were valuable moments of my high, and I had just wasted a considerable amount of them unnecessarily avoiding what I assumed was going to be an idiotic proposal.

"Fuck man, why do you stoners insist on wasting so much God damn time getting to the point? Next time, just whisper in my ear, 'shrooms', don't even say 'hello'. I swear to God, we could have arrived at this point in the conversation ten minutes ago."

"Yeah, you're probably right, but we are here now. So what do you think?"

I sat quietly evaluating what was assuredly an offer with a hidden clause. It had been my experience that mushrooms and speed were a terrible combination. A fast-paced, distorted perception of reality wasn't a pleasurable high. The last time I made this mistake, I spent six hours sitting on the front steps with my head in my hands mumbling, "This is too much; this is too much". The entire world was painted in ultraviolet colors. Stable objects began twisting and turning, spinning and dancing.

They moved uncontrollably, changing color the entire time; a truly nauseating ordeal.

"Are you interested?" Chase asked again.

"I'm figuring that out, give me a second."

I was interested, but I didn't want Chase to know this. I shrugged my shoulders indicating my lack of excitement. Sure, in a few days from now it would be nice to have a bag of 'shrooms, but this transaction wasn't going to enhance my current circumstance making the show of ambivalence easy.

Besides, I hadn't yet heard the catch, which I was sure was coming now that he had my attention. "I guess I could be, but like usual, it depends on how hard you are going to try to fuck me on the deal."

"Fifty an eighth."

I laughed in his face, "Chase, please, Nikki doesn't even get to fuck me that hard. Fifty for an eighth? Should I give you the money and wait here while you go get it too? Sell that shit to some drunken cheerleader," I told him as I started to stand up.

"Alright, alright?" Chase said as he cracked a smile. "You can't blame me for trying. Thirty-five."

I stared at him for a minute before I sat back down. "What's your angle, Chase? Why do you need me in on this?"

"There is something I need."

"No shit, there always is."

"It's not a big deal, it's just I only have fifteen dollars. I was hoping we could split an eighth. You'd get the bigger cap, or stem, whichever you prefer."

I looked at him a little taken aback. For the first time in our (unfortunately) long history, Chase had actually made a reasonable request. I had assumed that he was going to say something along the lines of, 'I only have ten dollars can we split an eighth?' But this was respectable. This I could do, and not even mind doing.

"I can do that for you, Chase. I just need to make sure the other two don't mind me spending the money." I told him as I stood up.

"Really, you don't mind? I mean as long as you can get permission?" he asked in a somewhat mocking tone that annoyed me.

"Don't push it, Chase." I told him as I left and made my way over to Nikki and Lenny. Nikki was in her customary position, focused on a group of young girls who were sitting at the table next to her. This was how she amused herself. For hours, she could contentedly deliver a stare so heavily laced with disgust that it even made me squirm. Occasionally, she would feel the need to emphasize this glare with a mocking grunt or exasperated sigh, but this only happened in response to comments she found exceptionally stupid. The young girls would fidget nervously; their postures would stiffen while they tenuously attempted to sneak-a-peak at their accuser.

Lenny on the other hand, was unaware of anything happening inside the coffee shop. He was staring out of the window at the clusters of people congregated outside as if wolves had raised him and human interaction baffled him. As far as I could see there was nothing of real interest going on out there, but he was content. His preoccupation was so engulfing, he barely acknowledged me when I took a seat next to him. There was short moment of acknowledgement, but then he refocused and forgot about my existence.

"Listen to this shit. These two girls are really onto something. Did you know that there is an 'emotional Armageddon' happening right now in this country?" Nikki asked loudly.

"No, I was not aware of that Nikki."

"The fat girl, wait, they are all fat; so that doesn't really distinguish any of them. The one with the stupid bow in her hair that is supposed to distract me from the fact that she is fat and eating multiple donuts; well, she is really smart, it's amazing."

I turned and looked at the group of girls. Nikki's words had frozen them stiff. "Jesus, Nikki, can you forget about them for a minute? I need to talk to you."

"I just love it when people speak in psychological jargon. It's so interesting. I especially love it when they do it in public. I feel like I'm being educated."

Nikki then simulated the act of vomiting. Her loud exclamation point seemed to bounce off the table, hit the walls, and grab everyone's attention around us. The spinning heads pushed my focus away from our table. For a brief moment I had to pretend that Nikki was just some crazy lady I had happened to sit down across from. I wasn't interested in causing the girls any more grief then they had already endured. I had more important matters to discuss anyway, but now I had to wait until all eyes returned to their original positions.

"Listen, just forget about them for a second and look at me," I requested, even though my focus hadn't fully returned to the table. I waited another minute for her to surrender voluntarily.

She of course didn't, so I had to turn, grab her arms and pull her from her focus. She wasn't happy about the interruption and her judgmental glare landed on me. "Don't look at me like that; I'm not fat and I'm not wearing a bow."

I continued to pull her arms straight. She wiggled for a brief second, but finally she leaned forward and turned her head so I could whisper my proposal in her ear. She wasted no time considering it. She shrugged her shoulders, rolled her eyes, and then pulled herself free from my grasp. She refocused on the girls, letting me know that this issue didn't warrant a conversation.

It wasn't quite the reaction I was hoping for but I didn't consider her disinterest an objection. I took a quick look over at Lenny. He was still gazing out the window trying to understand the humans. I decided not to bother him. I was confident his reaction would be the opposite of Nikki's. Lenny loved distorting his perception. 'Shrooms were also a natural entity. God had made them, according to Lenny, and he must have done so for our pleasure.

As I stood up, Nikki shifted her focus. "Make it quick; don't fuck around with that idiot," she ordered. I nodded hesitantly, knowing that situations of this nature were never quick.

I turned and waved Chase forward. He jumped out of his seat and hurried his way down the aisle. We exited the store and made a hard right, cutting in front of the large glass window.

Lenny caught a glimpse of Chase and me walking together and his back straightened. He frowned liked a small child too short to get on the amusement park ride. I shook my head slightly, while puckering my face, fully explaining that this moment was not about two old schoolyard chums reuniting for a final night of glory.

Chase and I took another right, down the alley next to the store. A gust of cool night air, funneling between the buildings, slapped me in the face, widening my eyes and nostrils. A slight slant in the path caused our pace to quicken. My feet pounded against pavement while my heart raced to keep up. I felt like a caged animal, finally freed and trampling across open space. We hit the conjoining alley and took another right into a small parking lot. This was the stoner's spot. They would sit back here on milk crates, next to an old dumpster that stunk of rotten milk, and smoke enough weed to disregard the fowl stench and pathetic scene.

When we arrived, there were two men sitting on milk crates, leaning against the dumpster, enjoying the back alley scene. Gary Stine, who everyone knew simply as 'Stine', was one of them.

The repulsion I felt towards this man rivaled that of the old milk stink. He came from a good family of considerable wealth and was well-educated, but he spoke and dressed like an illiterate bowery bum. His usual apparel smelled as if it rarely saw the washing machine, consisted of ripped, out-of-style stonewashed jeans, a faded heavy metal band t-shirt, and beat-up high top tennis shoes. He wouldn't say much, but when he did speak, he was always vulgar and offensive.

The other kid was Derek Proper. Life dealt this kid a short deck of low cards. At eighteen he was already balding significantly. He had the face of a pug; his intellect and personality didn't make up for these deficiencies. I didn't like the kid much. However, his enthusiasm in regards to my presence made it hard to completely hate him. I just wished he wasn't so hard to look at.

"Jay Jay, where you been kid?" Derek shouted out, as we approached.

His voice was like fingernails on a chalkboard. My back tightened, my shoulders raised, and the sense of freedom I had previously enjoyed evaporated. I considered turning and walking in the other direction. If I spun fast and walked even faster, my arrival would be forgotten, just a figment of their imagination. Even if it was pondered and they felt slighted, their feelings weren't really a concern. It was a difficult decision. The agony of meaningless conversation and faked interests was looming if I remained.

"Fuck it," I told myself quietly as I stepped over to the men.

I shook both their hands and faked a smile. I then took a large step backwards and tilted my head upwards in an effort to clear myself of the dumpster's stink. My attempt failed. A thick cloud of sour milk stench created walls around me so there was no escape. I wondered if there was actually a weed plant potent enough to facilitate the disregard of this intolerable situation.

"How you have guys been?"

"Good man, real good," Derek, answered, as he pointed at Stine. "Gary and I, we started a new band. It's a hardcore, heavy metal band; it's good shit. Stine's drums are really coming along, and we got this kick ass singer named Trevis. That's a cool ass name for a lead singer of a band, don't you think?"

I opened my mouth but nothing came out. I had no interest in hearing about another band they had started. So instead of faking an enthusiastic response, I simply turned my attention to Stine and nodded in appreciation for the skills I was positive that he didn't possess. He returned the pleasantry, but he knew how little I thought of him. His feelings were mutual, founded on somewhat substantial reasoning. In a drunken stupor, I had accidentally had sex with someone he was dating.

This girl's legs split for a warm breeze, but for some reason he held me responsible for an incident that I barely remembered.

"You smoke these days?" Stine asked, as he produced a miniature bong.

"No, I'm good," I told him.

I didn't need a hit of weed. I needed a snort, clean air, and a situation that didn't include two men foaming at the mouth like rabid dogs while watching a bowl get packed. This was hard to witness. Derek's eyes were bulging, his left foot tapped lightly in anticipation. Chase licked his lips repeatedly while refusing to blink. My stomach was now turning, and not just from the stench which was burning my eyes and nostrils. Lenny and I were attentive while observing the proficiency Nikki displayed while pulverizing large pills, but we didn't resemble pigs waiting by the feeding trough like these guys.

The sound of rapidly approaching footsteps echoing off the side of the building interrupted my thoughts.

I turned nervously expecting another unfortunate surprise. A smile pushed my cheeks high as I realized the person barreling toward me was Jesse Martin. He was an old friend, and an important guide in my formative years. He taught me the differences between prescription drugs. ADD meds are great; prescription weight loss pills are good; anything that ends in -icillin is worthless; and scripts that claim to cause drowsiness are always worth a shot, but be careful.

These were rules to live by. I was happy to see him. He offered a welcome distraction and possibly an option that might relieve me of the donut shop boredom for the night.

"Yo, yo," Jesse yelled, as he headed straight for me.

He gave me a handshake and half of a hug. He then turned and eyeballed the other three, but didn't bother with formalities. I appreciated that about Jesse. He stood about five foot five and wasn't scared of anyone. He didn't pretend he liked you if he didn't, and he wasn't concerned if you were six feet plus and demanding acknowledgement.

"Is this really happening, or are you three just back here jerking each other off like usual?" he asked.

He walked straight over to Chase, snatched the bong out of his hand, and pushed him to the side.

Chase hadn't smoked his turn yet and Jesse didn't care. Chase's face tightened. His eyes popped and focused intently on Jesse as he inhaled a large load. Jesse then handed the bong back to Stine.

"So, what's up with you, son?" he asked, turning his attention. I started to answer, but he interrupted me. "Who let you out of the cave tonight? Where's your little sidekick?"

"Which one?"

"Shit, does it matter? I'm surprised to see any of you trolls out in public. Anti-social mother-fuckers."

Jesse was a party kid. He loved the scene and he didn't care whose scene it was, as long as there was the potential for a good time. He moved from group to group without being hassled, even though his appetite for drugs was known. I attributed this to his size since it definitely wasn't his attitude. He was an arrogant little prick and he had no qualms discussing his opinion of you, yet people tolerated him. The majority would hand him a beer and raise a glass upon his arrival.

"Let's talk over here, away from these fuck-heads," Jesse suggested, as he grabbed my arm and led me away. "You holding anything good tonight?"

Jesse was the only person that would get an honest answer from me. I knew if he was asking, he was doing so with fair intentions. As far as the rest of the scene was concerned, I was never holding and always high. On occasion, I might develop certain needs, forcing me to deal with these people.

It would amount to nothing more than a frustratingly juvenile negotiation where eliciting equal compensation inevitably resulted in a futile charade. Jesse didn't play this game. If you were holding and he desired, he would overpay for the favor.

"I got some Dexies on me."

"Really?" he shook his head in disappointment. "Shit, I was hoping you had some Codeine or Percs. I'm looking for a soft lay down. You know what I mean?" He paused, cocked his head, and stared straight into my eyes for a moment. "You could use a soft lay down yourself. What day are you on anyway, kid? It looks to me that you haven't slept in at least two."

"Day three actually, but who's counting."

Jesse shook his head. "You three are fucking nuts, you know that right?"

"That's what they tell me."

"I hate to ask this, 'cause I know you're going to say 'yes', but I got to do it." He paused, reconsidered and then continued. "You want a boost?"

"A boost, huh? What are we talking, coke?"

"What else?"

"What's the price?" I asked, hoping that he was trying to sell.

"Come on, man, you know me; when am I ever looking for cash?

Speed for speed, a fair and beneficial trade for all."

"Fuck, I was hoping you wanted my money and not my good shit."

Monetarily, this trade was a fairly easy decision. Cocaine was expensive. My speed was stolen. However, cocaine was sold on every street corner in the ghetto. People held onto their Dexedrine prescription with closed fists. It could be months before I stumbled upon another bottle like this. The high I was on right now was steady and required a snort here and there to maintain.

Cocaine was time consuming. The high it produced was amazing, but only lasted twenty or so minutes, so it took some work to sustain the feeling. The low was my biggest concern. Cocaine produced a craving that reduced people to the likes of zombies, seeking to feed a hunger that could only be satisfied by more.

"You know I want to and should say no."

"A hundred mils per twenty-bag?"

"Damn."

I exhaled hard and shook my head as I considered the factors. This was a standard trade and there was no point in trading if you just came out even. Normally, I wouldn't have considered this exchange. The infrequent availability made relinquishing a hundred mils for a twenty bag of anything, even cocaine, a stomach-turning proposition. I considered renegotiating, then determined that it was counterproductive to insult a friend, especially one that was a decent source.

"How many bags are you trying to get rid of? At least two, I hope." I was dissatisfied with the even swap and bothered by the inevitable consequences. I decided if I was going to do it, I might as well do it right. I knew one bag wasn't sufficient, two bags weren't really either, but it was a good start.

"That's perfect; I have two," he answered, as he pulled the bags from his pocket.

Out of the corner of my eye, I saw the potheads squirm and then stand to get a better view. I turned slightly and looked. Jesse noticed my reaction and quickly spun ninety degrees. He took a few steps forward and stared at them down until they diverted their attention.

"Take a seat, this doesn't concern you," Jesse ordered and they obliged.

"You got them trained like dogs."

"That's insulting to dogs."

I smiled and then took another glance over at the idiots to double check their obedience. They were making a conscious effort to hide their curiosity and focus their attention elsewhere. I was grateful for this; it alleviated my paranoia. I removed my shoe as I always kept my stash underneath the sole of my left shoe. Accessing it was a bit of a hassle and it made people, like Jesse, cringe, but I felt secure that it could survive a routine pat down by authorities. Your average drug consumer would rather store their goods in an easily assessable place; this way, if the blue and red lights flashed they could ditch their stash in a pinch.

"Fuck man, toe speed? The price just went up."

"I'm clean."

"Man... You don't even sleep, so I know you aren't showering. You and that fucking shoe, I know I never taught you that."

We finished the transaction then Jesse turned his attention back to the three stoners who were pressed against the wall waiting for permission to move. Jesse wasn't going to permit this. He was frustrated by the waste of time, now that he acquired goods from me, he was anxious to go enhance his high.

"So, what the fuck? Is this shit happening or did you assholes just drag me down here to sit by a fucking dumpster and inhale rotten milk stench?"

I watched them squirm. Their eyes shifted to avoid contact. They were hoping and praying that they hadn't initiated a situation that would never come to fruition. Jesse stared, waiting for an answer. It finally came in the form of two headlights slowly approaching.

"Is this it?" Jesse asked, but he got no response.

The car's slow approach made me somewhat uncomfortable; I figured that it was the connection checking the scene. There were five people, more than there should ever be at a meet, but I imagined that anyone who sold mushrooms to potheads on a regular basis would have become accustomed to situations such as these.

"Something is fucked up here," Jesse remarked, which forced me to reevaluate my assessment.

We continued to stare into the blinding lights of the car. It continued to roll slowly down the alley. The unusual brightness hindered my ability to accurately assess the situation and I could see trepidation in Jesse's face. This made me nervous. I trusted Jesse's instinct; if he was worried, so was I.

"No, fuck this," Jesse exclaimed.

Jesse turned to run, but before he made his first steps a spotlight hit us. The blue and red lights started flashing and the doors to the car swung open. Two men jumped out with guns drawn.

They seemed to aim them directly at me and only me. My body went stiff and my feet sunk into the concrete. The wheels in my brain began to spin. The trade that Jesse and I just made magnified the intensity and I could feel the handcuffs tightening around my wrists. "Do not move; put your hands in the fucking air!" two voices shouted in unison. "Fucking potheads," I muttered to myself as I raised both hands into the air.

"Don't you fucking move; stand fucking still; put your hands in the air" one of the cops screamed again.

"How can I not move and put my hands in the air." Jesse whispered to me as he smiled. I was glad he was finding this amusing.

It was an unnecessary and contradictory request. The initial shock of a gun being pointed at you will guarantee your stillness for a moment. I couldn't move, and after assessing the situation, I decided it was bad. Holding Dexedrine would raise questions, especially when the name on the bottle was Elaine Gould. Cocaine meant I just won a trip straight to a cell. No questions would be asked, no explanations would be taken into consideration and charges would be immediately filed.

"What the fuck are you doing back here?" one of the cops asked as he slowly inched his way toward us.

The other officer remained behind the car. Both men were rotating the aim of their guns from person to person, keeping us paralyzed for the moment.

"What are you kids doing back here?" the officer standing behind the car repeated.

No one answered. We were all working on the same equation. There were two cops and five druggies and how can this equal freedom. That's all I cared about. The one constant that we all agreed on was that these cops weren't going to shoot a local teenager running down the alley behind A&M Java. No matter what was making our pockets heavy, a dead white kid was an unacceptable headline for our town's paper. If I made the decision to run, it didn't seem practical that the officers would sacrifice a four-person arrest for one, unless they assumed that I was running because I was the heaviest bust. There was no reason for them to believe that, so they would probably hold steady.

There was a variable in this scenario that had to be considered. The decision to flee may incite mayhem. It was unlikely, but possible, that if I ran, the others may split in opposing directions.

The cops would be forced to pursue. They would be aggressive in their chase, and as the instigator of this pandemonium, I would be made the focal point. I didn't like that outcome.

The advancing cop seemed to realize that we were all doing the same calculation and questioning his ability to contain the situation. His eyes were wide. He rapidly shifted his focus in an attempt to maintain order. He sped up his approach and, for some reason, it led straight to Stine. His judgment was based solely on appearance, and by these standards it was plausible that Stine was the heaviest bust.

"None of you fucking move," the cop shouted as he made his way past Jesse and me.

The cop grabbed Stine by the hair and dragged him past us. He threw him onto the hood of the car and kicked his legs apart. Stine became angry and tried to stand. The cop again grabbed him by the hair and slammed him back down, where Stine's face hit the car.

"Don't you fucking move," he yelled at the back of Stine's head. He then did a half turn, shooting Jesse and me a glare. "Don't even think about fucking moving, you little pieces of shit."

He turned his attention back to Stine and squatted. He began patting Stine's leg. Halfway up he found something of interest and stopped. Stine was done, and he knew it, so like a desperate donkey fighting to avoid restraints he bucked wildly. He struck the cop right under the chin with his right heel. The unexpected blow knocked him backward, flat onto his back. His head continued and slammed hard enough against the pavement to echo loudly. His eyes shut, thus reducing the cops in the equation to one. Stine wasted no time taking advantage of the situation; he bolted down the alley. The officer standing behind the car followed Stine.

Jesse and I didn't pause to consider our options. In unison, we ran up the hill to the donut shop, leaving Chase and Derek behind. Every man for themselves was an acceptable decision. Besides, I didn't care what happened to them, I was free for the moment and I wanted to remain that way.

We made it back up to the store, but we knew better than to stop. I paused briefly to knock on the store window. Once I established eye contact with Nikki and my dilemma was conveyed, I retreated to Jesse's car. Before I could get both legs in, Jesse was buckled into his seat, had the key in the ignition, and the car was moving in reverse. I closed my door and Jesse shifted into drive and hit the gas.

We didn't make it far before Jesse was forced to slam on the brakes. Small clusters of people scattered about served as an obstruction delaying our departure. We couldn't afford this; in no time, this place was going to be crawling with little pigs searching for the big feast.

"Drunk fuckers, move!" Jesse pressed on his horn. This startled the people within the small crowds. At first they stared angrily, but after Jesse laid on the horn for the third time, they began to comprehend the sense of urgency. Hesitantly, the crowds dispersed, and we were able to finagle a path. Our progression didn't last long. Before I could relax and exhale, a drunken imbecile appeared from out of the darkness. His sudden emergence forced Jesse to slam on the brakes and I reclaimed the sigh of relief I was about to emit.

"Mother-fucker, I don't need this." Jesse screamed as he tried to wave the man out of our way.

Jesse laid on the horn. The man reacted by hammering the car with closed fists. This angered Jesse and he slightly touched the gas pedal. I appreciated this. The man didn't. He stumbled backward several feet. Jesse wasted no time. He took advantage of the space. He made a sharp left turn, ignoring the curb. We hit it hard then bounced up and over it; unfortunately, Jesse had forgotten about the steep grassy decline located just beyond.

"Fuck!" Jesse screamed, as he realized the extent of the downward slope.

Jesse slammed on the brakes; a pointless, reactive response. We slid to the bottom of the hill, skidded over the sidewalk and bounced onto the street. Luckily, the blue and red lights hadn't arrived in time to witness this. Jesse took a quick right onto Route 7. This was followed by an immediate sharp left turn through a red light. He had an agenda, and that agenda was Cranberry Park. It was an obvious decision. The park was located across an invisible line that determined police jurisdiction. Unfortunately, it was located at the top of a long and curvy street, which we would be traveling on at a high rate of speed with little light.

Cranberry Park

I sat in the passenger seat. The roar of the engine shook my hands, which clung to the side of my seat as if it were a life preserver. Jesse's foot pressed the pedal hard against the floor. He held a tight grasp on the wheel as he achieved an excessive speed. I tried to close my eyes and ignore my imminent death, but each time the car slid into the opposing lane and touched the grass on the other side of the road, they would involuntarily pop open to investigate.

"Yo man, I think we are cool. No one is chasing us. You can slow down."

Jesse had no interest in slowing down. He was scared and overestimating his ability to safely maneuver the car. We bounced back and forth across the street like a pinball ricocheting off the side bumpers, applying the brakes only when the overgrown brush and shrubbery scraped paint. I winced as the hard pavement turned to soft gravel. The long arms of the tall trees reached out and swatted at the car every time we lost the road and tore up the grass. My legs would stiffen and brace for impact as we approached each mailbox. My jaw would then drop as I watched them pass by just inches away from my window.

"Yo, yo, yo," I screamed, realizing that the street was coming to an abrupt end.

Jesse straightened his arms and slammed on the brake with both feet. We began to skid. We hit the adjacent street and a small dip, which launched the car into the air. The conjoining road was suddenly inches below as we soared into the entrance-way of Cranberry Park. A large patch of loose gravel served as an insufficient landing pad and our flight turned into a slide. Jesse spun the wheel to the left, but a thick, and unavoidable concrete barrier that guarded visitors from idiots engaged in imaginary pursuits, was rapidly approaching.

My eyes closed tight and I began asking for forgiveness and making apologies for a life of opportunities squandered. I made peace with a God that I was willing to call upon, but not willing to admit that I believed in. I even resorted to lofty promises of a revised lifestyle. A loud crash interrupted my rebirth. I now imagined death sprawled out on the front of the car. A bloody body, an innocent enjoying a casual stroll through the park, was now a mangled hood ornament.

The car came to an abrupt stop, but I didn't. The sudden halt launched me out of my seat. My knees indented the leather dash and my face crashed into the cool glass, wedging my chest between the two. A loud exasperated gasp opened my eyes. I pushed myself backwards and into my seat. I turned and looked at Jesse. He was dazed.

"What? What'd we hit?" I asked, refusing to turn and look.

I remained focused on Jesse's facial expression. He remained stiff and wide-eyed until, finally, he shrugged his shoulders and coughed out a peculiar laugh. I relaxed, exhaled, and found the courage to turn and look. A demolished barrel of trash was wedged between our bumper and the concrete wall. It cushioned our impact and possibly saved our lives. I chuckled loudly and then started renegotiating my contract with God, making deductions and adding clauses.

I expected Jesse to mimic my amusement or at least relax a little, but his arms were still flexed and his grasp remained tight on the wheel as he was focused on the steel can. He was engaged in morbid reflection, imagining the possibilities that included our death. I had made lofty promises before the end result of the crash was determined. It was an involuntary reaction based on the possibility of my own demise. Rehashing, questioning, and evaluating what might have happened was an unacceptable, idiotic endeavor that could only result in an unnecessary conclusion.

"We are here!" I shouted.

"Fuck, I guess we are."

Jesse reached down and put the car in reverse. He slowly backed away from the wall. The trashcan was dead but the car seemed ok, except for a slight crinkle in the hood and a bent bumper. We took the left we meant to take initially and parked in the first available spot. "You okay?" I asked.

"I'm fine, I guess."

We exited the car and Jesse made his way to the front to examine the damage. I stood silently glancing around the park. His concern was obvious, but I was more worried about our loud arrival.

There was a group of men standing around a small fire with beers in their hands. Their eyes were intently focused and looking for an explanation. Apparently, they weren't drunk enough to disregard a vehicle soaring a few feet above ground and crashing into a wall like I had hoped.

"Yo man, that was fucking awesome," someone shouted from the small group.

"Fuck me," I muttered.

Two men, who couldn't contain their enthusiasm, broke from the pack and began to approach. I cringed and looked over at Jesse, hoping he would intervene. He was on a knee, playing with the bumper of the car and unaware of the evolving situation. I was about to be congratulated for his misjudgments and I didn't want the credit. I opened my mouth, about to yell for him, when an angry voice shouting my name interrupted.

I turned and was greeted by four knuckles. They landed just underneath my chin. My head jerked backwards. I stared at the stars, wondering if this was recompense for the earlier promises I had every intention of betraying. A second tightly-closed fist struck me in the cheek, splitting the skin. The final shot landed directly on my temple. My knees buckled and the world went black as I felt myself falling. I bounced off the ground and covered my head with my arms. Remaining still and playing dead, I hoped that the attacking bear would lose interest.

After a few minutes of stillness, I uncovered and opened my eyes. Jesse and our two new friends were struggling to escort an infuriated young man away. His name was Kevin Kovacs and he was trying to settle a debt that I created years ago. By the look of determination still in his eyes, it was apparent that three blows to my head weren't sufficient payment. It was three against one, but he wasn't giving up. He shook free from the men's grasp, then faked calm just long enough for his captors to relax slightly; then he charged like a bull towards a matador, in an attempt to break the barrier they created. I stood up and watched as it took all three to restrain him again.

"How'd it feel, you little punk-ass bitch?" Kevin screamed as the men pushed him backwards.

Kevin glared at me, obviously waiting for an answer to a question that seemed somewhat self-explanatory. However, the scowl on his face and his tightly closed fists explained that he desired a response

more complex than "not good." The dissatisfaction in his glance hadn't diminished. He would charge again and again if I didn't satisfy his desire for due acknowledgement.

"I'm not going to lie; you got me good, and it hurts, bad. I'm thinking that we are more than even," I told him, as I spat out a small amount of blood.

"Fuck you," Kevin responded, but after a short moment of consideration, he finally turned and stormed in the other direction.

Jesse and the guys watched Kevin carefully, making sure that this wasn't another ploy, before they turned and came my direction. They were smiling and obviously proud of their accomplishment.

There were now an abundance of topics for these men to discuss and I shuttered at the possible length of conversation it would take to cover the events. My gratitude for their assistance was quickly evaporating, and being replaced with contempt. It took a pronounced ignorance to watch a man almost die, get his face pulverized, then think that he might want to relive the ordeal for entertainment purposes.

"Fuck man, you okay?" Jesse yelled.

I didn't answer, but I made sure that I initiated eye contact, and sent a nod of appreciation to each person prior to arrival. As they drew closer, I extended my arm. I hoped that a handshake would be adequate. I desperately wanted to get on with the night without a discussion. "Fucking Kevin Kovacs," Jesse concurred.

"Yeah, no shit. Thanks for the update."

The curtness of my response wasn't meant to offend Jesse like his face suggested I had. These men begrudgingly accepted my silent offer of appreciation. I could see the curiosity in their eyes, but it seemed they weren't going to prod me for details. Jesse was trying to engage me in a conversation that was avoidable and he needed to shut his mouth.

"Wasn't that whole thing like four years ago?"

"Seriously man, my head hurts, and I don't want to talk about this, but yeah, it was a while ago."

Three years prior I broke his brother's nose in the middle of gym class. I had no real explanation. Being slightly drunk, but not drunk enough, made me irritable I guess. I demanded that he pass me a ball. He refused. His refusal enraged me and I commenced a quick-paced, single-focused approach. I didn't have a violent reputation, so he didn't even bother to assume a fighting stance. I insisted again and he repeated his refusal. Then I lunged. The knuckle of my middle finger landed flat on the bridge of his nose. A snap echoed, and blood flowed from both nostrils, to mouth, to chin, and finally, the floor. The two of us stood in shock of what just happened. Girls began screaming and the boys remained still and wide-eyed. The teacher rushed me to the principal's office and I was asked not to return to that school, while he went to the hospital to fix an already ugly face.

Lenny's Cutlass suddenly appeared, interrupting my recollection of the day. The car bounced into the parking lot and came to an abrupt halt. Nikki and Lenny jumped out. They casually walked over with inquisitive looks on their faces. They were expecting a re-enactment of our unplanned departure; however, the swelling of my face took precedence. Nikki hastily grabbed my chin. The contact made me wince and I involuntarily jerked my head away.

"Baby come on, easy with that."

"Jesus Christ, Jay, you can't catch a break can you?" she asked.

"If you can get me the fuck out of this situation, that's the only break I need," I told her, as I turned to Jesse. "Yo, do you want to come with us?"

"Where?" Jesse asked.

I looked over at Lenny's car. Jesse shrugged his shoulders and turned his attention to the two men. I followed his lead. I shook their hands again, but still remained quiet. Jesse glared at me. He expected some gratitude. I disagreed. These men upheld a civic duty and that didn't warrant a ceremony or the pinning of a medal. They got a nod and several handshakes, but in the interest of time and my high, I decided to oblige.

"Gentlemen, thank you for your help, maybe at a later date we can share a beer and relive these moments."

"Really?" Jesse responded, suggesting that my gratitude was insufficient.

"Can we do this please?" I asked him.

"Yo guys, thanks for your help earlier, really, it's appreciated. Don't mind this fucking prick, he's not right on a good day," Jesse told the men.

"You fucking done?" I asked.

"Yeah, I'm fucking done."

We abandoned the good Samaritans, and retreated to the sanctity of the Cutlass. I established eye contact with Nikki and tried to convey that there were motives behind my invitation to Jesse.

Nikki was extremely selective in regards to new admissions. Her expressionless response and slight shake of the head informed me that she wasn't happy.

"Where do you want me?" Jesse asked as he opened the front passenger side door.

"That works, you are our guest."

"Now you decided to be cordial?" Jesse asked, as he got in and shut the door. Nikki shot me a look from across the roof of the car. I nodded, acknowledging my understanding of the probationary period she had established for visitors. Jesse had just been rude, which wasn't a cause for immediate expulsion, but it wasn't a good start. Her tolerance was conditional. The ability to obey her rules determined the length of stay. Unfortunately for our guests, Nikki was the only one privy to the guidelines. As far as Lenny and I knew, there were a variety of offenses that one might commit which would cause removal. When it happened, Nikki would make a motion and they would be tossed to the curb, it didn't matter if that curb was lining an unmarked street in the middle of the ghetto. We left people stranded in some precarious places and there were times we didn't even know why; and we didn't really care.

"Fuck, I feel like shit" I said while taking my seat in the back.

Jesse turned and stared at me. He shook his head, and then asked,

"Why do you got to be such a stubborn prick? Those guys saved your ass."

"Should I have blown them?"

"A genuine 'thank you' would have done it. Have you ever thought that maybe if you weren't such a dick, people would stop punching you in the face?"

"It's something to consider, but it doesn't change the fact that right now I feel like shit."

"You just had your face tenderized. You're supposed to feel like shit," he told me, which was an obvious statement, but ironically, my internal discomfort far exceeded the external.

"What are you thinking?" I asked, directing the question to Jesse. "I'm definitely thinking powder over pills," I replied, answering my own question.

"Powder? I thought you were getting 'shrooms?" Nikki asked.

"No baby, it didn't work out."

"Oh, that's too bad," Nikki sarcastically added, while smiling.

"This is how I figure it. You throw me two more of those magical capsules you're holding and then we can cut four fat lines from three bags. That ought to straighten us out real nice," Jesse proposed.

I started doing the math in my head. We had two bags and three people; this meant we would each receive a little over thirteen dollars of cocaine. If we included Jesse and a fourth bag, our allotment would be fifteen dollars' worth. The street value of Dexedrine was five dollars a pill. We were receiving six dollars of cocaine for ten dollars of speed. This was a sucker's deal.

"I'm not exactly sure why we are wasting time bartering. This all seems reasonable; can we get on with it?" Lenny asked excitedly.

"Pay up then, if you're in a rush" I told him. "I'm eight fucking deep on this one already."

My attack was unwarranted and it surprised not only me, but everyone in the car as well. A deafening quiet emphasized this discomfort. Lenny's head hung in embarrassment. Oblivious to the details of the preceding transaction, he was overly excited. I thoughtlessly trampled an innocent moment of childish jubilance and I felt ashamed. Nikki accurately read my face and Lenny's posture then unexpectedly interrupted the awkwardness by reaching into her bra and retrieving her stash.

"Fuck, enough with this bullshit. Lenny…" Nikki yelled, as she handed Jesse two pills. "Jay is sorry he yelled at you; get over it. He just got punched in the head."

"Okay." Lenny answered, but he was still unwilling to turn his head.

"Jay, you can't be a dick to Lenny, just 'cause you got punched in the head."

"You're right, I'm sorry." I admitted while looking directly at him. He finally turned, our eyes met and he sent me a slight nod letting me know I was forgiven.

Jesse was confused by the situation and didn't know where to look. He continued to glance nervously through the back window, waiting for someone to acknowledge the transaction and tell him to proceed. Nikki placed her hand on his shoulder, leaned over him, and into the front seat. She opened the glove box and sat back down. We all waited patiently for Jesse to continue. It took him a minute to figure out what we wanted him to do. He finally saw and pulled out a small mirror we had hidden. He stared at it with mixed emotions.

"What? Did you think we would be snorting off an old beat-up owner's manual?"

"You fuckers are too much."

"Flip it over."

Jesse turned the mirror over and found a razor blade and a straw securely attached to the back. My eyebrows rose as he turned and looked at me. There should have been a merit badge awarded for this type of preparation. Jesse clearly appreciated it. He enthusiastically retrieved a bag of cocaine from his pocket and emptied it onto the glass. I, in return, took off my shoe, forcing him to frown. I handed him my bags and he added them to the mix. He then took a split second to appreciate the quantity.

"This is going to be a good blast. This fucking car needs a new vibe. I don't know where you three are, but I can tell it's no place I'd like to visit."

"No fucking kidding," Nikki answered.

"That bad, Nikki?"

Nikki didn't bother to answer. She was busy focusing on Jesse's hand as he divided the drug into four lines. She was usually in charge. An obvious tension emanated from her and Jesse noticed.

He slowed his process and became meticulous in his division. When he achieved acceptable symmetry, he raised the glass up for Nikki examine. She stared for a moment then nodded approvingly. Jesse took the show of respect a step further by extending the glass in her direction.

"Ladies first, always."

Nikki quickly accepted Jesse's gesture with a smile, but she wasn't smiling because she appreciated the show of respect, like he believed. She was afforded the opportunity to further assess his division and ultimately choose what she perceived to be the thickest line. This made her happy.

It didn't matter how miniscule the difference, more was still more, in her opinion. I understood the mentality. Jesse didn't, but he already accepted Nikki's smile graciously and was sitting comfortably in his seat, waiting. Nikki, surprisingly, took Jesse's misinterpretation into consideration and spent only a small amount of time on her evaluation. She even attempted to hand him the mirror after she ingested her portion.

"Just keep it in the back, we don't need to keep passing it back it forth."

He was right; it was an unnecessary risk. I sniffed my line then forwarded the glass to Jesse. He repeated the process. Finally, Lenny was pinching his nose while licking the glass clean of evidence. We remained silent and waiting. It didn't take long for the drug to take effect.

Within two minutes, my toes had curled up, my jaw locked, and my tongue was randomly searching my mouth with enthusiasm. The hair on the back of my neck stood straight, emphasizing that this was an excellent decision.

"Shit, that's much better already," Nikki whispered into my ear. I turned and looked at her. Her eyes were shut tight, but her mouth was slightly open. I watched as her tongue licked her lips several times and then disappeared. "My whole mouth is numb. This is some good shit, Jesse,"

Nikki commented without opening her eyes.

"Did you expect less?" Jesse asked.

"You got anymore?" Nikki asked.

I wasn't surprised by the question, but I was interested in Jesse's answer. I searched his face, but he was making a concerted effort not to react. He barely moved since the question was posed, and he was blatantly allowing it to linger unaddressed. This was either due to apprehension or he was being miserly. It was possible that the inquiry disgusted him, which was probably on Nikki's list of offenses that warranted immediate termination.

"Fuck, I feel so good. Do you have anymore?" she repeated, but this time the pitch of her voice had a slight whine to it.

I turned and looked at her. She was sitting straight upright and her focus was locked on Jesse. With two fingers I pushed lightly on her rib cage trying to grab her attention and redirect her stare. I needed her to stop. She was acting like a spoiled little child that hadn't even fully enjoyed the treat she had gotten and was already making demands. I wasn't opposed to the idea of another line, but she was conveying a sense of desperation, which could be manipulated.

"Jesse, I'm totally serious." she insisted, while pulling her pills from her bra. She then handed one to Jesse. "Totally serious, and this is a down payment," she told him, as she retrieved second pill for herself, twisted the top off of it and snorted.

This broke Jesse's statuesque pose. He cringed, but immediately looked down in an effort to hide his disgust. Lenny became an interested observer in Jesse's reaction, and Lenny wasn't pleased. He turned to look at me, and I acknowledged a fact we both realized; Jesse's plane was going down, it was on fire, and his seat was about to be ejected. Nikki would wait for an answer but the clock was definitely ticking, and Jesse's moment to scratch his head and carefully weigh his options was almost over.

"I've got one bag left. Give me four more pills and I'll give it to you, but I want a line" Jesse told us, as he re-engaged and focused on Nikki. The scale tipped in the right direction but as I feared he was taking advantage. "That's the deal."

Jesse's curtness and unreasonable demands angered me. Nikki retreated backwards into her seat. You didn't have to be a math whiz to recognize the lopsidedness of this trade. Nikki's silence wasn't in consideration of the proposal. She was deciding whether or not Jesse had just worn out his welcome. Lenny realized this and retrieved his stash.

"I'm good for it. I feel decent right now, but I'm sure I could feel better."

Lenny handed Jesse four pills, in fear that our silence would offend him and cause him to retract the offer. He then spun his head around and checked everyone's expression, looking for approval. I tried to fake appreciation but I was aggravated. Nikki had a similar response. Jesse didn't care what we thought. He opened the glove box and retrieved the mirror, but this time Nikki leaned forward and snatched it from him. She was done being polite.

Jesse was surprised, but he was paid handsomely, so he shrugged it off. Nikki's open hand extended in his direction concluded her insult. Jesse pulled out what he claimed to be the last bag and hand it to her without much hesitation; leaving me to believe he knew he had been an asshole, and felt slightly remorseful about it.

"Excellent," Nikki exclaimed.

"Nikki, are you sure you don't want to wait just a little and make it last?

I don't know about you but I'm feeling pretty good."

"I'm sure, but thanks for checking."

Nikki's tolerance for Jesse was now paper-thin and she wasn't going to make an effort to hide this fact. On a good day, her respect for him was minimal, and she definitely wasn't looking for unsolicited advice from anyone. Death was the highest high; it was pure and complete. That was her reality. It was a reality that no one else understood and she had no desire to lend ignorance an opinion.

"But we are still going up, Nikki. Why don't we wait and see how high we get."

"I'm well aware of high I am, but you're more than welcome to wait. I couldn't care less."

Jesse's face tightened as he watched Nikki cut out four even lines. She reexamined her work for a short moment, pushed a miniscule grain from one line to the other and then offered the mirror to Jesse. Nikki's opinion of her ability to create equality allowed her to disregard her desire to snort first. What seemed to be a peace offering was actually a dare that I hoped Jesse would misperceive as generosity. Jesse remained still as he tried to gauge her intent.

"When in Rome, fuck it."

Jesse took the mirror from Nikki and sniffed his line. He then handed the mirror back to her, knowing that this was the appropriate decision. She snorted, pinched and passed the mirror to me. I repeated the process, and once again, Lenny concluded by ingesting and then licking the glass clean. He tried to hand it to Jesse, who was obviously disturbed by the thought of Lenny's saliva, but eventually he took the glass anyway.

We sat in silence, realizing the drug was failing to achieve the previous result. The lines were considerably smaller, so it was understandable, but I was still disappointed. I looked over at Nikki, her eyes were open and she continued to pinch her nose and inhale. She concurred with my assessment and was making sure every last particle was traveling where it should be and not stuck. She emphasized the sentiment by licking her pointer finger, sticking it in her nose, and inhaling.

"Is it just me?" Nikki asked. She was directing the question at me, but she gained everyone's attention. Nikki didn't wait for a response; she was disappointed and she wanted a resolution. She reached into her bra and pulled out her stash without offering an explanation. Jesse's eyes grew wide. He grabbed Nikki's arm as she was twisting the top off a capsule. The sudden attack caused her to drop the pill and it fell to the floor. They remained still and staring at each other.

"Are you fucking serious? You're going to kill yourself."

He continued to hold her arm tight, but he was shifting his focus between Lenny and me, begging for someone to stop the insanity. He had no idea. If not careful, he would soon be the smaller cat tied to the larger cat and then thrown over clothesline. Nikki's eyes were cold and vacant; she was teetering on the edge of psychosis. A flinch of Jesse's hand, a slight twist of his wrist, and she was going to claw his eyes. I felt obligated to interject, but at this moment we were three faceless men.

"Are you scared of death, Jesse?" Nikki asked, glaring. "If you are, then it would be in your best interest to let me go," Nikki threatened.

Jesse dropped Nikki's arm, but continued to stare at her. "You know what, fuck this. Watching three suicidal freaks is anything but a good fucking time." Jesse told us, as he turned and opened his car door.

"Jesse, wait."

I reached over the seat and grabbed his shoulders. I tried to pull him backwards but he shook free of my grasp. He stood up, turned and did his best imitation of Nikki. He had seen more than enough. He slammed the door shut and we watched him walk away.

"Fuck that kid, right Jay? He wanted to fuck up our high."

Nikki leaned over and placed her head in my lap. She was shaking and scared. I reached down and stroked her hair my fingers. I was happy that she at least recognized me and wasn't completely debilitated by the experience. She finally closed her eyes and her tremor ceased. I took a deep breath and tried to relax. I shut my eyes and continued to comb her hair. It was not only soothing her, but me as well.

"Fuck, Jay, I still feel good. We're not going to let him ruin that, are we?"

"No, baby, absolutely not."

I opened my eyes to gauge Lenny's opinion. The side of his head was pressed hard against his window. He seemed to be watching something outside, but aside from a few people, there wasn't much of interest to see. He was in the midst of an argument with his Catholic conscience. Given the circumstances, I was sure he was losing the fight. I needed to interrupt before he was convinced that a major life change was in order.

"Lenny, what's going on up there? Are you worrying about the chicken or the egg question again?"

Lenny turned and smiled at me, "It's the chicken; it's got to be."

"Why Lenny?"

"'Cause if it were the egg, there would still need to be a chicken to sit on it. An egg by itself is an omelet."

"You know this is the way it should have been the whole time. Inviting people into the car never works out well, they don't get it." I told him.

"I hate that stupid chicken question." Nikki exclaimed, as she sat up.

"Can we please go for a walk, or a drive? I don't want to be still anymore."

I peered out of my window. The surly degenerates assembled around the bonfire grew, and there was now a keg involved. If we forfeited our sanctuary, their approach was unavoidable. This didn't appear to be a viable option. I wanted calm. I wanted comfort. I wanted the seclusion of Lenny's walls, and the warmth of his bed.

"Maybe we could go to your house, Lenny?" I asked.

"Why would you make a suggestion that's not even a possibility?" Lenny immediately responded.

"I don't know, wishful thinking."

"Wishful is still possible, that's stupid thinking."

"Okay fine, we could sneak into my house, maybe."

"That's even worse than my house. Jesus-freaks are bad, but sober drunks? Come on, Jay, do better."

"Wait, just hear me out, I was thinking we could climb up the tree next to my window and sneak into my room." I suggested, realizing immediately after how absurd the thought was.

"That's brilliant. Three kids who are high on cocaine and speed, climbing a tree that leads to your room, but also sits directly in front of the bay window of the living room, where an undetermined quantity of sobered drunks play cards. Absolutely brilliant; what could go wrong there?" Lenny asked, as he mockingly placed the key in the ignition.

"How about your basement, Lenny? Couldn't we sneak in there unnoticed?" Nikki asked. Lenny took a quick look at the clock and shook his head 'no'. It was still fairly early.

"Why don't we go get more coke? You know we want it and we need to waste time. That procedure takes forever."

This suggestion opened eyes. It was practical and self-serving. I was shocked that it was coming from Lenny and not Nikki. It was a terrible idea, but nonetheless, it was an idea that was going to surface eventually. I glanced over at Nikki. She was onboard. A smile stretched from ear to ear as she eagerly waited for me to cast the deciding vote.

"You both realize that we have to come down at some point. It's been days. Is that an option we should consider?"

"Tomorrow, we will accept our inevitable demise. Tomorrow, we will drink vodka and we will forbid the furthering of this dreadful amphetamine abuse. Tomorrow, we will drink through the low and back to normalcy. But not tonight; tonight we will get high and stay high."

"Was that a speech?" I asked.

"It was. Did you appreciate it?"

"You're an idiot."

"A very high idiot, I know."

"Let's not think about that." Nikki added. "It's counterproductive to think about what will happen. That fear will ruin what is happening. We can escape the end of this run for a little while longer, isn't that the point?"

"So Nikki gets smarter on cocaine and you turn into a moron? Is that what just happened?" I asked.

"That would appear correct."

"Jay, what do you think?" Nikki asked.

"All right, sure, let's go prolong an inescapable reality."

Nikki clapped her hands and hugged me. Lenny smiled, placed the key in ignition, and started the car. We were now zombies, looking to feed on more. They were excited about the feast we could afford, but once the money ran out and the drugs were all gone, this scene would turn black. We would become desperate; willing to eat whatever we could find, including each other.

Veteran's Island

Our destination was undetermined, but the objective was clear…buy cocaine. We needed a phone to do so and I had confidence in Lenny. It was this naïve sense of faith that afforded me the opportunity to rest my eyes. The accumulation of stress and the physical abuse had exhausted me.

I was too high to sleep, but my body wanted to shut down. I remained motionless, staring at the back of my eyelids and indulging in the sense of relaxation induced by the hypnotic glide of the Cutlass. I felt myself drifting, and I accepted my departure without resistance.

"Destination, please?" Lenny asked, interrupting my peaceful moment.

"A phone, just find us a phone, any phone that isn't surrounded by people we know." I told him without opening my eyes.

"So, not the phones at A&M?"

"Please, no."

I tightened my eyes and fell back into the darkness. It was nice to be still and not have to think. I wanted Lenny to drive forever, but the ride came to an abrupt halt a few moments later.

I jerked forward. My eyes opened and bright abrasive lights devoured my tranquility. I shook my eyes wide. Lenny had somehow managed to discover a traffic jam instead of a phone. We were bumper-to-bumper.

"What the hell?"

I turned around and glanced through the back windows. Nikki was sprawled out, several long strands of hair were in thin braids and she was about to complete another. She saw the panic in my face and her hands froze. She dropped her current project, sat up and began her own investigation. Sitting directly behind us was a pair of headlights hindering my attempt at to find a recognizable landmark. I twisted and turned, but all I could find was a sea of people filtering through a long line of cars. They created a multicolored blur of roaming congestion, wandering aimlessly, but in the same general direction.

"What the hell is this?" I blurted out. I was baffled. I shut my eyes for only a few minutes. "Where the fuck are we?"

I extended my assessment past the cars and towards the horizon. A massive body of water sat directly in front of us. I followed the skyline.

In the distance to the right stood a collection of what were once tall buildings, but were now decaying structures. To the left, a long row of recently built town houses lined the waterfront.

"Veteran's Island? Why the fuck are we at Veteran's Island?"

"What?"

"Why the fuck are we at Veteran's Island? It's not a complicated question, Lenny."

Veteran's Island was a slender mass of land that protruded into the marina. It was a beautiful spot if you ignored the surrounding geography. Early in the evenings, when the sun was just starting to set, rays of light would skip off of the still water, infecting the thick marina layer, creating a luminous fog. During the summer, the sea wind interrupted the sweltering day with a cool refreshing breeze. Mothers pushed strollers down the path that bordered the water's edge, while fathers taught their sons how to catch and throw a ball. It was a picturesque display of middle class America, one that we unanimously declared an undesirable scene.

"We're moving now," Lenny exclaimed, ignoring my question. He pressed on the gas and almost rammed the bumper of the car in front after it moved a total of three feet.

"You are kidding, right? When the fuck did you make this decision?"

"What's the matter with you? Why are you yelling at me?" Lenny asked, as his head snapped in my direction.

"I've asked three times, why the fuck are we at Veteran's Island? You haven't answered me, so I'm figuring you went deaf sometime between the park and here."

"We needed a phone; there are plenty of phones here."

I looked around, "That is true, there are phones here, but, when you saw all these cars, how did you still think this was a good idea? What the hell are all these people doing here anyway?"

"It's the SoNo Arts Festival, Jay. I felt like getting festive. Where's the problem?"

"Jesus Christ, Lenny, you idiot!" Nikki added.

Lenny's disclosure and Nikki's emphasis threw me into a state of panic. I spun around in my seat, frantically confirming his admission. As a child my mother had dragged me kicking and screaming to this event each year. She would hold my hand tightly as she pulled me from booth to booth, sampling mediocre fatty foods drenched in sugared sauces, which would stain her face. We would then take our full bellies to the middle of the island and sit on dry grass in front of the main stage while the sun beat down on us. Local musicians with more courage than talent would try to re-create the classics. My mother would bob her head, wave her arms, and join in during the chorus. Her moaning closely resembled the sound of cats in heat on a hot summer day, rather than actual singing. I would search the crowd, embarrassed, hoping there were no witnesses that recognized my face. It was an inconvenience as a child, but right now, it was a situational nightmare, and Lenny had just dropped us right in the middle of it.

"You did this on purpose Lenny?" I asked.

Lenny ignored my question. He was concentrating on a recently vacated parking spot. After pulling in, reversing slightly, spinning the wheel, and jerking forward to a stop, he finally accomplished geometric perfection. He emphatically twisted the key, killing the engine, and unlocked the doors to announce our arrival. Nikki remained still. I twisted my body ninety degrees so I was facing him. We remained in silence, unwilling to embrace his decision. Our reaction aggravated him. He sighed loudly as his head dropped and scratched his scalp in frustration. Finally he had gotten it all out and he looked up at me.

"What's the problem, seriously? You said we needed a phone, there are phones here."

"We needed a fucking phone, not a God damn carnival."Nikki shouted, as she moved forward so she could throw a disapproving glance at him.

Her interjection twisted Lenny's head towards the back. His stare ricocheted between the two of us. "I am failing to understand where the hostility is coming from. Can you use your words and tell me why you are upset instead of just shouting obscenities at me?"

"Lenny this is a fucking nightmare. Look at all these people." I answered as I pointed.

"We needed a phone, I got you a phone. Yes, there are a lot of people, but I also brought us to a place where we can kill some time, and maybe have a little fun while standing around waiting for phone calls to be returned."

"You seriously thought this might be fun?"

"I did. I also thought that three kids standing by a phone in the middle of a festival looks far less suspicious than three cracked-out junkies waiting for a call on some street corner."

The legitimacy of the statement forced Nikki to think. I was still shaking my head, but only because I was saving face. He was right, to an extent, but my gut was whispering. There was more to the story. He just fired a loaded gun full of logic he had been aiming at me since he made this decision. I searched the vast sea of faces, wondering what Lenny was up to and if this cloak of indisputable rationale was camouflaging a self-serving act.

"It just seems like it's going to be a pain in the ass to get out of here."

"We just got here. We are high and we have drugs. Let's have some fun while we make our call.

We don't always need to sit in a dark corner and hide."

"You know, there are going to be cops everywhere." Nikki added.

"Maintaining order, they're precautionary only. We can blend in; the sloppy drunks will steal most of the attention."

"You have an answer for everything tonight."

Lenny fidgeted with his keys while anxiously staring, waiting for the jury to come to verdict. He was determined to attend this event and there was no persuading him otherwise. He may have had ulterior motives, or maybe this was just his effort to exert some degree of control. Most of the time he played third fiddle to Nikki's and my wants and needs. He never complained. He happily stepped on the gas, spun the wheel from left to right, and applied the brakes when warranted. He was a great chauffer, and if he needed a personal night, who were we to deny him that.

"Okay Lenny, go enjoy your festival. Nikki and I will handle the call."

"What?" Lenny asked, as he squinted at me confused.

"Go have fun. Nikki and I will take care of the rest."

"Really? You're not going to come with me?"

"Don't be sad. We are going to go call Anthony, and then we are going to come find you. You find the fun and wait for us."

I wasn't convinced there was any fun to be found in the midst of the chaos, but I had already experienced the annoying mediocrity and drunken hassles many times. These sorts of situations were unavoidable and I wasn't exactly enthusiastic about leaving the car. Nikki was already pouting like a jealous little sister watching her older brother get his way. This break would be a blessing. A focused agenda would keep Nikki's mouth shut and buy Lenny some time to enjoy his sabbatical without having to listen to his sister's nagging complaints. More importantly, I could skip playing the parent trying to balance her desire to be the favorite against his sudden urge to be recognized.

"I'm telling you this can be fun, but I think we should stick together."

"I'm open-minded, but I'm not sold on this little detour of yours. Let us take care of what we came here for, and you do what you need to."

"What does that mean?"

"I don't know exactly what it means, but I can't wait to find out." I answered, still suspicious of his intentions.

Lenny shook his head and then opened his door accepting the fate that he constructed for himself. Nikki and I watched as the chaotic scene engulfed him. He was now part of the blur of color and it felt ominous. I climbed into the back and placed my hand softly on Nikki's knee. She pulled away and scowled. She wasn't used to Lenny's needs being a consideration and she was going to keep sulking until her discontent was illustrated beyond a doubt.

"You ready for this?" I asked.

"I don't want to go out there. Look at all those drunken idiots stumbling around. Tell me you aren't pissed."

"I'm okay with this. I needed a break from him and now we get to be alone."

"You're full of shit; you hate this as much as I do. And don't try to sweet-talk me, you suck at it."

I laughed for a moment because she was right and we both knew it. This seemed to relax her and she pushed my arm up and around her. She then scooted closer and nestled her head in my chest. I looked down at her partially braided hair and smiled, realizing that this was probably a good time to get higher. Since Lenny had inconveniently docked our boat at the port of drunken mediocrity and run into town to go whoring, it seemed only fair that Nikki and I be compensated.

With my free hand I reached for my shoe. Nikki straightened and our romantic moment came to an end.

"Good call." She told me as she pulled out her stash.

"Wait, I have those two pills left over from the split. Lenny owes us something for this bullshit. I think that's fair, don't you?"

"Even better call."

I handed Nikki one of the pills and we twisted, snorted, and pinched our noses. Nikki waited a minute before she pulled a second pill for her stash. I nodded and we repeated the process. This was a potentially lengthy excursion we were about to embark upon. If we were very lucky, it would remain on the slightly annoying side, but the mutation into extremely aggravating seemed more than likely. A little boost would help us maintain a measure of sanity, oddly enough. Maybe we could even find some of that fun Lenny had alluded to.

"Now are you ready?" I asked, as I opened my door.

"Fuck, it's cold out there," she exclaimed as she reached over me and pulled my door shut. "I say we stay here, give Lenny time to do whatever bullshit he needs to do, and when he gets back, we leave. Fuck going outside."

"How about we make the call we came here to make and then come straight back? This doesn't have to be a big deal. I'll leave the car unlocked."

"We can get it done fast?"

"Yes, babe."

"And we can stay away from the crowd?"

"Of course."

"I'd really like to punch Lenny in the face."

"I know, baby."

We got out of the car and began roaming. We had one specific need, a phone that could receive incoming calls. We bounced around the outskirts of the festival like little children on a treasure hunt. All the phones we saw were either useless or dismantled. Nikki's enthusiasm diminished once the instruments of the band could be heard. With each step closer to the stage, the vast collection of imbeciles seemed to multiply and the level of intoxication settled at belligerence. We were now fully immersed. In protest, Nikki dug in her heels and forced me to stop.

"I'm done," She yelled.

"There are only a few more phones left, Nikki."

"Seriously, Jay, we need to stop. There's too many people, this is too much, I can't . . ."

"Two more phones, give me two more phones." I didn't wait for a response. I tightened my grasp on her arm, and forced her to continue.

I tried to maneuver quickly and efficiently through the maze of people, knowing that Nikki's tolerance was about to expire. The crowd continued to thicken and instead of weaving through it, I began throwing elbows and clearing a path without realizing my grip on Nikki's arm had become unbearably tight. This made her nervous and she again stiffened her legs and pushed her large heels into the ground. I spun and stared at her. She was frightened and needed convincing if we were going to complete this goal.

"Baby, what's the matter?"

"I don't like this. You are angry and there are too many people. I'm not comfortable. I want to go back."

"Give me one more phone. I'm positive that's the one." I told her, as I pointed past the stage at a phone in the distance. "If that one doesn't work, we can walk the long way and go back to the car."

"I don't even see a phone. What phone are you talking about?

"It's through the crowd, by the far parking lot."

"Jay, I don't want to walk all the way over there for a stupid phone that's probably broken. I really don't want to do this anymore at all."

"I know, neither do I. Just give me this final phone and we can quit; then punch Lenny in the face when we find him."

Her eyes conveyed a lack of faith, but we had come too far to just give up. I grabbed her hand and we carefully made our way through the rest of the crowd until it finally thinned and I was able to let go of her. We approached the phone slowly, like two kids who had endured a long block of rejections while selling Christmas wrapping paper. This was the last house on the street, and if the answer was no, we had to walk back down the street empty handed with our heads hung low. I lifted the receiver and looked; it had an incoming number, but it wasn't the first. I bent down to listen for a dial tone. I turned and smiled. Nikki's enthusiasm didn't match mine. She rolled her eyes as she watched me frantically search my jeans for change. I was unprepared for this moment, and my now inside-out pockets illustrated that ironic fact well enough to force a laugh from Nikki.

I dug deep into my back pockets, but all I found was useless paper money.

"You're kidding me, right Jay? Please tell me you have some change! Or are you planning on calling Anthony collect?"

"This is fucking bullshit." I told her as I slammed the receiver down several times.

"What happened, baby? You found your phone, but now you can't use it?"

"Why are you mocking me? Do you have a quarter or not?"

"No, I don't, Jay. I don't carry change." She told me with a wide smile. "Can you go get change?" I asked as I tried to hand her a dollar bill.

"Where the fuck do you want me to do that?" She asked as she pointed at the large crowd.

"Please, Nikki," I begged, as I again extended my arm and tried to bully her into to taking the money. She shook her head at me. She wasn't going to consider accepting the money.

"You're the man. You're supposed to take care of shit like that."

I took a quick glance around. In the distance there were some vendors under tents. I wasn't comfortable leaving Nikki alone by the phone and if she headed in that direction it was going to be on a one-way ticket. In the nearby parking lot, a small group of large black men were gathering. They were drinking 40's of malt liquor while gangster rap blasted from huge speakers hidden in one of their trunks. To the left of the phones a few yards away, three homeless men were sitting on a small hill searching the grass for cigarettes that hadn't been burned down to the filter. This was the best of three bad options. One of the men was holding a rusted tin can and I could only hope wasn't full of used cigarette butts. "Fuck." I exclaimed.

"This is really stupid."

"I'm aware."

"What are you going to do?"

"I'm going to go ask that bum for change. You watch the phone."

"Watch the phone do what?"

"Really?"

"What should I expect the phone to do?" She asked as she chuckled at me.

"I'm glad you are finding this amusing."

"I'll make sure the phone doesn't do anything, and you go make some new friends." Nikki told me, as she waved me away.

I shook my head then took my first steps in the direction of my new friends. The men noticed my approach. One of them stood up and met me halfway with crossed arms and a tight face. I tried to side step this first line of defense and make my way directly to the treasure chest, but this man had no interest in my desire to limiting human interaction to mere necessity. He mimicked my intent, creating a barrier I had no choice but to address.

"Seriously, man?"

"Can I help you?" He asked.

"Can you help me? I need change. Can your buddy take care of that for me?" I asked, pointing to the man on the ground holding the can.

"We need social change. Can you help me with that?"

"What? No, I can't help you with that."

"Did you know...?"

"Yo man, you got change or cigarette butts in that can?" I yelled, interrupting the useless information that was about to be vomited on me.

"There's no cigarette butts in here, it's money." He answered as he stood up and scowled at me like it was beyond the realm of possibility that his can could be full of used cigarettes.

"That's great news buddy. Why don't you get over here and make a deal with me. I'll turn your coins into paper.

"He makes the deals." The man told me while pointing at the one standing in front of me.

"You make the deals?"

"That's right, I'm the dealmaker."

"You have an official title even."

"That's right, I'm the dealmaker."

"That's great, just great. Listen, dealmaker, I don't have a blueprint for social reform, but I can give you five dollars for ten quarters."

I didn't need ten quarters, but I hoped that the lopsided proposal would expedite matters. The dealmaker's eyes popped in recognition.

He stared at me for a moment, making sure I was serious. I nodded enthusiastically, explaining I realized the ridiculous offer. He turned and made his way over to his friends. There was a short one-sided discussion followed by the shaking of heads.

The coin holder's face was tight. He was obviously confused by the grossly beneficial deal, which should have been beyond dispute. Unfortunately, solving simple mathematical equations was not a part of these men's daily routine; they were too busy planning social reform.

"Boys, c'mon now, I'm paying five dollars for less than three dollars in quarters. I know that math makes sense to you," I yelled.

My encouragement produced no results. There might have been a slight hesitation in the process, but it was momentary at best. The two men resumed their assessment which included the counting of fingers and searching the sky for answers. The dealmaker continued to shake his head and lobby on my behalf, but apparently, we overestimated the other two men's faculties. The extent of their lunacy was obviously beyond my understanding, and I feared there was some sentimental attachment to these shiny pieces of metal. Maybe these were special quarters, quarters that possessed powers rendering this negotiation completely arbitrary.

"Jesus Christ, boys, what's the fucking problem over there? I'm offering you five dollars in return for two dollars and fifty cents," I shouted at them, as I took a few steps in their direction.

"You're offering five for ten. Why would I take five, and give you ten," the man holding the can told me.

And there it was: the gap between logic and insanity. The dealmaker turned and looked at me. He shrugged his shoulders and raised his hands into the air as a motion of surrender. He couldn't bridge the gap. The man holding the can tightened his grasp and glared at me with flared nostrils. He had sniffed out my ruse and was more than a little angry that I tried to slip one past him.

"Fuck it. Hey buddy, I'll give you five dollars, for four fucking quarters. How do you like that deal?"

The man holding the tin smiled. For some reason this made perfect sense to him. He enthusiastically dumped out a handful of change and fished out four quarters. He handed them to the dealmaker, along with a couple of cigarette butts, which were hiding

beneath the coins. I gave the man five dollars, took my four quarters and threw the butts onto the ground. The third man immediately ran over, picked the filters up and placed them back in the change bucket.

"Fucking idiots," I said to myself as I turned and walked away.

"Hey, he only gave me one; I gave him four, and he gave me one." I heard the man shouting.

I knew better than to turn and acknowledge the man's dissatisfaction. In fact, I knew enough to pick up my pace. I made my way back to Nikki, who had a peculiar look on her face. This worried me. I double-checked the phone's dial tone while staring at her. Her teeth were clamped down on her bottom lip and there was a slight sway in her posture.

"What? Fucking laugh already, stop holding it in."

"The phone tried to get away, but I stopped him." She told me, she was now swaying noticeably and amused by herself.

"Really? That's what you came up with?"

"Really? Did you just pay five dollars for four quarters?" She asked, as she began to laugh.

I ignored the question. I returned to the phone and placed the call, which was actually a beep. Anthony, our cocaine dealer, didn't accept incoming phone calls. He only accepted pages. He would then return the summons when he reached the nearest pay phone. On weekdays, we would sit around twiddling our thumbs watching the clock tick for hours on occasion. However, it was Friday night and business was to be expected, so Anthony would be prepared. He was probably circling the boulevard in his gangster mobile, ogling woman and waiting.

"Jay, Jay," Nikki yelled, as she tapped me on the shoulder.

I stood firm, convinced that she was only asking for my attention so she could mock me with another not-so-witty, unfunny joke. The tap turned into a grasp and Nikki forced my redirection. I twisted and was facing a rapidly approaching, very large woman with determined eyes. She was big and she was black. After each heavy step, she would lose her balance, tilt, but not fall, and then over-compensate with an equally wide stride. I cringed. Her awkward zigzag advance illustrated a level of intoxication I was not prepared to deal with. I turned back around, grabbed the receiver tight, and pretended that she was just a figment of my cruel imagination.

"Move, mother-fucker. I know you ain't using that damn phone," she demanded. A heavy hand then landed on my shoulder. She attempted to pull me backward but I stiffened and barely budged.

"Move, mother-fucker; I need to use that phone to call my kids," she repeated her demand, adding an explanation that made no difference to me.

I turned and stared at her, "You don't need to use this phone."

"Don't tell me what I need, white boy."

"There are plenty of other phones that you can use." I told her, as I waved my arm in a large circle.

She indulged my direction for a moment, but quickly disregarded my assistance. "I don't see any other mother fucking phones."

"You better look harder 'cause you aren't using this phone. I'm waiting for a call."

"It's a public phone; this ain't your goddamn living room, nigga."

"Listen bitch, your problem is not my problem. My problem was solved when I found this phone. I suggest you take your fat ass on a walkabout and resolve your issues somewhere else."

She opened her eyes wide. She tilted her head to the side like a confused dog struggling to comprehend my demand. After a short moment of contemplation, she made a grab at the phone, which I blocked with my elbow. Her hand skipped off my arm and smacked me in my damaged eye socket. A painful sensation traveled through my entire body. My toes and fingers immediately curled into tight balls of frustration. My eyes bulged, my teeth clenched, and my nostrils flared. I was now the bull staring at the matador and I was ready to charge.

"I will slit your fucking throat if you try that again; I swear to fucking god, test me." I warned her, and I meant it, even though I had nothing to slit her throat with. "I'll fucking slit your throat, you fat, disgusting, bitch." I repeated, emphasizing a point that probably didn't need emphasis.

She didn't move. She continued to stare, unwilling to believe me. This infuriated me. My muscles tightened. My leg twitched involuntarily as the thought of kicking her in that protruding belly flashed as an option.

Finally, I decided to spit. It wasn't a conscious decision; my head jerked back and then forward. Saliva projected forcefully into the air. Its flight surprised me. The shock of the splatter kept her paralyzed for a moment before she began frantically wiping her face. I crossed my arms, straightened my posture, and widened my eyes, making a plea of insanity.

Nikki bellowed out an ominous cackle, serving as an exclamation at the end of my insanity plea. This accelerated the conclusion of the interaction. The woman turned and cast her white flag into the air, before wobbling her way back across the field. I smirked, proudly, as she vanished into the crowd.

"Holy shit, that was awesome. I can't believe you spit in that woman's face."

"Yeah, I'm not sure what happened there."

"Well, it was great. I like it when you take charge."

"I don't know if spitting in a woman's face qualifies as taking charge."

"I liked it and she deserved it."

Anthony's call finally came in, interrupting our meaningless debate. I answered eagerly and began the usual dialogue, which was anything but normal. Anthony was paranoid, and like most paranoids, he overindulged his delusions; developing elaborate schemes to ease his mind. Police surveillance was a legitimate concern; I got that, but some of the precautionary measures seemed absurd. Code words were used and the majority of the conversation was spoken in Spanish. I guess Anthony assumed there weren't many Spanish-speaking cops. There weren't many white, suburban junkies who spoke Spanish either, but I learned.

"*Tiesto, que pasa, hermano? Soy necesitar algo blanco peluca.* One hundred forty, and soon if possible." This was all I could say. 'What's up my brother? I need white wigs'; at least that's what I thought I was saying.

Before I could receive confirmation of my order, I felt Nikki's hand on my shoulder again. This time she was pulling hard, with a sense of urgency. I spun and found her pointing at a skinny black man who was stomping across the field.

He was just a little guy, but his fists were closed and he was ready. Our glances met. He pulled his arm back into the locked and loaded position. He then aimed and began sprinting at me, like a warrior charging into battle. Daggers and spears shot from his eyes. They landed at my feet in an act of war. He expected me to put down the phone and answer for the injury I caused, but that couldn't happen. Instead, I waited. I waited until the first missile was almost launched, then I swung violently upward like a desperate heavyweight fighter with only enough strength for one final punch. With phone receiver still in hand, my fist circled up; knuckles and hard plastic landed underneath the man's chin with such force it lifted him off of the ground and into the air. He landed on his back and bounced into a dead stillness. I waited for a moment, making sure that he was going to remain there, before I turned and placed the receiver back to my ear.

"*Hola, hola, que pasa, hermano*, can you hear me?" Anthony yelled.

"Have you seen any good movies lately?" I asked acting as if there hadn't been an interruption.

"You want it?"

"What? When?"

"I'm going to the movies in an hour. If you are okay with the color of your wig, I'll meet you there for the show."

"Okay."

"One hour." Anthony replied, and then hung up the phone.

I shook my head and stared at the buzzing receiver. I missed part of the conversation and this worried me, but I knew Anthony wouldn't set the rendezvous if he weren't able to fulfill my request.

I hung up the phone and turned my attention back to Nikki. She was focused on the unconscious man sleeping on the ground; luckily the site hadn't traumatized her. A strange Cheshire-cat grin beamed while she stared, gloating. This relieved some of my stress. We had one hour to find Lenny, get back to the car, and get to Blockbuster. We would have to venture into the maze of people and search, so I was grateful Nikki didn't require a lengthy therapy session to deal with my necessary act of violence. I reached down and grabbed her hand, hoping that she wasn't going to fight too hard and waste our time.

"No Jay, I can't." Nikki cried, while shaking her head and staring at my hand.

"We have to find Lenny, and fast."

"Fuck."

"This fucking idiot is going to wake up soon and I don't want to be here when he does."

"Let's just go back to the car and wait."

"We don't have time to wait."

"Please, Jay."

"We need to go through the crowd to get to the car anyway. Hopefully Lenny will pop up somewhere and surprise us. Keep your eyes open and fingers crossed."

"He could be anywhere, that asshole."

"I know babe, but everything has worked so far."

"Is that what you call this? Working out?" She asked as she looked at the man.

"That could be me."

"I suppose."

"You ready?"

"Do I have a choice?"

Nikki was hesitant, but she wasn't going to force me to drag her. I did have to tug slightly to get her started, but once we were walking, we quickly made our way back to the stage and into the sea of faces. I again did my best to accurately assess the open canals and maneuver. The intense effort this took exhausted me and I lost my patience. Once again, I found myself barreling through the seemingly endless stream of people while searching for just one.

"This isn't working." Nikki screamed.

"No shit."

"I don't want to do this anymore."

"We have to."

"No, we don't. Fuck this."

Nikki let go of my hand and began shoving people to the left, pushing people to the right. I followed closely behind like a grateful Israelite watching Moses part the red sea. Many of her victims shrugged off the contact; some opened their mouths, but by the time they could vocalize their complaint, the wall of water had collapsed behind us and we had disappeared. We reached the stage and stopped. I continued to watch her, impressed by the proactive nature of what I hoped was the start of a plan, and not the extent of it. She pushed her back tight against a small concrete wall that kept the fans from rushing the stage and she stared into the audience. I tried to follow her glare, but it didn't seem to land on anything of relevance.

"What now, babe?" I shouted.

"We wait."

"For what?"

"For Lenny."

"How does that work?"

"We can see more people like this."

"You think?"

"If you stop staring at me and turn around."

I spun around and faced the crowd. My eyes skipped across the collection of faces. I was trying to quickly evaluate and disregard, but my focus landed on a small woman who was full of intoxicated energy and bouncing her way towards us. I didn't recognize her, but she seemed excited to see either Nikki or myself. I was curious, but I wasn't positive that I was accurately assessing the situation, so I repositioned myself in an uninviting stance and stared into the distance as if I hadn't noticed her.

All ninety pounds of this little girl slammed into me. Her arms wrapped around me and she spun me straight. She landed a misplaced kiss on my chin and began fondling my ass. I stared down at her, confused. I didn't know this girl, but I did find her to be attractive. This forced an involuntarily smile, which was promptly returned. "What's up?" she asked, continuing to smile.

I was suddenly aroused in a way that was uncommon after a three-day high; however, I wasn't sure if telling her that my dick was up would be an acceptable answer to that question, so I remained silent. I continued to stare down at her, overwhelmed by the amount of pleasure I derived from the simple contact. Sexual tension oozed from her pores as she slid her thumbs underneath my pant line. She was eager to remove all barriers that separated us. She began to rub herself against my arousal and I glanced around considering my options.

"So besides that, what's up?" She asked again, with a devilish grin that I was suddenly hoping would get me in trouble.

I still didn't have an answer. Nikki noticed and had a very clear opinion that differed from mine. Our disagreement was made clear when she dug her claws into my shoulder blades and violently removed me from the situation. She then stepped toward the girl. The pain she had inflicted upon me wasn't a satisfactory conclusion. This girl trespassed, and Nikki's glare explained her need for retribution.

The girl, frightened by the sudden appearance of Nikki, attempted to flee. I bit down on my lip and cringed. Nikki needed only three bountiful steps to catch up with her. Once within arm's reach, Nikki grabbed two fists full of hair. I winced, as I envisioned a simplistic act of violence. I was wrong. Nikki spun. She twisted and turned. The girl's feet lifted off the ground and her legs floated parallel to the ground as her direction was reversed. Nikki then released; her attention was focused on the four-foot concrete divider and launching the girl over it. It was a creative punishment, but Nikki's determination didn't parallel her strength. The little girl soared through the air, failing to achieve the necessary height she needed to clear the barrier. She crashed into the concrete like a bird into a glass window, and tumbled to the ground.

"Jesus Christ, Nikki," I screamed.

I didn't waste time surveying the scene for appalled witnesses. The few glances I caught assured me that there were plenty. The uniformed rental cops were reaching for radios and they would quickly assemble and mount an approach. Without a word spoken, we ran. We ran hard and fast, barreling our way through the arms of the mob, pushing and shoving. We paid no attention to the women, children, and elderly we left in our wake. We just ran. We ran toward an unrealized destination with desperation. Finally, when we reached the water's edge and there was nowhere else to run, we stopped.

"Are you alright?" I asked panting, gasping for air.

She didn't answer immediately. She was bent over and wheezing, but eventually she looked up and smiled. She took three long breaths before she straightened, and began to laugh. She laughed like she had just seen someone fall out of a window. She was clutching her stomach, and by the end, tears were streaming down her face. I was glad she was enjoying the moment, but a manhunt was assembling. The dogs would be searching and we were standing in a wide-open space, vulnerable.

"Nikki, are you done? 'Cause we should get the fuck back to the car before they start looking for us."

"That was fun."

"I'm glad you enjoyed yourself."

"Who was that bitch?"

"I have no idea."

"Really?"

"Yes, really. Can we go now?"

"Really?"

"I swear to fucking God."

"You don't believe in God."

"Please, Nikki."

"You're full of shit."

"Why are you angry at me?"

"'Cause you liked it."

She shook her head and began walking the path along the water's edge. I followed close behind, remaining silent, allowing her to kick rocks while mumbling to herself, uninterrupted. The degree of frustration was baffling and misdirected. The final straw wasn't my fault, and I was not responsible for the weight that broke the camel's back. Nikki and I were both pawns in Lenny's strategic maneuver. He was the puppet-master and his show had bombed. Nikki finally realized this and grabbed for my hand.

Our walk stopped abruptly when we noticed a body lingering outside the Cutlass. I strained my eyes and realized that there were two people and they weren't exactly waiting. Lenny was busy. He had his arms wrapped around a petite blonde and was jamming his tongue down her throat while she groped his ass. The puppet-master had made another terrible decision that in no way could be misconstrued as happenstance. The picture was now complete; Lenny had orchestrated this so he could accidentally bump into his ex-girlfriend, Anya. Nikki had just finished fuming over the previous Goldilocks, and this scene would undoubtedly reignite that fury. Even under perfect circumstances, Nikki despised this girl. Anya was a full-time psychotic whore with a part-time drug habit who picked Lenny's pockets any time hers were thin.

"What the fuck is that?" Nikki asked.

"Don't jump to conclusions, babe."

"There's only one conclusion to jump to. I'm not hanging out with that bitch."

Anya and Nikki were two very different types of girls. Anya was flirtatious and not embarrassed to take advantage of any man, especially Lenny. She knew how to expose just the right amount of skin. She flaunted her small, but ample breasts. She stood at angles that accentuated her curves, and sat in suggestive postures; postures that created the illusion of possibilities. Her insinuations were rarely subtle, but always in abundance. The accumulation equaled raw, overwhelming, sex appeal.

"Maybe she is just keeping him company."

"That bitch is not part of my night."

"Yo Lenny!" I screamed.

Nikki had already begun stomping her way towards Lenny when he heard my voice and spun around. He had a wide satisfied smile initially, but the scowl on Nikki's face dropped his cheeks. He took several hurried steps toward us while waving his hands, gesturing for mercy. I grimaced for him, hoping that he saved some of that impenetrable reasoning for this moment.

"What the fuck is this? Is this why you dragged us down here and almost got us killed?" Nikki asked, being overly dramatic.

"Killed?" Lenny asked, as his focused shifted between us.

"Not killed, but there were some issues." I told him.

"A lot of fucking issues, but none bigger than the issue of why that fucking girl's with you."

"Relax, lower your voice."

"I will not."

"She is holding and it's something that can really help us."

"What is she holding Lenny? Laxatives?"

"Quiet." Lenny demanded, as he grabbed Nikki's hand and placed two blue pills in it. Nikki stared down and scoffed.

"What the fuck am I supposed to do with this? I don't have an eating disorder."

"It's Xanax."

"She owes me more than two pills. And you're a fuck for this."

"A fuck for what?"

"Lenny, stop. Both of you stop, we don't have the time for this." I interrupted.

I motioned toward the car, not wanting to waste another second on this debate, but they held firm. Nikki was angry. I understood why Nikki was upset, but Lenny had a point as well. We would be scratching and crawling the walls soon enough. If Anya had enough Xanax, she was worth the inconvenience. I didn't have the time required to guide them to common ground, so I grabbed Nikki's hand and gently lead her away from her fixation. If she needed blood, she could take it in the car, but I wasn't going to miss our meeting with Anthony so Lenny could dance around Anya's sensibilities.

"Let's fucking go Lenny, we are meeting Anthony in fifteen minutes."

"Really?" Lenny asked, as he followed close behind.

"Yes, really, but if we miss that meeting, that bitch of yours is getting kicked to the curb." I whispered backwards at him.

I opened the car door for Nikki, placed my hand softly on her back and unnecessarily guided her into her seat. Just to clarify where my allegiances lay, I leaned forward and tenderly kissed her lip. As she closed her door, she continued to watch me, batting her eyelashes like a flattered but embarrassed little girl.

I straightened and found Anya, who was anxiously waiting for my approval. I nodded as I spun my pointer finger in small circles to motivate. They both jumped in and I ran around the car and climbed into the back-passenger side door Nikki already opened for me. I checked the clock, and then banged on Lenny's headrest. He turned the key, pressed the gas, and reversed.

We were going to make this meeting and a heavy blast of cocaine would solve all these issues. The tight knots of stress that had accumulated and wedged themselves in between my shoulder blades would dissolve and we could all live happily ever after, at least for a few more hours.

Wild Bugs

We were five minutes late to the meet, but Anthony's patience granted Lenny a stay of execution. Nikki had been focused on the clock the entire drive and as soon as the little hand met the big, she began sharpening her guillotine. The blade was pulled high when we turned into the back parking-lot where Anthony's jeep was waiting in the corner. We made the transaction, Lenny lifted his head from her chopping block, and Nikki secured the rope she was so eager to release.

"How'd we do?" Lenny asked.

"Feels right."

"Should we take this party back to my house?"

I still had a light grasp on a few resentments so I ignored Lenny's attempt to elicit excitement, and I double-checked the package. Everything seemed normal. It was surprisingly heavy, which should have raised an eyebrow, but I was focused on the turn of the wheels which would eventually put the memory of the festival behind us. We were en route to Lenny's room. We had enough cocaine to keep us high for the rest of the night, even with Anya onboard for the ride. I relaxed in my seat and enjoyed the sense of calm now resonating.

"Do you think we can stop? I'm starting to feel a little sick." Nikki whispered.

Nikki and I had endured multiple waves of attacks at the festival and although we had emerged victorious, our aggressors had managed to deplete our energy and reduce our highs. Nikki was now slumped in her seat; her head was pushed against the window and she was clutching her stomach. My skin had gone damp and my pulse was slowing, as the chains of reality tightened around my ankles and tugged me downward. My optimism wasn't a sufficient antidote, and a thirty-minute drive without a snort seemed like unnecessary torture that could easily be avoided. It might even jump-start the party Lenny had suggested was about to happen. "Lenny, we need to stop for a boost," I announced.

There was no response from the front of the car. Lenny discreetly twisted his head just enough so he could see Anya. They exchanged a short glance, followed by the simultaneous shake of their heads. Lenny refocused on the road ahead, determining that my demand was a request. I afforded them another minute to reconsider. They appeared content to ignore me and continue to drive, so I moved forward and leaned in between their seats. My glance remained on Lenny who was doing his best to ignore me. He wouldn't turn, but he couldn't help sneaking a peak from the corner of his eye.

"Is there a problem?" I asked, as I slapped him in the shoulder.

"No, Jay, there's no problem," he told me, still refusing to turn and look.

"So you'll stop?"

"Should I just pull the car over right here? Is that what you want?" he asked, as he tauntingly applied the brakes.

"I want you to not be an asshole and find us a spot."

"It's just ridiculous."

"What's ridiculous?"

"We are fifteen minutes from my house."

"We are thirty minutes from your house."

"Even so."

"Even so, what? I feel like shit right now and I'd like to fix that."

"Okay."

"Okay?"

"Is this what we are doing now? You are just going to repeat whatever I say?"

"And if it is?"

"It's fucking retarded."

"You know what, instead of saying, 'okay', you should be asking me how fucking high every time I say jump."

"Okay."

"Fuck you. Find us a spot."

Lenny scowled at me and then took an immediate right-hand turn onto the first available street. He hit the gas and cranked the wheel. The car whipped around the corner with enough speed to throw me backwards into Nikki. He took another quick turn but this time it was a left. Again, he pressed the pedal to floor and spun the wheel. The car skipped through the turn and Nikki and I ended up on the other side. The road then straightened. I sat up and extended my arms so I could grab him by the neck, but a loud cackle stopped me. I turned and stared at Nikki. She let out a second peculiar sound, which forced Lenny to ease up on the gas.

"More, Lenny, more." Nikki screamed.

"What?" Lenny asked.

"More!" Nikki screamed again as she kicked the back of his seat.

I continued to stare at Nikki who was now clapping her hands loudly. Lenny hit the gas and Anya let out a quiet moan as she grabbed for the door handle. Lenny ignored the next bend in the street. The rims of the Cutlass scraped along the curb as we bounced up and over it onto a small lawn. Lenny kept the engine roaring as we headed toward a slight embankment consisting of small plants and flowers. He cut the wheel in the middle of the garden and the car slid into a turn, chopping the heads off most of the daisies and daffodils. A cloud of fertilizer stink followed us as we left tire tracks across the rest of the yard on the way to the driveway.

"Okay, okay, enough." I screamed.

Lenny let off of the gas as he turned and looked at us, "How high?"

"What?"

"You say jump, I say how high."

"Jesus, Lenny."

"Are we good?"

"Yeah, Lenny, we are good, just find us a spot; preferably away from here."

For the next several streets, Lenny kept his hands at the ten and two o'clock position of the steering wheel, abided the speed limit, and stopped for three seconds at all signs. The only time his eyes left the road was when he twisted backwards to confirm that we drove far enough away from his destruction. I nodded and smiled, reconfirming that all hard feelings died with the daisies.

Lenny refocused and continued to drive until he found us a poorly lit, somewhat secluded, street. He parked and we all doubled checked the area. There was a house a hundred yards ahead, and two houses behind, but neither posed a threat.

"This will do, don't you think?" Lenny asked.

"It's close to perfect."

"Can we make this fast though? I'm feeling a bit edgy."

"Says the guy who just murdered a bed full of flowers."

"I take no prisoners."

I laughed and then leaned forward over Anya, who was stiff in her seat and still clutching the door handle. A hiss snuck out of my mouth as my eyes involuntarily rolled to the back of my head.

I opened the glove box and retrieved the mirror. As I sat back down, I realized that the straw wasn't attached to the back. This annoyed me. I assumed it was somewhere in the front rolling around on the floor. Anya was now quietly observing the stars and I didn't want to interrupt her by creating an issue that would induce complaints or suggestions. I shrugged off my disappointment, pulled a bill from my pocket, and rolled it nice and tight. Nikki puckered at the sight, but my closed eyes and the almost unnoticeable shake of my head informed her not to make an issue out of it.

Four evenly cut lines, this was what I was attempting, but the process proved to be more difficult than it should have been.

There was a slight shake in my hand. This wasn't uncommon and wouldn't have been an issue except that the drug was strangely moist, almost sticky. The powder seemed to clump together as I attempted to spread and divide. What were supposed to be sharp equivalent lines resembled a string of disproportionate sized pearls.

"Jay, what are you doing over there?" Nikki asked.

"Nothing. I'm just trying to get it right."

"That's not even close to right," Nikki responded, as she squinted and evaluated. This was her job and I was failing at it.

"Those don't even look like lines. What's wrong with you?"

"It's not me, it's the powder. It's sticky for some reason."

"Jay, don't sweat over equality, let's just get this done so we can get out of here."

"Sure, Lenny."

Nikki's scrutinizing eyes caused me to sweat. The shake in my hand became significant and the harder I tried to create parity, the more my lines resembled dotted zigzags. Nikki's loud sigh finally forced my resignation. Unwilling to admit incompetence and hand her the glass, I decided to snort. I stuck the bill in my nostril and inhaled hard. The moist clumps of powder didn't travel with ease. The damp drug clung to the sides of the dollar and accumulated until the passageway was completely clogged. The majority of the powder trickled out and dropped onto the mirror.

"What the fuck are you doing?" Nikki asked.

"The roll is too tight," I told her, as I unraveled the bill, scraped the powder off and re-rolled the dollar.

"Fucking Christ, Jay."

"You're making me nervous," I told her as I reformed my line.

"You are making me embarrassed so you should be nervous."

I snorted again, even harder this time. I managed to get the majority up and into my nose, but not all of it remained there. A clump of powder fell from my nostril and landed in my lap. My face turned red as I stared down at my dust-covered pants. Nikki's eyes widened with judgment. Lenny and Anya had also turned completely around and were bearing witness. Lenny smirked and fought to restrain a chuckle that would have gotten him slapped.

"What the fuck is wrong with you? Is your nose busted?" Nikki scolded.

I didn't respond. I swiped the powder off my lap with two fingers, licked them clean while handing the mirror to Nikki without looking at her. A loud snort, filled with determination, followed. Nikki's head snapped backwards and she pinched her nose as she handed the mirror to Lenny.

My face turned even redder with the realization that a simple pinch would have saved me some embarrassment. Lenny obviously learned from my humiliating display and approached his line in an unusual manner. He took one short snort, then he paused to pinch and inhale for a few moments. He then snorted the remains and secured it. Anya, who had grown impatient, reached for the mirror and pulled it awkwardly from Lenny's hand, causing the poorly formed line to spread across the slick glass. She examined the mess, but didn't see it as a problem. In preparation, she inhaled deeply and exhaled hard with the rolled dollar still in hand but away from her nostril; then she went for it. Her head swept back and forth across the mirror sucking up the scattered clumps of damp powder. Her head jolted back and she clutched her nose with her entire hand. I couldn't fight the urge to sneak-a-peak, in the hope she hadn't been successful. Disappointment, combined with my sense of embarrassment, moved me backwards in my seat.

"You should lick that thing clean before you put it away," Nikki told Anya, who had her hand on the glove box.

Anya froze. She turned and squinted at Nikki not convinced. "Really, you want me to lick the mirror?" she asked.

"Yes, I would like you to remove the drug residue from the mirror," Nikki responded, while shaking her head.

"Really, that's kind of gross."

"Oh my god, Lenny, please."

"Give it to me," Lenny told her, as he reached over, yanked the mirror from her grasp, and began licking it. "This doesn't taste right. It actually tastes terribly wrong," he told us as he wiped the mirror with his shirt and handed it back to Anya.

I took a large gulp of the drug that was dripping down my throat. Lenny was right. My face struggled to get away from my mouth, as I gagged on an unusual sourness. A few moments later, a potent chemical taste crawled up my throat and sat on my tongue. My teeth tried to scrape the tainted film away so I could swallow it, but the flavor continued to intensify. I closed my eyes and swallowed again, even harder. This time I choked, and coughed the drug up. A small portion slipped past the seal of my lips. I smacked my face with the back of my hand and wiped it away before anyone noticed. We sat in silence for the next couple of minutes while everyone searched for an explanation.

"Something is not right," Lenny repeated.

"Just wait."

"For what?"

"I don't know, but wait."

My eyes were wide, but only in an effort to adjust to the cesspool now in my mouth. The dreadful taste wasn't my biggest concern though. I had eaten the fungus that grows off of cow shit willingly and happily on more than one occasion because it produced amazing results. Right now, my worry was that there were no results. My gums weren't numb like they should have been. My tongue was circling my mouth in a desperate attempt to get away from the taste, not in excitement. The hairs on the back of my neck lay flat and uninterested; my mood was steadily declining.

"What the hell did we just inhale?" Lenny asked.

"I don't know."

"It wasn't cocaine."

"It has to be."

"If it was, it was cut with something it shouldn't have been and a lot of it."

"That fucking taste is killing me."

"I think we got beat."

My initial reaction to Lenny's accusation was to shake my head emphatically 'no'. His response to my response was to show me the palms of his hands at different angles. I didn't find this interesting so I covered my face with both hands and tried to rub the taste away, while I considered Lenny's opinion. Anthony wasn't some street corner hustler selling baby laxatives in twist bags. He was a legitimate drug dealer and we dropped fistfuls of money in his lap many times. There was no reason to believe that he would jeopardize our relationship.

"We didn't get beat, Lenny."

"I don't feel anything."

"It's Anthony though, he wouldn't do that."

"I don't know, Jay. I don't feel anything either. Maybe just a little bit nauseous, but nothing good." Nikki added. "I know, me too," I admitted.

"I think Lenny is right, I hate to say it."

"Anya, how do you feel?" I asked.

She was again searching the sky for stars. I continued to watch her, knowing that she was the most accurate barometer. We had been high for days and it was possible that our bodies were overly saturated. A sponge can only absorb so much before it becomes useless, but that doesn't mean that water on the counter isn't still wet. Lenny noticed my stare and followed it. I watched his eyes grow and his mouth drop in disgust. I repositioned myself for a better look. Anya wasn't searching the sky she was cleaning the window. Her tongue hung out of her mouth and she was licking the window. A stream of saliva had begun to puddle on the ledge.

"What the fuck!" Lenny exclaimed.

"Give me the mirror."

"What?"

"Give me the mirror."

"For what, Jay?"

"Look at your girl, she is licking the window."

"What's going on?" Nikki asked, as she straightened and leaned past me. "That's fucking disgusting."

"Give me the mirror."

"Jay, I don't think this is a good sign. I'm not giving you the mirror."

"Anya, how do you feel?" I yelled.

"It's like ice cream, its cold and its good." She told us, as she continued to lick her cone.

"I could go for some ice cream." Nikki jokingly admitted.

"What the fuck is wrong with you?" Lenny asked, as he nudged Anya.

"Are you alright?"

Anya spun towards him, forgetting to pull her tongue in before doing so. A small amount of saliva sprayed Lenny. He frantically began wiping his neck and cheek with both hands. Nikki and I clutched our stomachs as we fell backwards hysterically laughing. We allowed ourselves a moment to enjoy Lenny's disgust before we sat back up and examined Anya. Her face was glowing. A smile spread from car to car. She was in a good place.

"Do you feel better after your shower?" I asked, still laughing a little.

"You spit all over me." Lenny exclaimed, still staring at Anya.

"Shut up," She told him as she returned to her dessert.

"Are you convinced now?"

"Convinced? She's eating an ice cream cone made of glass and she just watered my face. What exactly do you expect me to be convinced about?"

I stared at Lenny for a second trying to understand what he just said, but for some reason I couldn't. I kept rewinding the tape and playing it back, but all I could hear was loud static and it was coming from a blurry face. An overwhelming sense of confusion pushed me backwards in my seat. Nikki was watching me. She began stroking my arm as if she read my mind and was trying to soothe me.

"Jay, something isn't right man, my eyes are burning; they feel like they are on fire. Are they on fire, Jay? Can you check?" Lenny begged. His tone scared me. I still wasn't sure what he was saying but the sound of his voice jolted me forward and into the front.

"What?"

"My eyes, are they on fire?"

"I don't know what you are saying, I want to know, but I don't."

"Is there fire coming from my eyes?"

"Jesus fucking Christ, you two." Nikki exclaimed as she pulled me backwards and claimed my position. "Your eyes are fucking fine, Lenny, chill the fuck out."

"Are you sure?"

"Can you see me?"

"Yes."

"Okay then, you wouldn't be able to see if your fucking eyes were on fire."

"Are you sure?"

"I'm pretty damn sure. Do you think you can get us home?"

"I think so." Lenny responded but he remained perfectly still.

"You are going to have to put the key in the ignition and start the car, Lenny."

"Right."

"Jesus, it's like a fucking insane asylum for retards in the car all of a sudden, I swear."

Lenny put the key in the ignition and turned it. Nikki sat back in her seat and put her seat belt on which she never did. I didn't understand this, but I decided to mimic her. I sat still watching the back of Lenny's head. It was twisting and turning. I could hear him mumbling and it sounded like he was arguing with himself. Nikki finally leaned as far forward as her seat belt would allow and placed her hand on his shoulder. His head snapped in her direction. The strained look on his face didn't inspire confidence. "Do you need me to drive?" Nikki asked.

"No."

"You're sure?"

"I just needed a minute." He told her, as he turned back around. He remained still and seemingly confused.

"Turn the lights on, Lenny."

"Yup."

"Right pedal makes us go. Left pedal makes us stop."

Lenny flipped on the lights and shifted the car into drive. He pressed the gas hesitantly and without consistence. We jerked our way down the next three blocks like a car that was running out of gas. I placed my hand on Nikki's straight back and began rubbing it to thank her for overseeing the situation. Finally, Lenny's foot became stable. The wheels found consistency and the bull ride we had been on transitioned into a smooth glide. Nikki removed my hand and smiled, as she relaxed in her seat. I wasn't sure what she was thinking about, but I was eager to diagnose the experience. My eyes weren't hot, but the lines that created the world were blurred.

The car was dark, yet I could see color, and lots of it. The back of Lenny's headrest was always a deep red and it never moved. Right now, it was pulsating like a heart, and as each beat echoed and bounced loudly between the windows, the fabric changed color. It mutated from purple, then green, and finally blue. It remained that way for a few breaths and then it reversed the color palate, but by then I lost interest. I pushed forward and leaned against the back of Lenny's seat so I could peer through the front window.

"Jay, are you okay?" Nikki whispered.

"I think so."

"This is fucking weird."

"What color is your seat right now?"

"What?"

I ignored the question and focused on the bright headlights. Lenny was driving overly cautious. I questioned this silently for a moment until I realized that the beams of light were magnifying a peculiar sight, which explained his speed. Huge fluorescent insects, with large wings, were attempting a kamikaze style mission. One by one, like Japanese fighter pilots, they would nose dive into a spiral and smash into the glass, as if the windshield was the deck of some large naval carrier sailing the sea with reinforcements. The repeated thud rattled my eardrums and shook me nervous. The post impact fragmentation seemed to be happening in slow motion, allowing me to distinguish each miniscule body part as it exploded into the atmosphere and floated away. Their blood-stained teeth and razor claws, forced me to question their intentions. Fortunately, the weight of their little bodies seemed to be having very little impact. All that was being accomplished was the obstruction of our view by the fluorescent smear of death amassing on the window.

A loud crash interrupted my preoccupation. The car lifted up and into the air. Nikki and I bounced, hit our heads against the roof, and crashed back down. The fluorescent cloak that was covering the windshield vanished. In its place, a large mailbox appeared. The collision with the curb and the sound of glass shattering caused Anya to drop her ice cream cone. Her head snapped forward, and she peered, fearfully, through the front window. Lenny was speeding up the front lawn toward the side of their house and this time it wasn't for kicks.

"Lenny!" Anya screamed. "Stop!

Lenny stepped on the brakes with both feet. We began sliding, uncontrollably, toward a large oak tree in the center of the lawn, stopping well short of it. I turned and glanced over at Nikki. She was unfazed by the event. She took a short look out her window, shrugged her shoulders, and sighed; almost in disappointment. She then relaxed in her seat and returned to whatever fluorescent world she was currently living in. I could only see the back of Lenny's head, but I could tell he was trembling. It was rare when Lenny scared himself. He was usually a very safe and cautious driver. Even under the worst conditions, he was able to maintain focus, stay between the lines, and vigilantly comply with the speed limit. I wasn't sure how fast we were traveling, but the mailbox remained indented in the hood, so it was a safe assumption that we were traveling faster than we should have been.

"Are you alright?" I asked, placing my hand on his head.

"I can't see anything."

"Was it the bugs? The fluorescent bugs?" I asked, excited that we were on the same trip.

"What?"

"The bugs that were trying to smash through the windshield. I couldn't see either."

"Lenny, you should really get us off of this lawn." Nikki added calmly and without moving.

"I can't see," he repeated.

"Is it the bugs?"

"What bugs? Why do you keep asking me about fucking bugs?"

The dome light abruptly turned on interrupting my investigation into the bug phenomenon. It took me several moments to adjust to the abnormal brightness, but when my eyes finally did, I realized that Anya had opened her car door and was stumbling across the lawn toward the house. A chill of panic shook my spine. I didn't know whether to order Lenny to drive, or tell him to go get his girl. I just knew I wasn't stepping out of the car, not with those gigantic fluorescent bugs buzzing around with blood fangs.

"Lenny, your fucking girl!" Nikki screamed, but she didn't wait for him to respond.

Nikki's door swung open and she jumped out. Five long strides full of determination shook the ground behind Anya, who was stumbling her way indirectly towards the front door. The sound of Nikki's large boots thumping against the ground turned her head. She tripped over her own feet, fell, and bounced off of the ground. Nikki slowed, took three more steps, and then hovered over her for a moment. She stared downwards, shaking her head, watching this little girl who was now sobbing uncontrollably. Anya was understandably afraid of what might happen if she got back in the car, but the tears were a cry for mercy. She presumed Nikki was about to inflict pain and she was scared. We were scared for her.

"I hope she doesn't hurt her," Lenny whispered.

"You are a terrible boyfriend."

"Fuck that, I didn't tell her to get out of the car. She made that decision on her own."

"Terrible boyfriend."

To our surprise, Nikki didn't punish Anya. She simply leaned over and extended both her arms towards Anya, who hesitated from a moment but accepted Nikki's assistance. Once Anya was standing Nikki gently pushed her in the direction of the car, but Anya dug her heels in and twisted back around and toward the house. She made two small steps and then Nikki's empathy ran out. Nikki wrapped her arms tightly around Anya's waist, jerked backwards, lifting Anya up and throwing her over her shoulder, as if she was dealing with an out-of-control toddler. She then turned and trudged her way up the lawn. Lenny and I remained still, our eyes refused to blink as we watched them approach.

"Hold this bitch," Nikki told me, as she dropped Anya into the backseat and kicked the door shut.

Nikki proceeded around the car. I watched Lenny watching her. His eyes were full of fear. He reached for the lock, but before he could press it down, Nikki had already pulled the handle. His door creaked open and she stood over him. She afforded him a short moment to voluntarily give up his seat, but he remained still. Without a word, she grabbed a handful of hair and yanked. He squealed like a pig as she violently ripped him from the car. She jumped in and slammed the door closed. My face tightened as she reached for the shifter. Nikki wasn't a good driver on a sunny, summer day. She put the car in reverse and hit the gas. Lenny remained frozen in place, like a man who had just been mugged and couldn't decide whether to scream for help or silently thank God.

The Cutlass bounced back over the curb jolting everyone upwards.

Nikki hit the brakes and shifted into drive.

"Nikki, you can't leave him here."

"Fuck him."

"Shit happens in these situations, your words."

Lenny tried to take advantage of Nikki's moment of contemplation. He began sprinting up the lawn to the car. He had his hand on the door when Nikki hit the gas. We sped down the street for several feet, before she hit the brakes and skidded to a stop, pushed the shifter up and into reverse. She then turned and peered through the back; there was a slight adjustment to the wheel before she hit the gas. The wheels smoked, screeched and took off. We were driving at Lenny, forcing him to dive into the lawn and tumble. She hit the break again and shrieked to a halt.

"Seriously, Nikki."

"What?"

"Hold her, while I help him."

As soon as the car stopped, Anya began squirming and reaching for the door. I waited for Nikki to restrain her, opened my door and got out. I ran over to Lenny and helped him up. He brushed the dirt off his clothing while glaring at the car plotting his revenge. I wasn't really sure what to say so I just waited for him to walk. Nikki wasn't as patient. She pushed on the horn and kept pushing until we began to move. Lenny headed toward the back passenger seat. I gently placed both my hands on his shoulders and guided him to the front, knowing that I couldn't trust him to handle Anya. He shook me off and pulled the door open, while keeping his eyes on Nikki the entire time. She didn't wait for us to get comfortable or for our doors to close. Once both feet were in she hit the gas and we began speeding down the road.

"Nikki, can you see alright? Lenny asked.

She didn't answer. Her eyes remained focused on the road ahead. Her grip was tight, and her back was stiff. I was intently watching her as I dug my elbows and forearms into Anya's rib cage with aggression. The burden of guilt was on her shoulders and I felt no remorse as I applied pressure and used her little body to alleviate my hostility. She was squirming again, but now it was because of the pain I was inflicting. A little squeal for mercy forced me to let her go. I sat up and leaned forward into the front. We were speeding down the road and if she wanted to jump from a moving vehicle I would gladly watch her tumble down the street.

"Nikki, can you see okay?" Lenny asked again. He waited a second for her to respond and then he asked again.

"Lenny, I'd shut up if I were you." I told him.

"I just want to know if she can see."

"I can see well enough not to drive in the middle of some-one's fucking yard, you asshole."

"I'm not exactly sure if that's an adequate answer."

"Shut the fuck up, Lenny. Nobody cares at this moment if your question gets an adequate answer." Nikki informed him.

"It's a legitimate question. It's my car you are driving."

"Seriously, Lenny, I'd shut up." I told him again.

"Where are you even going?" He asked.

"I'm getting Jay home and then I'm getting myself home. You and that dumb bitch can die in a fiery car crash on your way to your house for all I care. Actually, I'm rooting for that."

"I'm glad you at least recognize that you aren't welcome at my house anymore."

"Fuck your house and fuck you, Lenny."

"Shut the fuck up, both of you," I finally shouted.

I wasn't happy about the new direction the car was heading in. The party was apparently cancelled, and Nikki decided that we were now solo acts. Lenny wasn't going to argue. He was content to pout in the front seat like a toddler whose favorite toy was taken away. He was getting it back eventually and still had Anya to play with so our future was of no concern. I was about to be cast out onto an island of solitude. It was a fate that for some reason had been sealed by Lenny's idiocy and he cared not at all. He was willing to leave me alone in a yard and I suddenly wished that I made the same decision when I had the chance.

"What the fuck am I doing with you?" Nikki asked. I wasn't quite sure whom she was talking to, so I remained silent. "Jay, what am I doing with you?"

"I'm not sure?"

I didn't know how to respond. I wasn't sure what my options were. Lenny had uninvited me to his home. His blank stare and stiff posture made it clear he wasn't going to waiver. Nikki's plan was to go to her house, but I wasn't invited there either. I was counting on time to resolve our issues, but it would take more than sand pouring through the hourglass for Lenny's pride to heal.

"Are we being serious with this shit? After everything we've been through, are we really going to end the night like this?"

"It might be more than the night that's ending." Lenny threatened.

"That's a little overly dramatic don't you think, Lenny? What about shit happens in these situations? Isn't that the line you two sold me?"

"I'm done with these situations, and nobody is welcome at my house."

"What about that little bitch? Cause if she isn't going to your house,

I'm going to pull this car over and kick her ass out . . . right the fuck out."

"Neither of you are invited to my house," Lenny responded.

"Really, Lenny, it's like that? You're serious?"

"I've never been so serious."

"Ok," I responded, only because there wasn't anything else left to say.

Nikki continued to navigate the streets to my house in silence. I remained still in the backseat. My father would be home when I arrived, with a gang of sober and bored ex-drunks sitting in the living room waiting for any interruption that would help them forget about the dull, monotonous, string of events they now considered a life. I needed answers, and they needed to be good. The firing squad's rifles would be pointed and they wouldn't miss the mark.

The Talk Show

The Cutlass stopped at the end of my driveway just long enough for me to get two feet on the ground. I wasn't afforded the opportunity to make a final plea and there were no good-byes. Everyone sat straight waiting for the sound of my feet hitting the pavement. Once they did, Nikki pressed the pedal to floor and the car took off, screeching down the street. I watched the headlights turn and tail lights disappear, but I didn't spend much time mourning the sight. I took my first steps toward the house. Deciding I wasn't prepared, I looked for cover in the woods that bordered my family's driveway.

I remained still, standing in the woods, unwilling to cross the asphalt that divided the trees from the front yard. Fear coursed up and down my spine as I stared at the four cars that were parked in the driveway. Only two were ours, which meant there was a minimum of two men drinking coffee and smoking cigarettes in our living room. This number was an unlikely and overly optimistic tally. I had seen as many as seven people hop out of a compact car like circus clowns about to put on a performance.

My first attempt to move produced no results. My knees were stiff and unable to bend. My legs were heavy. My feet were rooted into the ground unwilling to budge. I was like a tree, protected and camouflaged by the dense forest that surrounded me. This calmed me. I extended my arms outwards as if they were branches. Small gusts of wind caused my limbs to sway. My fingers rustled like vulnerable leaves fighting with the harsh autumn breeze. I no longer needed to worry about seeing my father inside the house. I was a tree among trees and I finally had something to smile about.

A sudden and sharp pain in my elbow caused my cheeks to drop, the leaves to fall, and my branches broke hanging limp by my side. The gnawing sensation repeated. A large piece of flesh was torn from my thigh. My knees buckled, as my trunk bent. My head snapped back and forth as I searched for the culprit. A set of teeth then dug into my ankle. My eyes scanned the forest and landed on a large deer prancing into the darkness. He felt my stare and stopped, turned and returned the glance. My mouth dropped as I watched my blood drip from his mouth. He sniffed the air, laced with my stench. He then snorted at me, before he turned and bounced away. My forest of tranquility transformed into a collection of bright yellow eyes. These deer were hungry. They had the taste of human flesh in their mouths and they desired a feast.

I looked down at my feet, which had become part of the ground. I grabbed my pant leg with both hands and yanked one foot free from the soil. I placed it onto the pavement, and leaned forward pulling the second foot loose, then stepped forward. I was now on the pavement and released from captivity. I could move freely, but the yellow glow resonating from the collection of hungry eyes still worried me. Their appetites would supersede their desire to remain hidden; venturing out of seclusion, appre-hensively at first, they would overcome their fears, gain confidence and ultimately, I wouldn't be able to outrun a pack of bloodthirsty deer.

I still wasn't ready to go into the house, but I couldn't hide in the woods. So, I walked in a continuous circle, up and down the drive mumbling to myself, debating the situation. The radiant eyes mirrored my movement while creeping closer and closer to the edge of the woods. They were gaining courage and growing hungry. People were bound to exit our home eventually and if they observed my behavior, they would demand an explanation. Angry flesh-eating deer was a justification that could prove detrimental to my freedom.

I stopped pacing and walked a straight line toward the front door. As I crossed the front lawn, an image on the other side of the street caught my attention. It was my grandfather. He was picking tomatoes in our neighbor's garden. My grandmother was a few feet away kneeling and pruning the rose bushes. They waved and smiled at me. I waved back, curious what they were doing outside at this hour; more importantly, how they had escaped the six-foot grave they were in. I shook my head at this confusing turn of events, not wanting to stop and investigate. For their sake, I just hoped that the deer didn't notice them.

I entered the house and stood still in the kitchen. There weren't any loud voices embellishing mediocre stories. There was no arguing or even noise coming from the television. The smell of cigarette smoke was faint. I had gotten lucky and proceeded with confidence on a route that was supposed to lead straight to my room without a detour. I stepped softly through the kitchen and into the dining area, the echo of my feet hitting the floor seemed loud in the quiet house. I stopped and took of my shoes, discovering immediately that my effort was meaningless and my optimism was naïve. Out of the corner of my eye, I noticed my father and another man holding playing cards. I tried to continue past them but my father's voice stopped me.

"Jay, get your ass in here. We need a fourth for spades," my father demanded.

I searched for an excuse; my inner dialogue shouting a multitude of instructions, all of which centered on me running. Even if I had a reason locked and loaded, the sound of my father's voice caused my jaw to clench so tight that even breathing from my mouth was difficult. I stood there paralyzed, inhaling and exhaling loudly from flared nostrils. My father knew that I got high, but he had no idea just how high I got. My face and the blood spots that covered my clothing would raise questions. My inability to find a simple excuse to escape a spades game didn't bode well for the interrogation that was coming.

"Kid, did you hear me? Why are you still standing in there?" my father shouted.

I tried to turn but my knees were locked. I wanted to twist and acknowledge his demand, but fear kept me stiff. My internal conversation was still screaming for me to run for the front door, and it seemed that this was the only direction I was allowed to proceed. There was too much going on outside for me to consider leaving the house and the stairs were only ten feet away. I could ignore my father, buying me a slap at a later time, then casually stroll over to the staircase and disappear.

The bathroom door swung open and bright light hit me in the face.

My father's best friend, Smitty, stepped out. His large shadow engulfed me. Smitty was not only a tall man, he was muscular and now he was an unavoidable barrier limiting my options. Without hesitation, he grabbed my chin and began assessing the damage. I knew I looked terrible, but I suddenly realized that this could be my saving grace. Any odd behavior I exhibited could be attributed to the obvious trauma I had endured.

"Fuck, kid, what did you get yourself into?" He asked, not waiting for an answer. "Hey Jack, come check out your boy. Somebody tore him up good," he yelled, as he spun me around and pushed me towards the living room.

My father was relaxing in his oversized recliner with a mug of coffee in one hand, and playing cards in the other. A lit cigarette resting on the ashtray next to him caught my attention. It was emitting a mesmerizing, purple and blue stream of smoke. I squinted and followed it to the ceiling where it expanded into a dark magenta cloud, a moment away from showering the room with multicolor raindrops. I was interested to see what that looked like, but playing in the rain in front of these men would be unexplainable.

"What the hell are you looking at?" My father asked as he followed my stare up to the ceiling.

I shut my eyes tight for a moment and shook my head just slightly. When I refocused, the rain-filled cloud had vanished and the beautiful colored smoke had returned to gray. I exhaled and relaxed slightly. I needed to appear calm and keep my attention on the expressions in the room.

My father's face was tight and laced with disgust. He squinted suspiciously at me and I knew this wasn't a paranoid hallucination. The man next to my father, sitting on a metal folding chair, seemed disinterested in my arrival. He had six playing cards in one hand and a single card in the other hand he was anxious to throw down on top of the pile in the middle of the coffee table.

Smitty was still behind me acting as the unmovable barrier, keeping me contained for observation.

"What the fuck is wrong with your face?" my father asked.

"Nothing," I answered.

"Nothing?" My father asked. He relaxed, took a pull of his cigarette and continued, "It's always 'nothing' with you. That's the story of your life, just one big fucking nothing. Looks like that 'nothing' caught up with you tonight didn't it, boy?" He paused for a moment and waited for a response that wasn't going to come. "Sit down and play cards with your old man," my father demanded as he stamped out his smoke.

"Not tonight, my head hurts; I just want to lie down."

My father shook his head in submission and looked away. This wasn't an uncommon scene and his disappointment was the least of my concerns at the moment. He offered me temporary parole and I needed to take advantage of it. I tried to push my way backwards through Smitty, but he was standing firm, with his fingertips pressed in to my back. This forced me to spin around. A movement I wasn't prepared to make. My feet got tangled during the turn and I would have fallen, but Smitty grabbed me with both hands and pulled me up. He continued to stare down at me before he released me.

"I don't think it's a good idea for you to lie down."

"I tripped. Don't make an issue out of this."

"Why don't you just sit, you don't have to play if you don't want to, but sit for a minute."

"Yeah, kid, sit, it'll be good for you," my father added.

"Fuck man, I just want to go to my room."

"We don't always get what we want."

Normally, I would have sat down, refused to play cards and waited for their frustrated dismissal. I couldn't afford this luxury tonight. The purple clouds were ready to reform and shower. The large bay widow and the bright living room light shining out of it would surely attract the large fluorescent bugs. The loud thuds of their small bodies crashing into the glass and shaking the window would probably be more than I could handle. If I could remain composed through that, one dead grandparent or sadistic deer strolling casually across the lawn would send me screaming out of the room.

"Seriously, can we skip the charade tonight? I'm not going to play cards and we all know it."

"I really think he should stay down here, he could have a concussion or something," Smitty told my father, prolonging an unnecessary discussion.

"Jesus Christ, are you for real?"

"You never know."

Psychological abuse was a pastime for these men when they didn't have the numbers for a real card game or when they assumed that I was high. They would make me sit, watch me squirm, and wait until their scrutinizing eyes forced me to sweat. Then they would ask me questions that seemed more like riddles with no correct answer. When I couldn't decipher their gibberish, they would make assumptions about the extent of my addiction, point fingers, and make suggestions. This torture was equivalent to Chinese waterboarding, although I would have preferred it if they laid me down, covered my face with a rag and poured water into my mouth until I was convulsing and struggling for air. At least I could find a measure of excitement in the fear of death. Their routine was maddening and on a night like tonight, I was in no mood to play the puppet and let them pull my strings.

"Seriously, Smitty, are we really going to go through this charade where you pretend you actually care?" I asked.

"That's what you think is happening here?"

"It's either that or you're jealous 'cause I'm still out there living, while you're stuck playing cards with my father on a Friday."

"You have a big mouth, it's no wonder your face looks like that." "Are we done?"

"I'm done kid. You let me know when you are done and I'll be here for you."

"What does that even mean?"

"You'll understand when it's time for you to understand."

"Fucking riddles."

I didn't bother waiting for a response. He knew what he was doing, and I wasn't going to dance for him, not tonight. I cut the strings that controlled my feet and hands and I pushed past him with the amount of force that caused me stumble. It took me four more awkward steps into the dining area, before I regained my balance. I could hear Smitty chuckle in the background and I knew he was shaking his head. I didn't care; I walked casually over to the stairs and out of sight.

I stood at the bottom of a long, dark staircase. The absence of light created the illusion that the stairs extended indefinitely and I wondered if my body had the strength to make the journey. My muscles might surrender halfway up. I would go limp, and I would tumble backwards. I took a seat to rest before my attempt. My head dropped between my legs and hung there forcing the realization that I was absolutely exhausted. After several long, deep breaths and a short scalp massage, I stood up. I couldn't let the puppet-master find me unable to move without his assistance. I tried to take my first step, but my foot felt as if it had a concrete block strapped to it. I reached down and grabbed my pants with both hands, yanked them upward, and placed my foot on the next step. Over and over, I repeated this process, making my way to the top like a man with paralysis.

I hit the hallway at the end of the stairway and collapsed to the floor. I remained on my back, staring upwards long enough for the ceiling to begin move. There were no clouds or pretty colors. This time it just appeared as if the white plaster was breathing heavy and blowing kisses at me. I already had enough chemicals in my body and I wasn't interested in an asbestos laced smooch, so I flipped over and onto my stomach. I stared down the hall. My room was fifteen feet away. I positioned myself on my hands and knees and slowly crawled my way down to my door. I turned the knob and pushed, warmth oozed out of the room and my muscles turned to mush. I had to roll my way through the doorway.

I closed my eyes tight, pushed my back against the door and began to melt into the insanity of fluorescent colors. This vibrant infestation of my consciousness painted all my thoughts, ideas and memories. Purple people, I once knew, stood on a golden sidewalk waving hello. Pink dogs wagged their red tails excitedly, emitting orange and blue dust into an aqua sky.

The dust was then swept away by gentle gusts of warm wind, transformed into multicolored butterflies. They playfully chased one another through air, leaving streams of fluorescents behind. I walked on bright white clouds, wandering aimlessly through a beautiful world.

Then the ground started to shake. The fluffy pillows I stood on dissolved and I crashed into hard flat earth. My eyes grew, and my legs trembled, as a black cloud rumbled its way above the landscape, sucking the beauty from the sky, and striking down the life that wandered with thin bolts of lightning. The vibrations intensified, splitting the earth. What was left of the purple population and furry pink creatures fell into the crevasse. Black beads of perspiration drenched my entire body, as I watched my friends descend towards the middle of the earth where thick red flames reduced them to ash.

"Hey kid, you all right in there?" Smitty's loud voice asked from the hall, forcing my eyes to jar open. His flat hand pounding against wood shook my door and rattled my teeth. "Open the door kid." His request was followed by the abnormally loud screech of the doorknob turning.

"You've got to be fucking kidding me with this shit," I whispered to myself. Smitty's hand hit the door again but this time with a closed fist. A loud boom created by knuckles colliding with wood echoed between my ears. My whole body shook from the impact. An overwhelming sense of anger forced me to my feet. I spun, grabbed the knob, and yanked the door open with an amount of aggression that my damp hand couldn't control. I lost my grasp and the door collided with the wall shaking the entire room. I looked down to make sure the floor wasn't going to split, before I refocused on Smitty.

"Seriously, what the fuck?"

"You okay up here?" Smitty asked.

His voice was distorted and sounded like an out-of-tune radio frequency, full of static and hard to decipher. His lips were swollen, accentuating the individual cracks, strands of saliva stretched from top to bottom, locking his purple tongue behind bars. His eyelids had disappeared leaving just perfectly round balls, which pulsated with curiosity. His pinpoint pupils pierced through his cornea to prick me, causing my head to jerk backwards and move slightly from side to side. The sound of the small black dot being sucked back into place hit my eardrums and forced my shoulders to tense. His nose was extended and it twitched involuntarily, exposing his overgrown, loudly rustling, nose hairs. My face tightened and I swallowed hard in an attempt to suppress the nausea that was creeping upward. I started to inch away from this grotesque sight.

"What the hell is wrong with you?"

"I'm fine."

"Your face."

"I got into a fight. What do you want from me?"

"That's not it. What is that face you are making? You look like a half-retarded kid that swallowed something sour."

"Why are you harassing me?"

"I'm not here to harass you. I'm just making sure we don't find you dead in the morning."

"That's a little dramatic."

"You'd be surprised how many kids I've met just like you that aren't here anymore."

"I had a rough night. I got punched in the head a couple of times, but

I'm fine."

"You are on something."

"No shit, detective, but nothing that's going to kill me. Are we done?"

"Yeah, we are done."

"Good."

I closed my door in Smitty's face without a 'goodnight'. I sat down and waited for the floor to shake. His footsteps finally echoed down the hall and I shut my eyes, hoping that I would be catapulted back into that wonderful world of color. The loud knocks had jump-started my heart and all I could see was red, just a sheet of blood thumping. I opened my eyes, crawled over, and into my bed. It wasn't as soft as the clouds, but stretching out allowed my muscles to relax. I watched the ceiling, waiting for something magical to happen.

"Fucking Smitty," I whispered to myself.

My words seemed to linger above my head and rattle. I watched them shake for a moment, then they inserted themselves into the structure of the house and disappeared. I slid over and placed my ear against the wall. The statement continued to repeat as it bounced between two-by-fours on its way down to the living room. Finally, my words hit the bottom, and I hoped that they would dissolve; instead, they circled the room whispering into the men's ears. They exited through the opening in the fireplace. Like a neon sign flickering against a dark night sky, my annoyance flashed in front of the men, who were now mesmerized by the odd sight.

"Fuck." I shouted.

Big bold red letters shot out of my mouth and jumped into the wall before I could grab and restrain them. They plummeted downward and exploded into the room. Like a stock market ticker, the word 'fuck' pressed against the edge of the ceiling while circling the men below. My father's head twisted in disgust until the bulbs finally burst and disappeared. I jumped out of bed, grabbing my mouth. I searched the room for a different, less detrimental, hallucination to engage in.

Static voices began funneling up the walls. They filtered into the room, creating jagged lines that stretched from wall to wall. I strained my ears and tried to decipher. I could vaguely recognize what resembled an AM talk radio program being played in the distance. I closed my eyes and sat back down. The voices were faint at first, but the more I struggled to hear them, the louder they became until finally, they were recognizable. My inner monologue and imagination took control and I could clearly see what resembled a late-night television talk show.

My father was the host. He sat straight in his armchair, legs crossed, with note cards in one hand and a cheap, non-filtered cigarette in the other. He flicked the ashes from his smoke recklessly toward an undersized ashtray that sat on the table next to him, while he studied his questions for the night. Occasionally, he would look up and search for a crowd that should have filed in hours ago. He shook his head in disappointment.

On the couch, next to him, sat his first guest named Smitty. Smitty was a middle-aged recovering drug-addict. Smitty was an unattractive man in his early forties. Years of heroin abuse had taken its toll on this man's face. The portion of his skin that wasn't covered by thick stubble resembled the worn-out leather on the inside of an old catcher's mitt. Dark, purple rings surrounded tired, lifeless eyes. At first glance one might say that his teeth were a dull yellow, but upon closer review, you would notice a collection of plaque in the grooves, tinted brown. His nose hairs were almost as disgusting; it was difficult to figure out where they stopped and his mustache began. This did, however, make the empty seats in the audience understandable.

"My guest tonight is Smitty." My father announced to no one in particular. "Hello, Smitty, and welcome."

Smitty tilted his head and squinted at my father with a perplexed look on his face. Apparently, my imagination had failed to inform Smitty of his current status as a guest on the show. He finally shook off the confusion and leaned back into the couch. My father smiled brightly, as his attention skipped around the room. He then peeked down at his note cards. He studied them for a moment, nodded, and flicked them a couple times with his pointer finger, before tossing them into the air. Smitty's face tightened again as he watched the note cards fall to the ground. He looked up and into my father's large grin.

"So, Smitty, what's on the agenda tonight? Social reform, gun control, pornography maybe?" My father asked, as his brows raised and he scanned the room for interested eyes.

"What?"

"What's the topic of discussion?"

"Jack, that boy of yours is fucked up. I think this is the opportunity that we have been waiting for. We need to seize it."

"Whoa, whoa, slow down, partner." My father told Smitty, as he looked around the room almost embarrassed. "Let's not make this personal. It's a family show, my friend."

"What the fuck is wrong?"

"Language please, it's a family show, Smitty."

"Have you been drinking?"

"Smitty, come on now, you know better than that." My father responded while faking a laugh.

"Let's talk about something interesting, something that matters; let's give everyone a show tonight."

"I don't know what you are doing right now, or even what you're talking about, but this is our moment. I think we should call a 5150 on his ass, lock him up in the psyche ward for a couple of days to dry out, then take him up to the ranch and drop him off."

"And I think this is a good time to take our first commercial break." My father announced.

The curtain closed on the show and I could suddenly hear police sirens in the far distance. I moved over to my window and peered out. On a connecting street a few miles away, red and blue lights ricocheted off of the tall trees and colored the night sky. The men in blue were speeding through the neighborhood on a path that led straight to my front door. The faint roar of the ambulance's engine followed the blur of color. My father's talk show had been a premonition, not a hallucination. My body began to shake. It would only be a few moments before they kicked down my door, strapped me in, and wheeled me out. In the morning, I'd wake up in a hospital-issued gown and pair of green fuzzy slippers.

I stood and took a step toward my bedroom door and grabbed the knob, then realized the front door would be heavily guarded. Men might even be in the hallway waiting for me to see the lights and run. I leaned forward and pressed my ear against the wood. I squinted and strained. Smitty was whispering softly to another man, who was very large; the journey up the steps had left him gasping for breath. I released the doorknob and stepped back over to the window. Piercing static from police radios infiltrated my room. I cupped my ears and cringed as the noise bounced from ceiling to floor, striking me in the head. The sound was loud, meaning they had arrived. I bent down and grabbed the window frame, yanking upward. The dry hinge let out a squeal for mercy, but I had no time to be gentle. The red and blue lights took turns painting my face and I knew it was now or never.

I slithered out of the open window with relative ease. The slant in the roof surprised me as I stood and stumbled forward slightly. A blinding spotlight smacked me in the right side of the face. I turned to avoid it and again lost my balance. This time I overestimated the width of the ledge. My third step was into the dark night sky, now plummeting toward the hard earth; at least this time my feet were leading the way.

My heels hit the ground first. My knees collapsed, and I fell forward, slamming into the ground. Again, the air was forced out of my lungs, forcing me to gasp for breath. My eyes shut tight in anticipation of the impact, and remained that way while I attempted to categorize and understand my new pain. I finally sorted it all out and opened them wide so I could survey the yard. The red and blue flashes from both ambulance and police cars had blended together to create an ultra-glow, highlighting the entire forest, including some old predators of mine. The deer were waiting for me. They pranced back and forth trying to escape the sirens that echoed from tree to tree and landed on their delicate ears. Their mouths salivated as they struggled to decide if they should stay and possibly feast, or run and avoid mayhem. I patiently watched from the ground, knowing their decision may limit my options. They danced away from the brightness, knowing that if they remained they wouldn't be able to enjoy their meal with all this commotion.

I took a deep breath, and forced myself to my knees. Out of the corner my eye, I caught a glimpse of three shocked faces staring out of the window. I didn't need to turn and look. Their fingers were pointing in judgment as they screamed instructions to the men dressed in uniforms, who were still in the house and under the assumption I was in my room. Their approach would be aggressive and it was imminent. I jumped to my feet, forgetting about my broken body and depleted lungs. I began sprinting across the backyard. Adrenaline was now pumping through my veins and I was able to move across the lawn with little discomfort. I was heading for the woods, and although the bright lights where shining on them, I knew the forest well, and there were places I could hide. As I stepped over some thick shrubs that bordered the yard, I peered back at my driveway, realizing there wasn't an ambulance or police car waiting for me. The sky turned from blue and red to black. The air became still and silent. I stopped and reconsidered a decision that didn't need to be revisited. My father had just witnessed me falling through the sky. He watched me hit the ground and run. He was now aware that the extent of my insanity extended far beyond his initial estimate. There may not have been men at the house now, but if I returned there surely would be.

Threesome

I vanished into the woods, traveling with ease; jumping over the smaller bushes and shrubbery, ducking under the branches and spinning around the trees. I was a hunted man, chased by a pack of bloodthirsty hounds with an army of men looking to aim their rifles and claim their reward. I shot across the lawn of the adjacent house and hit the street. Then I stopped. I looked up and down the road realizing this was the extent of my plan. Lenny's house was a possibility, but it was far and my admittance was tenuous. I may have to hit my knees and plead, but eventually he would break. Nikki's house was closer, although not really an option. She would more than likely slam the door in my face. A childhood friend lived a mile in the opposite direction. If he were home, he would probably be awake and smoking weed in the basement. He was significantly closer, and a few pulls of a joint might take the edge off of this mystery high I was on; it was a gamble.

Lenny's house was the safest bet, but it was two miles away. The seven dark streets I had to walk would offer plenty of opportunities for the skies to part and the ground to open up. The ghouls and goblins would creep out from under their rocks and taunt me. Happy thoughts were a necessity. I would imagine rainbows and butterflies. I would concentrate on my feet, keep my head down, and ignore the lurking trees, hanging over the roads like skeletons. I would cover my ears and refuse to hear the whispered lies that the gusts of cold night air tried to deliver. I'd maintain a casual pace and in twenty minutes, I'd be under Lenny's covers safe and able to rejoin the purple people and walk my pink dog down streets paved in gold.

Forest Lane was the first street to conquer. Easy task. I took twenty large steps down this slanted street and was done. It was a good start. I made a quick right onto Deforest Road. This was another sloping street. I took advantage of gravity, and began to run. My feet slammed against the pavement, the noise echoed and startled me. I slowed and looked over both shoulders, sure I was being followed. Two dark shadows, one from each side jumped back into the woods and hid before I had the time to evaluate. I slowed my pace and continued to twist my head back and forth, peaking behind me. My awareness seemed to keep them locked in concealment and I confidently increased my speed. I took a quick right on Grey Stone Road and began creeping my way down this long, straight, street. My path was littered with small homes. Small homes meant short driveways. The driveways led to garages, and that meant spotlights. These lights remained on throughout the night. Normally, I hated this waste of electricity, but tonight I welcomed the interruption of darkness. The visibility enabled me to increase my speed and I moved with ease.

I hit Ground Pine and took a left. This was another long, straight street. Unlike Grey Stone, it was desolate. The road was comprised of four extremely large homes with an overabundance of land. The vastness of these estates negated the possibility of visual assistance. Through the trees, in the distance, I recognized small flickers of light, but nothing beneficial. I decided to keep my head down and focus on the ground. The street lacked curves, so navigating didn't require my concentration, allowing me to walk quickly. Left foot, right foot and road, this is what I was focusing on and it was working, at least for the first thirty yards.

Halfway down the street a sharp pain pierced my skin. It ripped through my muscle tissue on its way to my heart. My back straightened, my knees buckled, and I dropped to the ground. I massaged my chest. I rubbed my sides and my back searching for blood. My eyes scanned the street for my assaulter. Tall, lean trees, with long sharp arms lined the pavement. They were dancing in the wind and laughing at me, waving their jagged branches excitedly, and encouraging me to continue or retreat. It didn't matter which direction I chose, they just wanted another opportunity to slit me down the middle and gut me like a pig.

I stood up and stared, remaining still, unwilling to proceed. This angered a large maple, standing tall several yards ahead on the right. With a long limb that had been pointing at the stars, he swung at me. I ducked just in time. The branch slashed through the night sky and grazed the top of my head, scraping my scalp. I winced in pain as I began to run. The trees in the distance started cheering and applauding. They didn't care if I was successful or cut to shreds and left bleeding on the side of the road. They were just grateful for the entertainment. They jumped up and down shaking the earth. The black sky highlighted the long line of aggressors, waiting patiently to make an attempt at my life. My run became a sprint and I weaved my way down the street with wide eyes that assessed the effort of each thorny stem. Some branches swung violently at my head. I dropped and rolled, barely avoiding decapitation. Others tried to sever my legs from my body. I hurdled over these attempts like an Olympic track star. I dodged, dipped, and jumped over each stab that was made. Occasionally, I would misjudge and a razor-sharp arm would land on my skin, slicing it open. I ignored the pain and continued moving, leaping and ducking, bobbing and weaving my way down the street like an animated character in an unrealistic video game.

Then, out of nowhere, a small bald man dressed in a bright red sweat suit dropped from the sky and landed in the middle of the street. A mushroom cloud of dust engulfed him. When it cleared, I found a wide stare and a devilish grin that stretched from ear to ear. He began clapping so loudly that he distracted the trees and they became preoccupied with the noise. His kind eyes urged me to continue, but I stopped instead. The man began to wave me forward, but I refused to move. He gritted his teeth as he began a slow approach. As he drew closer, I noticed that his face was wrinkled. He was old and frail. He had a potbelly and skinny little arms. If it was his desire to do me harm, I was twice his size. Curiosity moved me toward him, and I found myself staring into deep emeralds. They were warm and inviting; it seemed as if this man had been sent to protect me.

"I have the antidote." He whispered into the air. A small gust of wind delivered his words to my ear and I smiled.

The man reached into his pocket and pulled out a bag containing a single fluorescent green pill. He held it in the air, like a carrot in front of a donkey. I picked up my pace. The man laughed tauntingly as he nodded in appreciation of my effort. He watched me closely and waited until I could smell him, then he dashed into the woods. I squinted at the residual glow of red and green that he left behind, considering for a moment the option of entering the forest after him. I shook my head, threw this possibility away, and resumed my journey.

The man reappeared twenty yards down the road. He was now waving his baggie with enthusiasm. Green dust sprinkled the ground and collected into piles around him. I didn't waste any time. I raced toward him, convinced that I could catch this old bastard who I felt was toying with me. He smiled and chuckled as he watched me. My arm was extending toward him when he suddenly dissolved into thin air, leaving behind a large red stain on the pavement. I squatted down and ran my hand over the mark. It was hot and releasing bright red steam that formed little clouds just below my nose. These clouds swirled around my head several times before they shot into the sky and floated away. The piles of green powder still remained and I reached down trying to scoop some up for further examination. The dust colored my fingers and hands, evaporating after. I stood and scratched my head, not knowing what to make of this one.

I continued down the street and took a left onto Tree View Lane. I felt slightly dizzy. My chest was tight and my breathing became shallow. I grabbed my heart; it was still excited and pumping vigorously, but my lungs couldn't fully expand, and each time I sucked in the night sky I could only capture an insufficient amount. I tried to ignore this and continue, but I was now dragging my feet through each step. A tingling sensation spread from my face to my arms and down to my legs. I stopped and watched as the world around me turned black.

When my eyes opened, I was flat on my back and halfway in the street. I collapsed and was now staring up at an endless sky. I tried to move my unresponsive legs. My hands were tightly clenched and unwilling to release. My arms dangled, like soft useless noodles, my body and neck were stiff. My focus remained straight north on the largest star in the sky. It was pulsating, slowly expanding with each beat, radiating warmth. A tear formed in the corner of my eye and rolled slowly down my face. "Death is the highest high you can achieve." I heard Nikki's soft voice whisper in my ear.

I closed my eyes and accepted my fate. The world turned cold for a moment and then warm. Large fingers of a white giant picked me up and held me securely in the palm of his hand. He raised me away from the street where my body still remained. I reached out for it. The giant smiled, shook his head back and forth and I knew there were no bodies where I was going. The deer would finally have their feast.

My giant released me from his grasp and disappeared, leaving me floating freely in pure white. I squinted one last time and found my body. I sent a little wave, before I turned and forgot about it. I widened my arms and spread my legs. I began soaring through magnificent brightness. People dressed in white gowns, sat on thick clouds and nodded in welcome. Not far away, vibrant, golden gates shined. They were open wide and a soft gentle breeze seemed to be pushing me in that direction. It was the beginning of Heaven and I was about to soar through it like an eagle. "Wake the fuck up. Wake the fuck up," I heard a voice shout.

Darkness swallowed the warmth and light. I spiraled through a black sky, waving the arms that seconds ago controlled my flight. Cold lips pressed against mine. Air pushed its way into my lungs. I coughed and choked as a heavy pressure hit my chest, followed by more cold lips. A lashing then struck me across the face, followed again, by the forced expansion of my lungs. My eyes popped open, just as a man's arm raised into the air. I closed them tight in anticipation of a second strike across my face.

"Wait, he's awake, he's awake. I just saw his eyes!" Mandy screamed as she pulled a young man off me.

A mess of color was all that surrounded me. I squinted and blinked. Slowly, the world came back into focus. Mandy Miller was standing on top of me. She was white with fear and staring down at me with a sense of disgust that forced me to look away. I had received this look from her plenty of times over the years and unlike most who would deliver that glare, hers never became palatable.

"Jay, can you hear me? Are you alright?"

I could hear her, but I was preoccupied with the men standing behind her. I glanced at each one, hoping for recognition and maybe some sympathy. They were dressed in blue and white leather jackets. They wore matching football jerseys; there wasn't an ounce of understanding in their stiff postures. Their arms were crossed, and the revulsion that resonated emphasized a unified opinion, which was full of hate.

"Jay, can you hear me?" she asked again.

"Yeah, I can hear you." I told her, as I started to move.

"Don't," Mandy ordered, as she placed her hand on my chest and pushed me backwards.

"Seriously, I'm good."

"Just stay there. We are going to call for help."

"Please don't do that."

Mandy loved me once. I was her first kiss and her last dance all through grade school. We passed notes during class in the day and spent hours talking on the phone at night. We spent three years together; holding hands to start, then eventually, would sneak into the woods to explore our pubescent urges. We smoked our first joint together while sharing a wine cooler. Her progression into the world of drugs stopped there, while mine continued with reckless abandon. She secretly hated me for forcing her to watch helplessly as I sunk further and further into the abyss that would become my life. She had no choice but to turn her back on memories that she cherished. She held onto the anger this caused so tightly that I was somewhat surprised that she stopped to save me.

"I just had a little too much to drink. I sat down for a second, and I guess I passed out. It's not a big deal," I told them.

"Dude, you were fucking dead," a boy, everyone knew as Flick, told me.

"Dead, is dead, Flick, so I seriously doubt that."

"No way man, you were fucking dead. You still look dead," Flick repeated.

I ignored him and tried to reposition myself. Flick, who now seemed interested for some reason, stopped me by placing his large forearm on my chest and digging his elbow into me. His glance over at Mandy explained that he was the one most likely to see her naked tonight, so this was an attempt to impress. He knelt down next to me and grabbed my arm. He placed two fingers on my wrist in an attempt to check my pulse, but he was checking the wrong spot. His eyes searched the sky as he pretended to count beats that weren't happening. This kid might end up in med school eventually, but he was no doctor at the moment.

"Yeah, I can barely get a pulse," he announced, looking at Mandy.

"That's because you're pressing on the wrong spot. Why are you trying to take my pulse anyway? I'm right here, I'm alive and talking to you," I said while shaking my wrist free.

"I'm checking to see how alive you are. What kind of shit are you on anyway?"

Before I could answer, another voice chimed in, "The kind of shit that makes you go to sleep in the middle of the fucking road."

"Like alcohol?" I suggested. "But I bet you guys have never passed out anywhere unusual."

"Just leave him, let's go," the man suggested as he threw his hands up in frustration.

"Jay, we almost ran you over, we could have killed you." Mandy told me.

I looked to my left. The front tire of a large SUV was five feet from where my head was once. She was right. This would have killed me, but I was already dead. I shrugged my shoulders and refocused on Mandy. She was ghost white and her mouth had dropped open. Her head shook as she imagined what could have been. I felt an urge to free her from this contemplation, only the truth was far too incriminating, so I kept my lips tight.

"It was a bad place to pass out, I admit."

"Jay, really? It's me. Be honest, what do you need me to do for you?"

"I need a ride to Lenny's. That's what I honestly need right now." "That's where you were going?"

"I took some pills before I left my house and I was drinking vodka a few blocks ago. I'm not sure what happened. I must have fallen and hit my head, but I wasn't doing anything that would kill me. Scouts honor."

"You were never a scout and you have no honor left." Mandy blurted out, uncovering some of the hatred she had buried years ago.

"I know you think I'm a piece of shit, and I can't disagree, but tonight isn't my night to die. I'm okay, I swear."

Mandy wanted to believe me, but she was shaking her clenched jaw back and forth. The two men I didn't know were pacing and kicking rocks, occasionally they would take a glance over to see if there was any progress. Their patience was thin from the moment the key left the ignition; it was gone now, but

Mandy was calling the shots. I needed to convince her and I needed to do it fast.

The street was beginning to vibrate. The trees were smiling and ready to resume the hunt. In the distance I could see bright yellow eyes. The deer had a feast planned and they weren't happy that it was going to be rescheduled again.

"Just help me get to Lenny's."

"Can we just get this fucking kid somewhere, or leave him? I don't care what you choose, I just don't want someone we know to drive by and see us in the middle of the street with a junkie." My new friend, with the opinions I liked, added.

I pushed my way through Flick's large forearm, and jumped to my feet. I looked back at Mandy. She was counting the rocks on the ground. The small crinkle in the corners of her mouth told me that she was revisiting the memories that we made, as her eyes skipped from pebble to pebble. She wiped away the tears and looked up. She still loved me. I still loved her too, unfortunately though, tones of purple and blue started to drip down from the heavens. These colors mutated at the horizon and trees were now swaying in front of a ruby red backdrop. They rubbed their branches together, eager to have another go at me. It would only take one stab to send me screaming down the road. These men were already displeased with the thought of me in their car and the offer of a ride would be tossed out of the window if I went sprinting down the road like a man on fire.

"So, can I get a ride?"

Two large crows, circling above, cackled for my attention. I glanced upwards. Their beady-eyed stare explained they were anxious to feast on my corpse, breathing or not, and beat the deer to the good meat. I took a step toward the car, forcing one to plummet. His beak was wide and his claws extended, as he soared downward. I ducked down just enough not to draw suspicion, but not enough to avoid the swooping bird's claws, which scratched the side of my head and my ear. My teeth and fists clenched, as I tried to shake off the pain and not look up. I made another move toward the car and the second bird started his dive. He twisted and turned as he plummeted through the red sky. I forgot about everybody that was judging me and focused on the creature's spiral. I slid several feet to the left and watched as the bird bounced off of the ground and then back into the sky.

"Little bastard, fucking crows," I said.

"What's that?" Mandy asked.

"Nothing."

I pulled the car door open, jumped in, and slammed it shut. Both crows swooped down and landed on the roof. Their claws scratched the ceiling above my head as they circled, looking for an entrance, deciding to create one themselves. Their long beaks tapped repeatedly on the metal that separated us, sending chills down my spine. I continued to watch the men outside, hoping that they would find acceptance for this situation before the birds were successful. Their faces were tight, they could tell this was important to Mandy, so they shrugged their shoulders and made their way to the car.

"Where am I going?" Flick asked, once everyone was seated.

"Abbott Lane, number three."

"But that's only two streets from here."

"I know."

"Just drive him." Mandy said. "God knows what can happen to him in two streets."

She was right. I turned and stared out the window. I could see yellow eyes watching us in the distance. Flick put the key in the ignition, started the car, and began to drive. I watched the deer bounce through the forest trying to keep up with us. The trees that lined the street were waving at me. They were sad that I had to go, but also thanking me for a good time. I was a worthy opponent and they appreciated that. I searched the red sky for my giant, but all I could find were regular size stars, and none of them were pulsating. We would meet again. There was no way around it. The car came to a stop a few minutes later at the edge of Lenny's yard. I opened the door and hopped out. I was about to thank the men and Mandy, but Flick hit the gas before I had the chance. The car sped down the street with the two crows still pecking on the roof and a half-opened door that slammed shut as they made their first turn.

I spun around and started walking up the drive. I kept my head down and my focus straight. Each footstep left a deep imprint in the hard pavement as it began to crack and shatter beneath my feet like old fragile glass. I raised and pressed both hands tight against the sides of my face, limiting my peripheral vision and ignoring any attention the noise would attract. I stepped as soft as possible but the driveway continued to crackle beneath me, perking the ears up of the critters hidden in the woods. They inched to the edge of the forest and were sniffing the air, about to pounce.

The driveway was shattered, but I made it to the side door before it broke. A sigh of relief escaped my mouth as I entered the house, bouncing up and down on the stable linoleum. I took a moment to search my body for bloody wounds that might stain the carpet. I lifted my shirt and ran my fingers up and down several times, but they kept coming up dry. I pulled up each pant leg, still finding nothing. I wiped my face and picked at my ears, also clean. I half expected this to be the case, so I shrugged my shoulders and made my way in to the living room. I sat down on the couch, shut my eyes; allowing the walls of the house to protect me as I considered how I was going to sell my arrival. Lenny would be angry, but hopefully our separation and some time alone with Anya had relaxed him. I would make a plea for mercy, explaining how the trees attacked me.

If I was lucky, I'd find him walking a pink dog and happy to see me. I would drop to my knees and beg if he required it.

The hypnotic tic of the small grandfather clock in the corner relaxed my body, and I sunk into the couch. The soft cushions wrapped around my waist and held me tight. I was tired and comfortable. I glanced around the room. The walls were still and the ceiling was the correct color. I considered just sitting still on the couch until the early morning, then sneaking out when the sun peeked out. The small chance that I may fall asleep and Lenny's mother discovering me pushed me onto my feet where I stepped lightly over to the stairs.

The old wood creaked with every step. Lenny's mother worked hard and slept like a rock, so my nerves remained steady as I continued to the top. As I neared Lenny's door, I began to tiptoe. I grabbed the doorknob but my hand was shaking notice-ably, so I let go. My heart was pounding.

Sweat dripped down the side of my face as I raised my fist to knock. My elbow locked in place forcing me to reconsider. My knuckles colliding with wood, even if it was done softly, would shatter his nerves and cause an anger that might force me back out to the street. My sudden appearance would frighten him, possibly to such an extent that he would attack me.

This dilemma kept me still and confused in the hall.

"Lenny," I whispered through the closed door.

I pressed my ear against the door. I could hear them wres-tling around under the covers. I grabbed the doorknob, twisted and lightly pushed. A large mass seemed to be playfully bounc-ing underneath the blankets. I took a small step into the room and I could hear Anya panting. I moved even closer and my eyes adjusted to the darkness. Lenny's hands had a tight grasp on the top of the headboard. His arms were straight and his flexing muscles pulled his body forward. He was breathing deeply as he thrust himself aggressively against her small frame. She began moaning, and scratching at his back as he continued to take the day's frustration out on her. Their moans grew deeper and more enthusiastic as he continued to violently penetrate her.

This noise hypnotized me and I was sleepwalking over to the edge of the bed without realizing it. I hovered over them, watch-ing as they grinded up and down. Lenny's final grunt released an abundance of tension. It was followed by a loud scream, drop-ping me to my knees. Their motion slowed and the room went calm. I pinched a corner of the blanket and lifted it slightly, but their sudden pause caused me to release my grasp and duck. They giggled as they complemented each other on an excellent performance.

I lifted the covers again, slid my hands underneath and began moving forward until I felt soft silky skin. I ran my fingers up and down Anya's calf waiting for an objection that never came. Now confident, I lifted the blanket even higher and crept underneath. My hand slid up Anya's thigh. My fingers pressed lightly into her flesh, as I massaged her leg. Her giggle said yes. Her quiver said now. She inched her way toward me, anticipating my hand reaching its final destination. I pulled back slightly and waited a couple of seconds just to tease. Her vibration escalated, she was begging me to continue. I placed two overlapping fingers between her legs, and penetrated her softly. Two feet hit my chest with enough force to push me to the floor. The blankets were torn from the bed and tossed into the air.

Lenny's dark shadow emerged and consumed me.

"What the fuck, Jay?"

I ignored the question and strained my eyes, hoping to at least catch a glimpse of Anya's naked body. My head bounced from left to right, but Lenny's tight fists kept obstructing my view. The bulging muscles in his arms, combined with his glare explained his desire. His flared nostrils blew smoke in my direction and I scooted backwards to remove myself from striking distance.

"Seriously, what the fuck is wrong with you?"

"Lenny, are you doing okay?"

"You just stuck your finger in my ass, so, 'no'."

The sound of laughter and the squeak of Lenny's wooden chair turned our attention to Anya who had her feet up on Lenny's desk. She was counting the stars in the sky again, but Lenny's announcement had caught her attention and her body now twisted awkwardly toward us. She was also fully clothed, which was disappointing. A wide smiled stretched from ear to ear as her bulging eyes anticipated the details of our romantic encounter.

"You think that is funny?" Lenny asked.

"I thought you didn't like ass play?"

"I don't."

"Now you know how I feel."

"Lenny, I'm not doing very well." I interrupted knowing that I should make my plea while he was distracted. "My father saw me jump out of my bedroom window. Trees and deer wanted me dead. Mandy Miller found me collapsed in the street. I think I died. I know I'm seeing all kinds of shit, really bad shit. I need someplace safe. Please don't kick me out."

"You seemed like you were doing fine when you stuck your finger in my ass." Lenny told me.

"I thought you were her."

"Is that supposed to make it better?"

"I don't know, but I wouldn't stick my finger in your ass on purpose.

I'm seriously not right."

"Jesus Christ, Jay, calm the fuck down."

"Are you going to hit me?"

"No."

"Are you going to throw me out?"

"I should."

"Lenny, be nice, you know you can't make him leave." Anya added.

"Wash your fingers and go to the basement. I'll be down in a minute and we can talk about the night."

My haste to close the window of opportunity on any reconsideration, caused me to slam the door as I hurried from the room. The noise shook the walls and I imagined Lenny's nerves. This was nothing compared to my fingers breaking his seal, so I wasn't extremely concerned. I made sure not to look back as I skipped down the stairs, smiling. Anya's compassionate plea explained her desires. I was sure by now, that she scooted the desk chair to the edge of the bed and was lobbying for the experience of three naked bodies massaging away the memories of this night. Lenny's lips would tighten as he shook his head and stared at the ground. Anya would scoot even closer and lightly press her breasts against the top of his head. Her hand would drop to his inner thigh, and slowly move upward until his desire outweighed his repulsion. He would make an attempt to bypass the negotiation that included my naked body.

I reached the basement and took a seat on the brown leather couch. I kicked my feet up on the coffee table and was ready to relax. I closed my eyes, stretched my arms, and wiggled my way into complete comfort. I directed my mind toward happy thoughts, all based around Anya's naked body. I imagined my fingers caressing the silky skin of her thighs. She smiled as she grabbed my head and jammed her tongue down my throat. I didn't mind her aggressive kiss and her thick, pouty lips glistened with spit. The motion of her head, circling my face was unpredictable. Her misplaced saliva finally became an aggravation I couldn't ignore and I grabbed a fist full of hair and spun her around. I licked my fingers and slid them forcefully inside her. This thought had me aroused and I contemplated storming up the stairs, letting my intentions be known. It was time to change the subject.

My mind wandered to Nikki. She was sitting alone in her room, clutching her knees, and rocking back and forth, trying to ignore the world around her. My tears began to collect and run wild as I imagined her backed into a corner, while the dark shadows surrounded and inched closer. They laughed as each took their turn slicing skin from a helpless captive. I was responsible for these figments. Failure wrapped itself around my neck and pulled tight. My eyes opened as I gasped for breath. I shook my head violently, but I couldn't escape the restraint, so I sprung to my feet and began circling the room. My thoughts continued to chase me and my walk became a skip, my skip increased to a trot, and finally I was jogging at a speed that forced me to wobble. I collapsed and slid across the cold floor.

I remained on my back staring up at the ceiling, hating Mandy and her friends for saving a life that I no longer wanted to live. I glanced around the room searching for something sharp that I could use to regain the freedom they had stolen. A garden hose or thick rope would also do the trick, but there was nothing. I sat up and took off my shoe. I dumped the contents out onto the floor. Six pills hit the concrete and bounced. A half-full bag of powder dropped and spilled. I stared down, wondering if this combination had the ability to kill me or just turn me permanently mad. I decided I didn't care.

I grabbed a pill, twisted the top off, and snorted. I sat there for a moment pinching my nose and inhaling. I reached for a second pill, but the door at the top of the stairs swung open, interrupting and forcing me to my feet. I stuck my foot back in my shoe, scooped up the drugs, and moved to the couch. I stuffed the bag and pills into my pocket, dropped backwards, and tried to appear calm. Lenny and Anya had the swagger of newlyweds being presented to the world, as they came down the stairs hand in hand. My eyes rolled to the back of my head, but when they returned, they widened. Both were holding a bottle of wine with their free hand.

"You ready to drink a little?" Lenny asked, as he raised a bottle of red wine into the air and took a seat in the folding chair across the table.

"Does it help?"

"If you are desperate enough to gag it down."

"I'm feeling pretty fucking desperate, you have no idea."

"Oh, I think I have some idea."

"Red or white?" Anya asked as she lifted her bottle up and took a seat in the old lazy boy next to me.

"Which is better?"

"They are both disgusting, at least the white is cold," she told me as she handed me the bottle.

I accepted, smiled, then tilted the bottle toward the ceiling and took a large gulp. I forgot about the sour taste and had overestimated my ability to swallow it. I choked, then coughed a large portion of the wine out and onto my shirt. Without hesitation, I lifted the bottle again, hoping that a successful swig might make everyone forget what they just witnessed. My tongue swirled the swill around in my mouth, allowing my taste buds time to adjust. I swallowed hard and managed only to gag a little.

"Rough night for you too?" Lenny asked, as he took a swig off of his bottle.

"The walk over here was a bit intense."

"You collapsed?"

"And almost died, twice."

"You can't do anything right today can you?"

"I guess not."

"So twice?"

"The second time, that asshole Flick, almost ran my head over with his car."

"On purpose?"

"No, it was kind of my fault, I was in the middle of the street."

"Dying for the first time?"

"Something like that."

"Well if you have to go, you might as well inconvenience some people on your way out, I suppose."

"You two seem to be doing okay."

Lenny's eyes grew wide as he shook his head emphatically, no. I smiled and nodded seemingly sympathetic, but taking pleasure in our shared misery, and grateful the night hadn't been all naked bodies and orgasms. He took a peek over at Anya and I followed. She was also shaking her head as she revisited some of the horrifying details of the night. She looked up at me and reached for her bottle without saying a word. I watched as she took a chug meant for a much larger person. She swallowed it with ease and then handed the wine back. I drank again, now convinced of their antidote.

"What did you see?" I asked.

"People…mostly shadows running around outside…and then footsteps on the roof. We heard helicopters in the distances; spotlights hit the window, followed by ambulances and police sirens."

"Yup, police surrounded my house and I had to jump from my window to get away."

"Jay, you need to stop jumping out of windows."

"You think?"

"One of these times you won't get back up."

"Would that be the worst thing?"

"Being dead?"

"I'm tired, Lenny."

My throat went dry and swelled. I started to cry and tried to hide my tears, but the dam was now overflowing. I faked an itch in my nose and tried to casually wipe myself dry. My vacant stare landed on the concrete wall as I struggled to pull in enough oxygen to calm myself. Lenny and Anya began to move. I feared that one might try to comfort me. The thought of human contact made me gasp. Footsteps headed in the opposite directions. A few clicks followed, and then the sound of a piano being played filled the room and brought an unexpected calm to my breathing.

"Jay, it's okay man, nobody is judging you."

I turned around. Lenny had three blue pills in the palm of his hand and was offering them to me. Anya found a handful of tissue, forcing them on me. I accepted her offer and cleaned myself up the best I could. Lenny leaned forward, grabbed my empty hand, and dropped the pills. He slid the bottle of wine in my directions and nodded.

"You'll feel better in a few minutes."

I threw the pills toward the back of my throat, took a nice pull of wine and fell backward with closed eyes and a tight grasp on the bottle. The music continued to fill the room, hitting my ears, and it was beautiful. I took another sip off the bottle and waited. I remained still and quiet, still too afraid of what might happen if I tried to speak. Warmth filled the room and for a split second, I thought I felt the fingers of my giant wrap around me. This raised my cheeks, but the feeling stabilized and to my disappointment I remained seated in this world.

"How do you feel, Jay?" Lenny asked.

"I feel better, a lot better." I responded with tightly closed eyes.

"Good."

"Lenny, I'm sorry."

"Shit happens in situations like these, right?"

"It's becoming redundant isn't it?"

"Life in general? Or just this night?"

"This life. Trying to forget it is becoming harder and harder, don't you think?"

"Don't start that talk, Jay."

I wasn't able to fully open my eyes, but the fluttering of my lids allowed me to recognize Lenny's smile. I reached up with my free hand, and rubbed my cheeks to see if I was also smiling and I was. Lenny's chuckle allowed me to give up on my attempt at sight. I placed the bottle on the table and allowed my heavy head to fall to the side. Moments later someone was tugging on my feet. My legs were placed on the couch and a layer of protection landed on top of me. I whispered, "Thank you", but I wasn't sure if it was in time. I continued to fight the darkness and enjoy the strange low; eventually there was no choice other than to succumb to sleep.

My deep slumber was interrupted early the next morning when the blanket that had kept me warm all night was ripped from my grasp and tossed to the floor. My eyelids tried to rise, but they weren't completely accepting and fought to keep their seal. A loud repetitive thud hit the side of the couch, shaking my eyes open. Lenny's mother hovered over me. Her hate-filled glare curled me up and pushed me away. Her fists were clutched tight. I covertly patted my pockets, trying to find out how much she knew. They were empty and I was in trouble.

"I don't want to see you in this house ever again." She told me, waiting a second for the response I didn't have, "You are done trying to kill my son."

"Okay."

She snarled and made a motion in my direction, but refrained, and looked away. She remained distracted only long enough to find a small measure of composure. I was now scared. Her deep breaths blew heat in my direction. One false move and

I would become a news story that would be repeated yearly, finally becoming a movie-of-the-week special.

"Put your shoes on and leave."

I didn't react. My shoes were dangerously close to her. She followed my glance and kicked the sneakers in my direction. I repositioned myself and tied my laces. I stood, keeping my head down as I scampered up the stairs. I paused in the living room. I considered running upstairs and shaking Lenny awake, but a full night's sleep killed my suicidal thoughts.

Country Song

I hit the street and began walking. The sky was still dark, but the bright yellow sun was starting to emerge and a beautiful red and orange horizon crept upward with every step I took. The songbirds had also come out and were perched in the trees that lined the road, but they weren't singing to me. Their chirps tightened my shoulders and made me cringe. The thin clouds of morning fog also seemed strange. They had a peculiar pinkish glow that colored my skin, making it apparent that the drug was still alive and coursing through my veins. It feasted on stress and Lenny's mother just produced the adequate feeding. I shook my head and kicked the larger street rocks, disappointed that my night of sleep had failed to end this experience. At least the effect seemed diminished. This allowed my attention to bounce from the horizon to the road, and refuse the audience that the chatter between my ears was demanding. The sky was beautiful, the air was warming, and there were large stones that needed repositioning.

That was all I needed to worry about.

I entered Nikki's house without knocking and made my way past the living room to the staircase. My hand was on the banister and my leg hung in the air ready to step, when the sound of someone torturing a small animal stopped me. Loud, piercing screeches echoed off of the walls and tumbled down the stairs. This was followed by deep bellowing moans. The noises met in the entranceway, mutated together, and danced around me, keeping me paralyzed. Then a sudden, and seemingly fatal, silence sent a chill through my body. A succession of squeals that were louder and more desperate shattered the quiet and motivated me to move. I turned around and started to leave the house, convinced that this was just another cruel hallucination that I wanted nothing to do with.

"Open this fucking door," Nikki's father screamed. "Open this fucking door, right fucking now."

His voice stopped me and I spun around. I heard a heavy fist colliding with Nikki's bedroom door. The sound repeated, shaking the walls and the floor. The cracking of bones pierced my eardrums, as the boom grew louder and louder. Her father's hand was a bloody ball of rage, smashing into a wooden barrier. More squeals resonated from her room, followed by another explosion. Her door was now covered in blood. His face, dripping with red, the carpet where he stood, saturated.

"What the fuck is wrong with you, Nikki?"

Her father's scream confirmed that his voice was real. I tightened my fists, determined to be the man that Nikki needed. I moved up the stairs, wasting no time, and making little noise. Pulsating eyes, spewing hate, landed on me as I reached the top of the stairway. His bloody fists shook, as he slowly moved toward me forgetting all about the door and his daughter behind it. There was determination in his stomp, but I held firm. I stared into his eyes and conveyed my own disgust. Nikki may have been with me when she took the drug, but I wasn't the reason she took it. We were now chest to chest.

"What the fuck did you give my little girl?"

"What the fuck did you do to your little girl?"

He grabbed me by the shirt and pressed me hard against the wall. I raised my arm to swing, but didn't. This was his right and I'd give him a moment to express his anger. His grasp tightened as his forearm pushed against my chest with bone-breaking force. He dug his elbow into my ribcage as his knuckles attempted to snap my collarbone. Enough was finally enough, and with both of my hands, I pushed with all the force I could muster. He stumbled backward a few feet, then regained his balance. His eyes locked on me, his head dropped and he charged. I slid and allowed him to pass by. A little extra push helped him hit the brick wall behind me sooner and with more force. The house shook as he fell backward and hit the ground. Blood gushed from a deep gash in his forehead.

He grunted and reached for his face. He should have been unconscious. His semi-debilitated state would offer the opportunity I needed.

As I watched him wipe the blood away from his eyes and smear it down the side of his face, I considered wrapping my hands around his throat. I started to bend and extend my arms, but no matter how much Nikki hated him, the sight of her dead, bloody father lying in the middle of the hallway wasn't going to help me calm her. I still couldn't resist giving him a long over-due kick in the ribs, before I turned my attention. I moved tight to the door, placed a flat hand on it, and slapped my fingers lightly against the wood, making just enough noise for her to hear. My hope was that she could differentiate between a bang and a tap, but she just whimpered.

"Nikki, are you alright in there?" I whispered, but there was no answer. "Nikki, please open this door and let me in," I begged. "It's Jay, please let me in."

I grabbed the knob, lowered my shoulder and was about to ram the door, when I felt a tug on my ankle. I looked down at her father. He had one hand on me and another arm was reaching up. His eyes were partially shut, and his groaning suggested he was putting the puzzle pieces together. I shook myself loose and stepped backward away from Nikki's room. Then, without much consideration, I stepped and lunged. I kicked the door with a flat foot, full of fierce determination. It exploded open and when the shards of wood fell, a horrific sight caused me to gasp for air.

Nikki was curled up on the floor of her room. Blood speckles stained the carpet around her. During the night she had repeatedly dug her fingernails into the flesh of her body and face, carving out deep red canals. Strands of her hair had been torn out. My beautiful girl resembled a rag doll, torn to shreds by snarling pit bulls fighting to establish dominance. I took a step into the room, but her scream combined with a violent shake stopped me. A sense of guilt, again, tightened around my neck. My head dropped and I saw that the commotion had awoken Nikki's father. He was now on his hands and knees, staring. He rose without blinking. My window of opportunity just slammed shut, but I took another step into the room anyway.

Two heavy hands landed on my shoulders. His fingers dug into my skin, and before I could even try to shake free, my feet were off the ground and I was flat on my back in the hallway. He turned, took two steps, hovering over me. My instincts raised my forearm to block the blow that Nikki's loud screech interrupted. He spun around and both sets of eyes watched in horror as Nikki tore a large chunk of hair from her head. She inspected it curiously for a moment before she tossed it to the ground.

"Nikki what the fuck." Her father yelled.

"Jay, what happened to me?" She screamed

Her father didn't afford me an opportunity to answer. He rushed into the room and scooped Nikki up like a little child. She began to claw and scratch at him like a wild animal. He tightened his grasp, restricting her arms and legs. She continued to squirm for a few more seconds then went limp. I thought it was over, but then two rows of white teeth opened wide, and her head jerked forward. She clamped down on the thin part of his upper ear. Her head shook back and forth as she grinded through skin and cartilage.

"Fucking cunt," he screamed, as he released her.

Nikki slammed to the ground and rolled away from him, crawling to the corner of the room and pushing her back up against the wall. I thought she was scared, but her wide-eyed glare was more vicious than fearful. Her blood covered lips spread into an evil grin, as she wiped the red from her chin and then licked her fingers. Her black eyes remained focused on her father as her smile mutated into snarl. A growling sound resonated from behind clenched teeth. She watched as his fists closed. Once they were tightened, she lunged toward him like one of the pit bulls that tore her to shreds. He stumbled backward and almost fell over me.

"You're fucking gone, you little psychopath."

I watched him turn and storm down the stairs. Once he was out of sight, I crawled toward Nikki. I could hear him stomping back and forth between the kitchen and the living room. He began ranting, but he wasn't talking to himself. He was barking orders, and making demands. The clock was again ticking. I stopped halfway across the room and searched Nikki's face for some form of recognition. There was nothing. I remained still and staring at her while she gazed through me. Tears formed in both our eyes, rolling down our cheeks. My sadness penetrated her catatonic state. She delivered a sad smile and for the next several minutes we sat there crying, searching for an explanation.

"Nikki, baby," I whispered.

"Jay, what happened to me?" She asked, as she examined her arms.

"I'm not sure," I told her as I wiped away my tears in an attempt to appear strong.

"They did it to me."

"Who did what to you?"

"The people that cut me like this. They put the eggs in my skin and I had to get them out before they hatched."

"It's okay, baby."

"But I didn't get them all, Jay. They hatched and the bugs started crawling underneath my skin. They are still crawling 'cause I didn't get them all. I needed to get them all."

She then dug a fingernail into a strip of skin on her forearm and scratched it off the bone before I could reach out and stop her. She raised the bloody flesh to eye level, examined it, and flicked it to the floor. I remained silent, because even after searching there were no words to say. My eyes returned to their sockets and I inched my way closer. Her tears again accumulated and streamed down her face. I opened my arms and extended them. She crawled in and I wrapped her up and held her.

"Jay, what did I do?" She asked as she stared upward for answer.

"I'm not sure, baby, I'm not sure."

"What happens next?"

"I don't know."

"Don't say that," she ordered, as she slapped my chest. "Give me a good answer."

"Baby, I really don't know."

"It's going to be alright though, isn't it?" She waited for an answer, but I refused to tell her the lie I so desperately wanted to whisper. "How bad is it, Jay?"

A loud commotion coming from the entranceway answered that question for me. Nikki began to shake as the sound of closed fists pounding on the front door bounced up the stairs and into the room. Her father stomped his way to the front door, opened it and began yelling out before a question was asked. Calm voices requested only the pertinent information and after a short conversation, a stampede trampled its way up the stairs.

Nikki's fingers dug into my back as her shake turned violent.

"Tell them 'no'," she begged me. "Tell them that you will take care of me. I only need you, Jay, just you. Tell them, Jay. Tell them please, I can't leave you."

"Baby, I'm sorry."

Dark shadows turned into blurry figments and my eyes adjusted to find three EMTs standing in the doorway, whose eyes were filled with disgust. Nikki's father informed them of the situation, and the jury came to a verdict without a trial. Junkies. That's all we were to these men and they treated us as such. Two men tore a screaming Nikki from my clutches, while the third man dug his fingers into my arms. I was forcefully tossed to the side. Nikki continued to scream and reach for me as they lifted her into the air and tossed her onto the stretcher without compassion or any consideration for her injuries. One of the EMT's pressed his knee deep into her chest, as a second yanked her restraints tight. Her sad eyes remained on my face, begging me to make it stop, but all I could do was watch helplessly from the corner as they wheeled her out, passing her smiling father.

"She's not coming back, I'll make sure of that," her father announced, as he turned and found me, "I hope you said your good-byes."

"Wherever she is going, she'll be better off away from you."

He was still standing in the hall, but the pleasure he derived from watching his daughter restrained was exchanged for his seething hatred for me. He didn't bother responding. He just shook his head and smirked at me, pretending I was foolish. I snickered back at him as I stood up. I tensed my muscles and puffed my chest, informing him that I was ready. He began laughing, because he knew there was nothing left to take from me. He spit in my direction, then turned and left the hallway. I waited until I heard his feet hit the last step, and made my way out of the room.

I ran out of the house and shot across the lawn just as the men were locking up the back of the ambulance, but not in time to find Nikki's eyes for a final good-bye. The front doors slammed shut and seconds later, the lights started flashing. The shrill sound of the siren wailing brought a heavy sense of permanence, forcing me to stare at the ground. When I looked back up, the ambulance was speeding down the road, seconds away from turning and disappearing for good.

Nikki was gone, but her father was now sitting on the top step of the front porch sucking on a beer like he was at a spectator's sport. I shook my head and scoffed, right before I returned the spit that he sent in my direction. He laughed and started to shrug off the gesture, but instead, decided to half-heartedly hurl his half-full beer in my direction. He did so without aiming or standing up. The bottle tumbled through the sky, but didn't manage to make it to the street. I snickered at the stupidity as I turned and started my departure.

I was once again kicking rocks, but this time I did so with a hole in my heart and no destination in mind. My lack of options demanded a creative solution. I began to think that maybe I should just find a set of train tracks to follow. I could catch a slow moving freighter that was headed south and ride it 'til the end of the line. I would start over, in a small town that sat on the sea where it remained warm all year 'round. I would get a job on a fishing boat. I would work hard and drink harder. I'd rescue a mangy mutt that followed me everywhere and buy a cheap truck so he'd have a window to hang his head from. I'd find a nice woman to shack up with who would massage my sore muscles and take off my boots when I was too drunk to remember. It would be a simple life, not much to brag about, but it would be mine.

"Hey. You," Lenny's mother screamed, pulling me from my fantasy. "I thought I told you I never wanted to see you at this house again."

I halted in the middle of the road and spun around in circles, shocked to realize that I was in front of Lenny's home. My feet stopped and my eyes landed on Lenny's mother. She was standing at the front door, foaming at the mouth like an attack dog that just spotted an intruder. The wild look in her eye made it clear there wasn't an acceptable explanation for my arrival. I had walked here out of habit and I couldn't have had worse timing. The car was warming up in the driveway and as I looked closer, I saw that Lenny was buckled into his seat. His head twisted back and forth emphatically, while his bugging, wide eyes continued to land on the front of the house. This sight scared me and I turned my attention back to his mother who had already begun her charge.

"Why are you here? Why did you come here?" She asked me, as she continued to wave both hands like I wasn't watching her storm towards me. "You're not welcome at this house. I never want to see you here again."

"You fucking said that already," I screamed at her, as I motioned for her to turn and go to her car. I was aware of our size difference and not at all scared. She didn't oblige my direction, but she did stop several feet away from me. We continued to stare at each other and in doing so, we realized the ridiculous nature of this charade. My eyes lost interest and strayed. I caught a glance from Lenny. He seemed proud of me for standing firm. I cringed at his odd smile and childish wave. This shift in focus was obvious to his mother and she interrupted the moment.

"I'm going to call your parents," she threatened.

"Do you need the number?"

"What is wrong with you?"

"Because your son does drugs, something has to be wrong with me?

What's wrong with your husband, lady?"

Her anger transformed into a deep sadness. She bit her lip and searched the trees and sky for an explanation to the truth that I had just smacked her with. I never molested Nikki and I didn't sneak out on Lenny in the middle of the night. I was guilty of having my own demons that I was trying to outrun, but that was it. I was no longer willing to be saddled with guilt, and ridden around the backyard like a pony because her son and I were running the same race.

"He's my son," She finally said, as she looked up at me with tears still in her eyes. "Just leave him alone, please."

I ignored her and began walking. I could feel her watching me, begging me for some form of acknowledgement, but my anger kept my head down. Lenny was also staring, but my need to deny that we had spent our last days together kept my focus on my feet. The car started moments later and I heard it pull down the drive. It turned in the opposite direction, like I knew it would, regardless. She wasn't going to risk me running down the street next to the car trying to free her son. She needed to believe that I was crazy and that by turning left instead of right, driving her son far away, was going to solve her problems. I didn't know where she was taking Lenny, but the sadness in her face told me he would be gone for a long time, if not forever.

This thought was overwhelming and it forced me to stop and take a seat on the curb. I wanted a fresh start now more than ever; walking the train tracks to a magical beach town offering me love, money, and a dog just for showing up, seemed unrealistic. I needed the Cutlass. I jumped to my feet and began jogging back to Lenny's. A sense of enthusiasm caused a childish grin, spreading from ear to ear. I would find the keys, hit the gas, and soar down the interstate. When they arrived home, I would already be in New Jersey, where I would sign the deed to the car and trade it in for my old, rusted-out pickup truck. Once I crossed the border to the south, I was bound to find a mangy street pup wandering aimlessly that I could rescue. The mutt and I would hang our heads out of the windows, while we cruised into Florida. We would drive until we found the poorest neighborhood on the sea, where most the town's people were illiterate, and my new best friend would appear smarter than the average person.

I entered the house happy, but as I passed through the kitchen and into the living room, the extent of Lenny's mother's determination punched me in the gut. My feet chased my head around and around the room, while I gasped for air. Everywhere I looked I saw boxes. Some were taped shut, while others were half full. The television, the DVD player, and the stereo were gone. Even the clock and the antique mirror were off the wall. My legs started to shake. My vision faded to black. My knees buckled and I hit the ground. My sight returned moments later, but my enthusiasm did not. I curled up into a tight ball and closed my eyes. I planned on remaining there until I was found and taken away, but the voice in my head continued babbling until it had rattled off enough small reasons to push me to my feet. I took a final glance around, kicked open a few taped boxes, then made my way up to Lenny's room.

I moved to the desk, ignoring his half-packed room. I tore each drawer out and tossed it into the air with no real purpose other than destruction. When I was done, fragments of wood and metal covered the floor and Lenny's keys were in my pocket. The ruin I stood over brought relief. I was now breathing easy and able to turn my attention to the boxes. One by one, I reached down and ripped them open. I lifted them above my head and shook the contents out. Then, just for fun, I jumped up and down on each box, rendering it useless. In an attempt to put an exclamation point on my demolition, I spun around the room like a tornado ripping down the pictures, posters, and even the mirror that hung on the wall. I took a moment admiring my work, before I exited.

I moved down the hall and into Lenny's mother's room. My high cheeks dropped when I discovered that there was no packaging to destroy. My thirty dollars was sitting on her nightstand, so I stuffed that into my pocket. I turned and started to leave, stopping before I hit the door. I couldn't resist embracing this new form of therapy I had discovered. I spun back around, stepped to the dresser, and tipped over the large mirror that hung above it. It hit the ground and smashed. Fragments of glass spread across the rug. They attracted the sun and created a glow, forcing my smile to return. I bounced back over to the nightstand, pulled the drawers, and flung them across the room like they were Frisbees. They hit the wall with enough force to create holes before they disassembled and fell. I grabbed a handful of jewelry that looked expensive, and considered kicking and shattering the sliding glass doors of the closet, when I suddenly needed to urinate. I started toward the hall but stopped. The sense of calm I achieved was derived from strange acts, so I let my pants drop to my ankles and I shuffled over to the bed. A devilish grin spread wide as I waved my stream back and forth, covering as much area as possible. I discovered the exclamation point I was looking for.

I skipped down the stairs and into to the kitchen. I was again excited about casting a steel line from the back of a small fishing boat and earning a mediocre wage that would support my drinking and buy the dog its food. I stopped at the liquor cabinet, pulled out two bottles and took a seat at the kitchen table. I was eager to get a jump-start on my adventure into alcoholism. I didn't want to look like a rookie when I hit the boat, so I un-capped the whiskey, because that's what real fishermen drank. I took a big swig and found out that not everyone was born with sea legs.

A burning sensation traveled half way down my throat, and then I choked, coughed, and spit the entire gulp out onto the table. I twisted the top back on, while trying to shake and pucker the taste out of my mouth. I grabbed the bottle of vodka, because every dream worthwhile takes a little bit of work, and I wasn't giving up on mine. I unscrewed the top, but as I lifted the bottle, my eyes landed on the hands of the clock above the sink.

It was half past noon. I had no idea where Lenny's mother went or when she was coming back, but I didn't need to be sitting in her kitchen, toasting to the destruction of her home when she arrived.

I skipped across the front lawn with a bottle in each hand and a smile that was taking pleasure in the wide-open front door that begged the attention of any passerby with questionable morals. I had Lenny's keys, liquor, jewelry, and thirty bucks in my pocket, 'so let the savage have at it', I thought, as I climbed into the car and started it. I adjusted my seat, fixed my mirrors and found a country music radio station that would put me in the mood for drinking whiskey while traveling through the south. I was ready to go, when I realized I didn't have the gas to go anywhere.

"Fucking Lenny."

I grabbed the bottle of whiskey off the passenger seat, unscrewed the top, and turned the country music up. I closed my eyes tight, tilted the bottle just slightly and slurped the small amount of booze that was waiting just below the opening. It burned going down, and it hurt even worse when it came back up, but after gagging twice, it was safely in my belly. I waited a minute and took a slightly larger pull, but this time I did so with my eyes open. This attempt went down a little easier and only had to be pushed back down once. My tummy was now warm and I took a moment to enjoy the feeling, listening to the man on the radio. He was singing about losing his woman. He wanted her back, but he didn't know where she'd gone. He wasn't even sure if she would take him back or if he could find her, but he was sure she had the dog. It was all very confusing, but it compelled me to take a large swig off my bottle of southern liquor, swallowing like a proud country boy. When it hit my stomach, I was still a little worried about the man singing, but my life was becoming clearer. My world without Nikki made no sense at all and it wasn't a place I wanted to be. Luckily for me, I knew where my woman was headed, and she would take me back if I could find her, so I put the car in reverse and stepped on the gas.

Whiskey and Fries

I arrived at the hospital, but remained outside pacing back and forth in front of the large, sliding glass doors. I searched the ground for the story that could explain my arrival, managing only to discover reason after reason why I should be speeding down the interstate rather than circling a small patch of the sidewalk. I despised this place. Inside, it smelled like death, with cleaning products sprinkled on it. The people disgusted me. The elderly made up the majority. They sat reading, while the scent of decaying organs resonated from their pores. Sick little children ran wild, rubbing their snot-covered hands on everything, while disease emanated with every breath they took. Then there was the awful moaning of the injured. The sight of blood and exposed bones from the wrong angle could buckle my knees and drop me. The displeasures in the waiting room were nauseating, but it wasn't the main deterrent. The educated minds and trained eyes, walking around in white jackets, posed the biggest threat. One curious glance could result in the forming of a committee, a unified diagnosis would follow, and before I realized what had happened, I'd be standing behind a locked door. This was the situation I was trying to save Nikki from and I needed to reach her before the key to that door was thrown away.

As I entered the hospital, I made a concerted effort to keep my focus straight ahead and on the heavy set, Latino nurse standing behind a long counter that separated the patients from the administration. She was chewing a piece of gum like it insulted her, while sorting papers into various files. My footsteps drew her attention for a brief moment, her eyes widening slightly, not out of shock, but in annoyance for the interruption I was about to cause. Her focus dropped back down to her paperwork before I reached her. She continued to ignore me as I made my final steps and I appreciated her disinterest. I may have bruises on my face and blood on my shirt, but I could walk, and seemingly in no imminent danger, thus making me less important than her need for organization. This disregard allowed me to proceed with confidence.

"Nikki Esposito, please."

"Can I help you sir?" the nurse asked, as she barely looked up.

"Nikki Esposito." I repeated.

"I'm not sure what that means, sir. You're going to have to be a little more specific," she told me, still focusing on her work.

"She's a patient somewhere in this hospital. Nikki Esposito, that's her name."

"You don't know what floor?"

"No."

"But you are sure that she was admitted to this hospital, today?"

"She was admitted this hour...just now probably."

The frustration in my voice was apparent. The nurse straightened and focused. Her eyes bulged as she examined my face. Lack of sleep, malnutrition, obvious drug abuse; I could see her silently diagnosing me and reaching a prognosis that wasn't good. She forced a smile, continuing to chomp out the remaining flavor in her gum. I could tell she was flipping through a mental Rolodex, full of options.

"Is there a problem?" I snapped.

"Sir, calm down, I'm just trying to get information."

"I am calm. I just asked you a question. How is that not calm?"

"You seem agitated and I want to help you."

"You could press some keys on that computer and tell me where to go.

That would help."

"What exactly was she admitted for?"

Her tightly crossed arms, squinted eye stare, and the way her tongue was moving her gum around the inside of her bottom lip made me nervous. The aggressive tone in her voice shattered my confidence and forced my focus to shift around the room. A security guard, leaning against the wall a few feet away, grew interested in us. I intercepted a short glance between the two of them earlier, but hadn't deemed it concerning. He was now standing upright and this had me wondering if Nikki's mother had informed them both of the possibility of my arrival.

"I'm not sure, I just know that she came in within the last hour or so."

"And you are positive it was this hospital?" She asked again. It was clear that she was stalling for some reason.

"Yes."

"How old is she?"

"Seventeen."

"Let me look, but I don't remember a young girl," she told me, as she turned her attention to her computer. I assumed Nikki had been rushed from the ambulance, through the waiting room, and was receiving immediate attention, but now I was searching the seats, wondering if she was still sitting in the waiting room. Her injuries weren't life threatening, but they were self-inflicted. It was possible they were making her wait as punishment. I was also looking for the 'good Samaritan' character present in almost every hospital movie scene. The guy who witnessed Nikki come in and couldn't wait to help me find her, not realizing I was the drug-addicted boyfriend responsible. This whole situation felt like that made-for television teen drama, I envisioned earlier in Lenny's basement. Nikki was now the star of the show and I found the story I was looking for in the parking lot.I was the distraught brother character whose sister had gotten involved with a bad crowd. She had been at a party, drinking, trying to fit in, and they pressured her into taking drugs.

"Sir, what did you say the name was?" The nurse asked.

"Nikki Esposito. She's my sister, and she had an accident of some sort." I blurted out, "I woke up to a frantic message from my father, saying that she was on her way here, but that's all I know." I told her, realizing that I was getting a little carried away with my new role.

The lady stared at me for a moment, processing the onslaught of information I had just thrown at her. She finally nodded and began banging away on her little keyboard. She continued to press on it for several seconds. Finally she stopped, but didn't respond. She just stared at the screen. I already knew how bad it was, so my concern was focused on conveying an appropriate response to the news she was about to deliver.

"She's on the third floor, CPW3."

"What exactly does that mean? I'm not familiar with those letters." I lied.

It was too late. Nikki was locked behind large steal doors and pacing the dirty, dimly lit halls of the psyche ward with the other animals society deemed unfit. The decision was made and it was obvious that while Nikki was being rushed to the back to have her cuts cleaned and bandaged, her mother was lobbying for her daughter's institutionalization. The men in the white jackets skipped the formality of a preliminary conversation with Nikki. Instead, they formed a small circle several feet away from her bed, took a couple of glances, whispered among themselves for a moment, and came to a unanimous decision. Nikki's transfer from the Immediate Care Unit to the psyche ward was signed. She would receive a sedative before this news was delivered and by the time the nurse showed up with the wheelchair, a long string of saliva would be dampening her lap.

"It means her condition is not critical."

"What is CPW3?"

"It means that she has been taken to the third floor."

"Obviously, it's not the three that's confusing me, it's the CPW."

She paused, then answered, "County Psych Ward."

"Oh."

I didn't want to overreact, so I remained still and silent. My focus shifted around the room, bouncing from person to person.

A vacant stare finally landed on the wall behind the nurse and remained there. I began to bite the nail of my thumb; the thought of my sister locked away in such a place was unfathomable. In reality, I was using each nibble to count the seconds. I didn't want to over exaggerate this moment.

"What does that mean exactly? What's wrong with her?"

"That's all the information I have."

"So she is in the psyche ward, but you can't tell me why?"

"Who did you say you were?" the nurse asked again, but this time I found a small amount of compassion in her voice.

"I'm her brother."

"I can have a doctor come and talk to you when one is available, or maybe you could call your parents."

I looked around at all the miserable sick faces and knew there was no way I was waiting in this cesspool of disease.

"Can I just go up and see her?"

"No, not until four. That's when visiting hours start."

"What do they do until four? Shock therapy?" I asked jokingly. The only response I got was a scowl.

Embarrassed, I turned and looked for a clock. My eyes were burning, and my eyelids were heavy and wanted to drop. I squinted through my blurry vision, but the vibrating hands telling the time melted together into one long, shaky black line and pulling them apart was impossible. A gnawing sensation was now chewing at my gut, suggesting that I was hungry; my body was damp with perspiration. This was all a good sign. I felt sick, the last of the drugs were being sweated out, my appetite had returned, and the possibility of unaided sleep had arrived. The trip was finally over and I was ready to eat a cheeseburger, drink some whiskey, and take a nap.

"It's 1:15," The nurse finally told me.

"I think I'll just come back."

"Are you sure?"

"Yes, I'm sure."

"Are you okay, sir?" She asked staring at the sweat that collected above my brow.

"I'm just a little overwhelmed. "I told her, as I wiped my forehead. "Do you want to take a seat? I can get you some water."

"I think sitting around waiting might be a little too much for me. I'm going to get something to eat and come back at four. Will you be here?" I asked, even though I didn't really care and wasn't sure why I had done so.

"I won't be, but you don't need to come to this desk. "She told me, as she leaned forward and pointed down the hallway. "Just take the elevator to the third floor and someone will talk to you."

"Thank you for your help."

"I hope everything works out."

I turned, walked away from the desk and past the waiting area. I was hungry, but also nauseated, so I kept my head down and focus straight, knowing that the sight of one broken leg with a protruding bone could put an end to my whiskey and burger dream. The glass doors slid open, fresh air hit my face and I began skipping across the parking lot. My keys were in my hand several steps before I reached the Cutlass and my head was held high. I just walked straight into the lion's den and I could drive away proud that I made an attempt to save Nikki, even though I wasn't positive that there would be a second try. I'd wait until after food, drink and sleep to make that decision.

I twisted the key, turned up the radio, and flipped the switch to the air conditioning. The cool air attacked my wet skin, my eyelids dropped and my head fell backwards into the seat. I reached for the whiskey, pulled the top, took a swig and relaxed. On the radio, a man was strumming on a banjo while hollering about his wife stealing his truck and running off with the dog. I started to wonder what was wrong with these southern women, when a bounce in my neck interrupted the thought. My eyes jarred open and I was staring at my lap. I shook myself awake. There was an order to the way the proceeding events needed to take place and passing out in the hospital parking lot was not first on list. I capped my booze, put the car in reverse, and hit the gas.

I had a particular burger in mind as I drove, but the squiggly lines that divided the street forced me to pull into the first fast food place I could find. After misjudging the curve in the drive-thru and scraping the Cutlass against the corner of the building, I was finally staring at a large glowing menu. Everything was dripping with sauce and cheese and I wanted it all. Unfortunately, my cramping stomach reminded me that it shrank considerably. My thin pockets also forced me to restrain my gluttonous desires. There were going to be more important needs when I awoke, so I ordered a kid's meal and an extra side of fries.

I found a nice, shady spot several blocks away from the hospital. I parked in between an old pickup truck and a beat-up Oldsmobile sitting on cinder blocks. The street was lined with boarded up, abandoned houses sitting on overgrown lawns and I was confident that the Cutlass wouldn't draw any unwanted attention here. I unwrapped my kid's burger and stuffed half of it into my mouth. The bread was stale. The meat was dry and chewy, but after two more large bites it was gone. I sucked down the rest of the whiskey and combined the vodka with my sprite. I leaned back in my seat and sipped on my cocktail as I enjoyed my double order of fries.

I woke up a couple hours later to the sound of metal tapping against glass. An old black street bum, wearing no shirt, was banging on my window with an empty beer can. His free hand was motioning for me to roll down the window while his yellow eyes remained focused on the half empty bottle of vodka on the passenger seat. I wasn't happy about the interruption, but pleased that my vision was no longer blurred. I ignored the man and raised my arm into the air; there was no shake in my hand. I wiped my forehead and it was dry. I felt refreshed. My mind was clear and focused on Nikki. I turned the key, put the car in drive, and hit the gas, without acknowledging the man's request.

I strutted through the glass doors of the hospital with confidence. There was a different Latino nurse, chomping on a piece of gum behind the long counter. I waved at her as I passed by. She puckered her face and searched her surroundings to see whom I was acknowledging. I laughed to myself as I continued down the hall. I was feeling good. I even smiled at an old, decrepit woman sitting by the elevator, but I made sure not to exhale too hard in her direction for fear she might turn to dust.

The elevator doors opened into a small, empty waiting room. I took a seat in a chair and began my wait. I was still feeling confident, but there was something about the white walls that tightened my shoulders. A small vent filled the area with cold, sterile air that left a taste in my mouth every time I took a breath. The tick of the wall clock echoed ominously off the walls, which were now pulsating. My chest tightened as the four sides of the room inched closer and closer. My shield of confidence had cracked. My legs were desperate to shake out some of the anxiety, so I leaned forward and pressed my elbows into my knees. I wanted to avoid looking like a man whose shock therapy hadn't worn off and needed immediate help. I was now sweating and the perspiration stunk of whiskey. My arms tightened against my body to conceal the stench my damp armpits were emitting. With a bare hand, I tried to wipe away the beads that accumulated above my brow, which didn't help. The moisture just smeared, and my entire forehead was now glistening under the fluorescent lights.

I was a complete mess, so I stood up and began to pace the twelve-by twelve waiting area. This looked far less suspicious than sitting still in a cold room, perspiring. I moved in small circles, staring at my feet. I counted the bleached tiles and examined the space between them, questioning the collection of dirt that somehow managed to survive the regularly scheduled sanitization. I listened to the clock echoing off the bare walls. The hard thump of my heart collided with the melodic tick and I began to breathe in unison. My pulse rate slowed, the perspiration ceased, and I began to relax.

A scream disrupted my tenuous calmness. My head snapped in the direction of the sound. I began searching, peering through the window that led into the ward. There was steel mesh between two panes of glass. This obstructed my view, so I moved closer. I pushed my face against the glass and tried to squint through one of the small squares. The sound repeated. This time it was laced with desperation. I pushed harder, anxiously examining the situation inside.

I could see several blurry figures all dressed in hospital-issued pajamas moving arbitrarily up and down a poorly lit hallway. Nurses dressed in blue, buzzed in and out of a large octagon shaped desk, sitting dead center. A person dressed in all white seemed to be circling aimlessly. There was man in a suit that appeared, said a few words to the nurses then disappeared behind a closed door. The chaotic scene was underwhelming only because it seemed to be happening in slow motion.

A loud buzz startled me and I jumped away from the glass .I straightened, pulled the wrinkles out of my shirt and continued to hold my arms tight against my body. The large steel door slowly inched open. Two brown eyes peered at me through the small crevice. I smiled and tried to appear calm as an overweight, gray-haired woman holding a chart, inched her way into the room.

"Who are you?"

"Lenny Esposito."

"Who's the patient?"

"Nikki Esposito; I'm her brother. She came in this morning."

"Okay, you can come in," she said, opening the door.

I walked over to the door while she continued to look me over. I kept a straight face, nodding just slightly in appreciation for her assistance. She returned the gesture, then placed a soft hand on my back and gently guided me. The touch sent a slight shiver down my spine that went unnoticed by the nurse. Even if she had, I was a distraught family member and a slight amount of anxiety was to be expected.

"You're the brother?"

"That's right."

"I don't remember your mother or sister mentioning you."

"Well, I'm sure they weren't thinking about me either."

The nurse nodded, as if she understood. "I'm going to need you to sign in."

She again placed her hand on my back and pushed me toward the octagon desk. The thump of my heart may not be cause for concern, but I was afraid the dampness of my shirt could raise a question I had no answer for. I signed the visitor sheet with my new fictitious name, which seemed appropriate. I turned and waited for my next direction. The nurse pointed and I followed her down the hall. My arrival drew the attention of the patients. They huddled together and stared. Their glances were heavy with intrigue, as they mistook me as a new admission. Whispers grew louder as they discussed my possible maladjustments.

We passed doorway after doorway. Most rooms were quiet. Loud singular voice chatter resonated from a few; I heard some moaning and screaming coming from one. The large man dressed in all white made his way down the hall and attended to this disturbance. Most of these people would spend the rest of their lives on this ward protecting their dark realities. These damaged psyches would never be fit to live in the real world again. I feared that Nikki fell into this category and sadness overwhelmed me. My body trembled, my eyes swelled, and I was forced to choke my tears down. The sudden change in my disposition caught the nurse's attention.

"Are you all right?" She asked as she stopped.

I continued to walk. The cease in motion registered a few steps later, and I halted. I turned and stared. She was compassionately studying my face. I appreciated her concern and smiled, took a few steps toward her, then motioned for her to continue.

"I'm okay. I've just never been in a place like this and it's hard to believe that my sister is here."

"This is a good hospital with good doctors. Your sister will be well taken care of here. I promise you that."

"It's just overwhelming," I told her.

"I understand, dear, but patients tend to feed off the emotions of their visitors. Be brave for your sister."

"I think I'm just a little anxious, but I'll pull it together."

She smiled and we proceeded down the hallway. Nikki's room was just a few steps later. It was the second-to-last in the hall. I figured this was a good sign. Suicidal patients and people that were violent and considered a danger to others would be kept the closest. The mildly depressed and the drug-addicts were most likely stored in the back. They caused the least amount of trouble and they weren't really a priority. I was happy that Nikki had been labeled appropriately.

"This is her room," the nurse told me, as she softly tapped on the door. There was no response. She tried again, this time with more force, but still there was no response. "She might be sleeping."

She tried a third time, but still there was nothing. She paused and waited, wanting me to suggest an alternative. I ignored her. She lightly pushed, nudging the door open. A dry hinge announced our arrival. This was greeted by a reluctant whimper. We took another step into the room. The squeal of the hinge amplified. Nikki let out a noise, which resembled that of a caged animal fearing torture

"Maybe this isn't the best time. I don't know that she can handle the excitement," the nurse whispered as she began to inch backwards.

I stood firmly behind her, halting her retreat. Her decision was final. She continued her attempt to push me backwards. I wouldn't budge so she shoved her elbow and forearm into my chest. My body got hot and frustration overwhelmed me.I swiped my arm across her breasts and grabbed her shoulder, forcing her out of my way. Stepping past her into the room, I stumbled and bumped into the door, colliding with the wall.

Another fearful squeal echoed from Nikki.

"This isn't a good time."

I ignored her again and took another step into the room, realizing that she had grabbed onto my shirt and was trying to restrain me. I twisted my body free. I had enough. The look in my eye must have explained my willingness to allow this to escalate. She stared, but decided not make another attempt at stopping me.

"This is unacceptable. I need you to come out of this room now."

I shook my head and moved further into the room. She retreated down the hall, so I knew my time was limited. I made my way over to the bed. Darkness impaired my vision, but I could distinguish a large mass underneath the blankets. I squatted down and began caressing what I believed to be Nikki's back.

"Baby, it's just me."

A sudden movement knocked me off my feet. I landed on my back and stared upward into black eyes that refused to blink. I remained still. I would allow her ample time to investigate. She continued to examine me, refusing to relax.

"Baby, it's me. Are you alright?" I asked, as I moved to a knee.

"Jay, is that you?" She was squinting at me as if I were an old acquaintance, a friend that she hadn't seen for years and hardly recognized.

"Are you alright?" I asked again.

"Jay, what happened to me?" She looked around the room. "Where am I? What is this place?" Tears filled her eyes as she surveyed her surroundings.

Although I had already seen it, the destruction of her face startled me. I was speechless. My mouth was open but nothing was coming out. I just shook my head and searched for an explanation. It scared her. She began to tremble. Her eyes closed, she turned away from me, and flipped on her side.

"Baby."

"Jay, I'm sorry."

"Baby, it's not your fault. I still love you."

I never said these words before. I hadn't realized I was saying them until they came out. Nikki flipped back over and faced me. She was smiling. She looked happy while tears were streaming down her face.

"You love me?"

"Yes, baby."

"You love me."

I reached out to touch her, but before I could, two large hands landed on my shoulders. I watched the happiness in her face turn to fear. Suddenly, I was yanked backwards and hit the floor hard. A knee landed on my chest as I struggled to move. Hands tightened around my wrists and locked them in place. Once again, I found myself staring upward into angry eyes. I tried to kick and he let go of one hand to strike me twice in the side with a closed fist. Just as I was resigning to my fate, the sound of shattering glass interrupted us. The man looked up and searched the room, Nikki was gone. She had gotten out of bed and gone into the bathroom while we were wrestling. A loud crash forced him to release his grasp on me. He stood up and ran over to the door, yanking it open. Nikki was lying on the floor, blood covering her face and forehead. She seemed to be laughing.

"Go get some fucking help. "He screamed at me.

I moved to my hands and knees so I could see what was happening. Nikki was staring directly at me. She smashed her head against the mirror and was bleeding. Red glass covered the ground around her. She reached for me as blood gushed from a deep cut she carved into her wrist. The man panicked and grabbed a handful of toilet paper, trying to wrap the wound. Within seconds it was saturated and useless.

"Go get some fucking help." The man screamed, as he wrapped more toilet paper around her arm.

"Baby."

"Run, Jay, run. I love you." She silently mouthed.

I stood up and looked at her one last time, then sprinted out of the room. I hurried down the hallway waving my arms at the women behind the octagon desk. They seemed puzzled that I emerged unaccompanied.

They stared, unconvinced by my plea for help.

"Are you fucking kidding?"

"What is going on?"

"My sister slit her wrists, she is fucking bleeding. "I screamed as ran into the desk.

The women stood and made their way out from behind the desk. I watched as they hurried down the hall to Nikki's room and disappeared. I ran to the door and tried to yank it open. It was locked and wouldn't budge. I moved back to the desk. I leaned over and began searching. I pressed every button I could find. Lights turned on, lights turned off. A couple of bells sounded, and finally a buzzer rang. This was the sound I needed to hear.I ran back to the door, slipped out, and disappeared.

A Final Boot to the Head

I sat in Lenny's car with the engine running, still in 'park'. I was staring at the steering wheel unable to think about anything other than Nikki's bloody arm reaching for me. I was choking on this image. My chest was tight and every breath I took hurt. I wanted to cry, thinking it might help, but the tears wouldn't come. So, I just sat motionless and wide-eyed, drowning in a sadness that would have sunk me if a hard knock hitting the car window hadn't broken me out of my trance. I looked up. A middle-aged woman was staring down at me, making a motion suggesting I roll down the window. Her kind eyes, nice smile and seemingly honest intentions, put me at ease, so I obliged her even though I had nothing to say.

"Are you okay in there?"

I continued to stare up at her not knowing how to answer the question. I opened my mouth and started to say something, but I couldn't speak. My chest had tightened even more and I was now gasping for air. My eyes began to fill with tears. My mind was racing and the weight of the guilt resting on my shoulders was unbearable. It was my fault and I had the urge to admit everything and unburden myself, but this wouldn't stop Nikki's bleeding. It wouldn't rescue Lenny from whatever hole his mother dropped him in. It would provide temporary relief for me, but I wasn't sure at what cost, so I remained silent and allowed my eyes to overflow and stream.

"Are you okay?"She asked again.

"I don't know."

"Are you hurt? Do you need help?"

"I'm not hurt."

"Can I walk you in or do you need assistance?"

My tears released the tension. I took a few deep breaths and then looked around. Nikki's fate was sealed. Even if I chose to walk up to the doors with this woman, hold my arms out, and turn myself in, they weren't going to let me near her. They would hold me, then ship me off to a separate facility. Nikki sacrificed herself for me and if I ended up behind lock and key, then all the blood she spilled would be in vain.

"I'm actually leaving." I didn't wait for the woman to question my response. I put the car in reverse and hit the gas, looking back at the woman as I pulled away. She was making her way into the hospital and I appreciated this. It was one less thing to worry about. Now I just needed some sort of plan. Alcohol would be the appropriate drug to help me forget.

In the sketchy area of the neighboring city there was an old, rundown restaurant called The Rastafa BBQ, which allowed minors to sit in the back alley and drink overpriced, watered down rum drinks. That's where I was headed. I knew a few of the kids that frequented the joint although they weren't the type of people you wanted to spend too much time with. They liked to drink, and when drunk they would become violent. A fight would inevitably erupt, either among themselves or between them and some innocent bystander. An extended glance could elicit an inappropriate amount of anger, which would then escalate into a brawl. Sometimes these altercations would include knives being used or a gun being fired.

I parked the car on the street and made my way into the restaurant. I kept my head down as I walked the narrow aisle between the tables. This was the ghetto, and most of the people dining had grown accustomed to the sight of homeless people and drug-addicts. Since I looked better than your average street bum and smelled about the same, no one took much exception to my arrival.

The young, black woman that was standing behind the counter did take a step back as I drew closer. She examined me for a moment and wasn't sure if she should take my order or request that I leave. I ignored her and looked into the kitchen. An old Jamaican man working the grill saw me, stopped what he was doing and came out to greet me.

"He's okay," he told the girl as he extended his arm.

We shook hands and he led me into the kitchen. We stopped once we were out of view from the customers. I pulled twenty dollars from my pocket and handed it to him. In return, he gave me a dime bag of swag marijuana, rolling papers and a bottle filled with rum and juice mixture.I didn't smoke normally, but this was the price of admission.I stuffed the weed and papers into my pocket and tipped my bottle in his direction as an act of gratitude. He nodded, shook my hand again, and then opened the back door leading to a long, poorly lit alley.

"Yo, yo, my mother-fucker. "Mickey screamed at me as I took a step into the alley.

Mickey stood up and stumbled his way over to me. He wrapped an arm around my neck and stared into my eyes. The interaction was a little too intimate for my taste and it caused my body to tense up involuntarily. Mickey was a scumbag who I wasn't exactly fond of. He also smelled worse than I did. He was dressed in his work clothes, which had been clean and fresh early that week, but hadn't seen the washing machine since. The day's dirt combined with his sweat created a grime that was still noticeable on his hands, arms and face. Some of this filth was caked into his beard. The sight was too much and I tried to pull away, but he continued his greeting by dragging me toward the table where he was sitting. This annoyed me and I shook myself free. He stared at me for a moment, insulted, but he knew we weren't close friends. We grew up at the park together, but had always been part of two separate social groups that never really mixed.

"Where you been, you dick?" He asked as he playfully punched me in the stomach.

"I've been around." I told him.

"Have a seat, we are celebrating tonight."

Mickey dropped back into the chair he originated from, but I remained standing, assessing the group of degenerates that were with him. I didn't recognize the three men. They were all wannabe thugs. Crooked hats, oversized clothing, and neatly styled facial hair. I felt like I had just been cast in a poorly produced rap video, playing the part of the man that stumbled into the wrong place at the wrong time. Their focused glances made me uncomfortable. I considered that I was about to get beat down and robbed. Mickey knew I was usually holding and his hospitality could be a ruse.

"Yo, what's your problem? Have a seat." Mickey demanded as he kicked a chair toward me.

"What are we celebrating?"

"You, mother-fucker. And my boy Johnny over here, just got out the joint."

Mickey wrapped his arm around the large man next to him and put him into a headlock. Johnny ducked out of the restraint and pushed Mickey away with an amount of force that almost tipped Mickey out of his chair and onto the ground. Mickey balled his fists and scowled, but was unable to intimidate. After his fake punch failed to scare Johnny, he resigned and reached over, grabbing a bottle of rum. He filled Johnny's cup before taking a swig off of it. He then turned his attention back to me.

"That fucking midget was by earlier."

"Midget?"

"Take a seat, what the fuck?"

I grabbed the chair from the table next to me and dragged it over. I set my bottle down and then took my seat. When I looked up, Mickey was already extending his rum in my direction. The dirt underneath his fingernails forced my face to tighten as I envisioned my lips visiting a place where his had already been. I considered refusing, deciding instead that I would be careful, not obvious, as I took my pull. I tipped the bottle toward the sky, keeping the opening a safe distance from my lips. A large gulp filled my mouth; I tried to choke it down, but the liquid forced me to gag. Mickey smirked. He didn't recognize the insult and in return, I smiled at his stupidity.

"Thank you."

"I heard you had a rough time."

"Who said that?" I asked, confused by the statement.

"Jesse, your little midget friend. Fucker was looking for a prescription. I told him to find you," Mickey said and then laughed. "He said it was your fault he was still awake. He also said that girl of yours is off her fucking rocker again. What's up with that?"

"Fuck that kid, it's always someone else's fault with Jesse."

This news annoyed me. I tried to shake it off, but I was feeling protective over Nikki at this moment. The mere mention of her name choked me up. I could feel the tears start to form in my eyes and this was the wrong place to show emotions. I grabbed my bottle and twisted it open. I placed it against my mouth, keeping my lips tight so they sealed the opening to the bottle as I tipped it up. I paused in that position, allowing the rum to shield my face from the men. Once my shoulders dropped and my eyes dried, I took a small sip. The men were looking at me cross-eyed when my focus returned. This reaction was preferable to the abuse I would have taken if I began sobbing like a little girl for no apparent reason.

"That midget drinks like a bitch, anyway. We had no use for him so we sent him on his way."

"How long ago was he down here?"

Before Mickey could answer, the Rasta from the kitchen came out of the back door. He was holding a pitcher of Jamaican

Rum. I fished out ten dollars and handed it to him. He looked surprised, but nodded graciously. He handed me the pitcher and without a word went back inside. I placed the rum down in the middle of the table. The men looked at it for a moment, then they too nodded in appreciation. "My contribution to this little party"

After all the other drinks were replenished, Mickey filled up a glass and handed it to me. I set my own bottle to the side. I would drink that later. We sat in silence. I wasn't sure what they were thinking about, but I was thinking of a plausible excuse to get out of this alley without offending anyone. I felt out of place and sensitive so I needed to be alone.

"Everyone, this is Jay," Mickey announced.

The introduction was slightly overdue and unnecessary. The men at the table all nodded with minimal enthusiasm. They tipped their glasses in my direction without offering a personal introduction.

"So, what brings you down to this little shithole?"

"It's been a rough day, a rough fucking day."

I regretted saying this immediately. I broke eye contact with Mickey and looked down at my shoes, hoping he would forget about that statement. He didn't care about my day, and this certainly wasn't the place to talk about what I had just seen. The booze loosened my tongue and my emotions got the best of me.

"I noticed that your face is fucked up. Is that why you are here? You need me to take care of something?"

I looked up from my shoes and stared into his eyes. He was eager and smiling, waiting for my response. Mickey liked to fight and he was hoping that I could give him a reason. I thought about sending him to Nikki's father's house. If anyone deserved a beating, it was him.

"You want my list?"

"Nah, not a list, just give me one name at a time and we will see how it goes. Just make sure that they are carrying a fat wallet though or at least something of value. You know what I mean. "He instructed me, as he winked and smiled.

"You're serious, aren't you?"

"Just start with your face. Who did that and where are they?"

I thought about that question for a minute. There was no money in killing a cat, so Muffin was safe.I could give him Brian Kovacs, but I had no idea where to find that kid. It was doubtful that Mickey would be willing to wait outside the hospital for the man in white.He was just doing his job anyway.Nikki's father was the only answer. I knew Mickey wasn't going to kick in the front door to a family residence and beat up a middle-aged father of three, so I put this offer in my back pocket. I would pull it out and use it on a different occasion; I was positive of that. "All I need is a name, Jay."

I nodded graciously at him and was about to take a rain check when a loud commotion spilled out into the alleyway.I turned.Four, large, under-dressed women were helping each other stumble their way toward us.The cheap dresses, over applied make-up, and three-inch heels suggested they were prostitutes. I had a hard time imagining that someone would actually pay for these disasters. Mickey disagreed; he stood up, knocking over his chair in the process.He spread his arms wide with excitement.

"The bitches are here."

Bitch wasn't the word I would have used to describe these women.They were obviously intoxicated and seemed anything but bitchy. They were laughing, smiling, and whispering in each other's ears while they made their way down the alley.My body shivered when the largest one pointed at me. She then split from the pack and stumbled toward me.Thick, fleshy arms wrapped around my neck. A wet kiss left a small puddle of drool and lipstick residue on the side of my face.I tried to shake free, but she held tight.

"You're mine." She told me.

Mickey looked down at me and smiled.He could read my face, which was laced with disgust.I again tried to wiggle my way free and stand, but I was no match for this woman.She circled around me and was now sitting in my lap, staring down at me.I wouldn't look up.The other three girls picked a man and did the same, leaving Johnny all by himself.This was his party.I hadn't even been invited.Hopefully that would be my ticket out of here.

"Mickey, your boy needs some love over there, it's his party".

Johnny was leaning back in his chair, arms crossed tight, and he was snarling at me like I had stolen his bone. My eyes widened, as I silently begged Mickey to intervene. His focus bounced around the table for a moment, ricocheting between Johnny and me in an attempt to escalate the hostility.He smirked and inched toward me.My eyelids now completely disappeared, and I shook my head just slightly, desperately trying to convey my desire to have this beast removed.Mickey laughed for a moment then grabbed the woman's hand and pulled her toward him.

"Darling, this boy here isn't part of the party."

"Well let's make him part of it."

"Unless you got a cock under that dress, he won't be interested." Mickey told her, as he stuck his pointer finger into a closed fist and pushed it in and out rapidly.

"Jesus, Mickey," I exclaimed. I didn't mind being gay to get out of the situation, he just didn't need to be vulgar about it.

"You're a fag?" She jumped out of my lap and stared down at me like she wanted to slap some sense into me. I shrugged my shoulders, and showed her the palms of my hands as an apology. She shook her head as she refocused and found Johnny. Anger was replaced by disappointment; her lips tightened, as she attempted to conceal her revulsion. I couldn't blame her, but the disgust on her face was slightly insulting. It registered with everyone sitting around the table and there was an awkward moment of quiet. Mickey became annoyed and placed his hand on her back, pushing her in Johnny's direction.

"Bitch, I paid you, now move it."

I watched the woman waddle her way over to Johnny and slip into his lap like she was getting into an ice-cold bath. Johnny didn't care, he started fondling her breasts, and I knew this was my cue to leave. I hopped out of my chair and took a glance around the table. I tried to nod to the men, but with my sexuality now in question they avoided the eye contact. I couldn't help but snicker at their arrogance. These obese hookers didn't even want to be in their laps, however, they assumed that a gay man, like myself, wouldn't be able to resist trying to grab some ass.

"What the fuck? Where are you going?"

"I don't need to be the gay ninth wheel."

"Fuck you, whose gonna run the camera?"

Mickey's question caught the attention of one of the women and she jumped up out of her chair, "Nobody said nothing about a camera, I don't get down with cameras."

"Bitch, shut up. Sit your fat ass down." Mickey yelled as he motioned at the woman. He turned his attention back to me."Yo, I'm serious. I want that name."

I nodded and smiled at his demand. I grabbed my bottle off of the table and gave the whole scene an unenthusiastic wave good-bye; I didn't bother to verbalize my intentions. I just turned and sashayed my way down the alley, wiggling my ass like an excited gay man who had just seen a boatload of sailors pull into port. Mickey laughed loudly to salute it.I opened the back door, grateful I had just been spared playing witness to another bad scene that would be burned into my memory.

I drove straight from the BBQ to Cranberry Park. It had been hours since Nikki's incident; it was a small town and the whispers had surely grown into a loud buzz of accusations and half-truths. There was always a victim and villain. The mangled little girl locked behind the steel door couldn't be both. The mob would be angry. The executioner would be searching for a neck. Under the weight of guilt and shame, I would happily offer mine to the guillotine. Even if I ran into sympathetic eyes, I was an exposed nerve. The slightest prodding would cause an emotional breakdown and uncontrollable sobbing in public, not an endeavor I wanted to engage in.

I circled the parking lot several times, hoping I wouldn't find a face or car that I recognized. Once satisfied, I parked the Cutlass where it was least visible. There was still a little vodka left, so I opened the bottle, tipped it upward and finished it.I tossed the bottle out of the window and high into the air just for fun.I watched it tumble through the sky and once it had shattered on the ground, I leaned over and turned on the radio. I tried to relax, but I just lost my woman, and I wasn't sure if she was even alive to get back, so the music saddened and angered me. I turned the aggravating noise off and leaned back in my seat, trying to enjoy the silence. I opened my bottle of rum and took a swig. I rolled a joint, although I wasn't a pot smoker.

Maybe it could help improve my mood.

I sat there smoking and drinking.

I woke up to the sensation of fingers lightly massaging my scalp.

Soft gentle eyes of a small dark haired girl landed on me. She continued stroking my hair, while beaming, as if this was the moment that she had been anticipating. I squinted at her, seeking recognition. There was none. My confusion seemed to amuse her.She grinned, which put me at ease, but the pleasure I was deriving from the experience filled me with guilt over Nikki. I didn't deserve to be happy, but if this girl could take my mind off of the scene at the hospital, I was going to let her. It seemed idiotic not too.

"Alexandra."

"I know."

"No you didn't," she responded, as she shook her head, play-fully. "But, its okay, I didn't expect you to. You can call me Alex, or Al, if you prefer."

"Why would I call you Al? That's a boy's name."

"My father wanted a boy. He has three girls. He calls me Al."

"Well then, I definitely won't call you Al."

She smiled. She had funny teeth that reminded me of a jack-o-lantern. They were jagged and pointy, but aligned so there were no gaps between them. I found this strange at first, but the more I stared, I realized that her smile was perfect. Her eyes were a deep blue, round and wide, with a sense of wildness in them. I felt lost and then found within the duration of a short gaze. She had freckles; they weren't overwhelming, they covered a small portion of her cheeks and spread over the bridge of her small button nose. Her dark hair collided with her rich blue eyes and pale skin, the contrast creating a beautiful balance.

"What are you doing in my car, Alex?"

"What are you doing in Lenny's car, Jay?" She asked as she again laid a bright smile on me.

"How do you know this is Lenny's car?"

"I know things."

I shook my head. This was one of those strange girl-answers that I didn't understand. Lenny never mentioned her before and he would have. The thought of the two of them together in this car made me oddly sad. This furthered my confusion. My mind kept skipping from her statement to my emotion, trying to figure out what each of them meant.

"Don't hurt yourself over there."

"What?"

"It's been a long day for you and you need to relax. "She told me as she handed me the bottle.

"Is that so?"

"I'm sure you've earned it."

These statements amplified my growing uncertainty about the situation. I took a sip of the rum and tried to forget about it, but I could feel a tension in my body. She was being deliberately vague, this was suspicious and it kept her objective unclear. I closed my eyes and tried to shake off the feeling, while my intuition was screaming. Something wasn't right, but she continued to smile and stare. I didn't want that to stop.

I opened my eyes and asked, "What do you know about me or Lenny?"

"I don't know anything," she told me as she reached for the bottle of rum. I handed it to her. She took a small sip and then gave it back to me. "There's only one red Cutlass and everyone knows who drives it.It's not a big secret."

"I guess that's true, but what do you know about my day?"

She smiled at me and looked around the car, "You were sleeping in a car that was full of smoke, on a seat that was partially on fire, so it's a fair guess that you had a long day."

I hadn't noticed, but now that she mentioned it, it was slightly smoky in the car. I looked around. There was a small burn in my shirt and an even bigger one in the seat between my legs. A small portion of the joint was still on the floor. I knew I passed out, but I thought I finished smoking before this had happened. Alex was now nodding sarcastically at me as my recollections painted a fuzzy picture.

"The whole car was filled with smoke," She told me. "I aired it out the best I could, after I extinguished you and your seat of course."

"Thank you."

"You are very welcome. It would have been a shame if you had burned up in this car. "

"There are people that would disagree."

"You can't be who you are and expect to be anonymous in this little town. I know you know this."

"I don't understand that statement, it worries me."

"This is the only moment that exists. There's no place for worry in it."

I could feel my face tightening as I tried to hide my suspicion. This young woman, who I had never met, seemed to have some preconceived notions that were oddly accurate. This made me uncomfortable. Either someone was feeding her information, or I was a moron that had been overlooking her. Either way, I was in no mood to decipher vague female codes and try to decide which case was true. It seemed unnecessary and it was giving me a headache.

"Stop doing that."

"Doing what?"

"Talking to me like that? If you have something to say just come out and say it."

"Why are you upset with me, Jay? I don't understand."

"Why are you here?"

She leaned forward and placed her hand on my thigh. Then she grabbed the side of my face and turned it so I was staring directly into her eyes. She inched even closer and placed her soft lips on me. She left them there for a few seconds before moving back to her original position.

"Was that supposed to be less confusing?"

"Are you confused? Cause you shouldn't be."

"Where did you come from? I don't get it."

"I've been around, Jay. It's not my fault you didn't notice me."

"Where have you been?"

"Really?" She asked, and paused to stare at me. I didn't respond because it wasn't a rhetorical question. "I was at A&M the other night when you almost got busted. I was here drinking when you went off into the woods with your dog and that little Jew girl. I have third period English with Lenny, when he shows. So I didn't come from anywhere, I've been here."

"Really?"

"Really."

"Shit."

I felt like an idiot. I tried to stare down at the ground, but she wouldn't let me. She grabbed my chin and forced me to refocus. She wasn't mad. She was smirking, and biting her lip, explaining that she had known I was an idiot before she got into my car and she was still here.

"So, why are you so worried? I thought you were the type that just enjoys what life brings you."

"I didn't know I was a type."

"You are definitely a type."She laughed.

"And what type is that?"

"You don't ask the right questions."

"I don't?"

"No."

She closed her eyes and leaned forward. I still wasn't convinced that I understood what was happening in this car, but I wasn't going to allow her to have control over this kiss. I grabbed the back of her head and pulled her close. I pressed my lips hard against hers. Our tongues met moments later and playfully chased each other. She caressed my body, while I explored hers. We eventually parted, but she stayed where I placed her.

"So, what's the right question?" I asked.

"Are you my type? That seems to be the only 'type' question that matters."

Dark shadows, followed by a bright light, suddenly interrupted the conversation. A tight restraint landed on my neck and ripped me from the car. I landed hard on the pavement. I tried to move but a shoe collided with my forehead and slammed my head against the asphalt. The world went black for a brief moment. I shook off the blow and searched for Alex's eyes, but instead, found a young man helping her from the car. I tried to move again, and just as I caught a glimpse of Alexandra walking away from the car, a boot struck me in the side of the face.The world again dissolved. I could feel feet hitting my body, but I made no attempt to resist.

When I awoke, three sets of eyes were staring down at me. They were full of contempt and waiting for a reason to continue. I remained silent. These men weren't trying to be anonymous. They were dressed in blue, football jerseys. If I cared, I could have taken numbers for later reporting. I just wanted to find Alex and confirm that she was part of my demise. My eyes scanned what they could see of the park and finally landed on her. She was sitting on a fence with a couple of men who were also sporting numbers on their chest. She was laughing, drinking, and unconcerned for my predicament. My beautiful moment was nothing more than a set-up. My head dropped and bounced against the pavement, but I couldn't even feel it.

"You ready for some more?" one of the young men asked as he raised my bottle of rum into the air and took a swig.

"Who was the fucking girl?"

"What?"

"Was that a difficult question?"

"Are you being a smart ass?"

"Considering the company, I imagine it would be difficult to take the crown as dumbass."

This angered the man wearing the number twelve jersey. He leaned backward, took a step forward, and kicked me straight in the ribs. I heard a loud crack, winced in pain, and grabbed at my side, struggling to conceal the agony he just caused. I began to cough. My mouth was already full of blood and by the time I was done coughing, my chin was a deep red. The eyes staring at me widened, the men took a step away surprised at what they accomplished. I used this pause in the action to turn on my side and spit the rest of the blood out.

"I think he is done." One of the kids decided.

"You know why this is happening?" Number twelve asked me.

"Could you narrow down the possibilities for me?"

"Fuck you, junkie. Next time you steal from a brother of ours, you won't get off this easy."

"Did I get off easy?"

"What did you say?"

"Who was the fucking girl? That's all I care about." I asked as I started to sit up.

"She is a friend of Marshall's, that's all you need to know."

I nodded, closed my eyes, and let my head drop. My bones would heal, my brain would stop throbbing, and the blood would be washed away, but knowing those eyes were never meant for me hurt more than the three combined. I began to stand. The men moved backward and made their way to the fence a few yards away where Alex was still drinking and enjoying her night. They took seats and forgot about me. Their point had been made, and they thought it was over, but it wasn't. They gave me hope, and then ripped it away from me. That was worse than a boot to the head.

My face was hot and my fists were tight as I got into the car. I sat there for a moment considering my options, but there was only one. Return to the Rastafa BBQ and give Mickey the name he asked for.I checked my review mirror. The men were enjoying my rum and they were doing so in my sanctuary. I didn't know any of their names, but I knew where they would be after they were done with my bottle. I put the car in reverse. I rolled backward and cut the wheel so I was perfectly aligned with the men.

They were busy laughing and joking so they didn't seem to notice.

I pressed hard against the gas. The pedal hit the floor and the wheels began to spin. They screeched and smoked for a second, grabbed a hold of the pavement and took off, screaming its way towards them. Their eyes widened as they scattered and dove out of the way. The rear tires slammed into the curb and bounced up and over it. I kept my foot on the gas and drove straight through the fence, which shattered into pieces. I hit the brake and the car slid for a few feet where it collided with a thick oak tree. I put the car in drive and again pressed on the gas. The wheels spun in the soft ground as I sped through the park, hit the street, and headed for the interstate.

I parked the Cutlass directly in front of the Rastafa BBQ and stumbled into the restaurant like a drunken, gutter bum, ricocheting from table to table, rattling glasses and moving silverware. My blood covered shirt and swollen face drew heavy stares with loud gasps. I maintained focus and tried to limit the destruction as I navigated the thin path to the counter. The young, black girl's jaw hit the floor and her eyes widened as she searched for the man behind the hidden camera who would tell her this was a joke. It wasn't a joke and my Jamaican friend, who had been so gracious earlier, hurried out to greet me. He grabbed me by the arm and led me through the kitchen without saying a word .He didn't ask for money, he just opened the door to the alley, pushed me out and slammed the door behind me. The loud thud bounced down the concrete strip gaining the attention from the men still at the table.

"Back again?"

I moved toward Mickey. My blurred vision affected my depth perception and I crashed into the table. The men's glasses tipped, clanked hard against the wood, then two rolled to the ground and shattered. The noise startled me. I over-compensated and took a large step backward, causing me to stumble. Eight eyes were on me, but only Mickey's were large. I stood there embarrassed, waiting for him to mock me.

"What the fuck, dude? You need to slow your roll. There ain't no need for all that." Mickey told me as he pointed at the broken glass on the ground.

"Sorry, it was an accident."

"Fuck, I'd send you inside for more glasses, but the way my man slammed the door on your ass, I don't think it'd be a good idea."

I didn't respond and took a seat at the table. The men continued to stare at me with half-open, glazed-over eyes. Mickey was making a big deal of my entrance; they were too stoned to care. My bloody, swollen face hadn't even registered with them. Mickey noticed it; he had done a double-take in the middle of scolding me. His examination continued as I made my way to the chair. There was a slight shake of the head and a frown, followed by a moment of contemplation. He was reluctant to say anything.

He was slumped in his chair, high and drunk, knowing I was about to dump a load on him that he wasn't sure he wanted to carry.

"So what the fuck, dude?" Mickey finally asked, as he leaned forward and grabbed my chin. He moved my head back and forth inspecting my fresh wounds. "Are you asking for trouble or is it just fucking finding you these days?"

"I've got a name."

"For what?"

"You said…"

"I know what I said, mother-fucker." He interrupted.

Mickey pushed backwards in his seat, lifting the front legs of the chair off the ground. He glanced into the night sky, looking like he was counting stars. I knew he was arguing with himself, regretting his earlier offer. He started evaluating the competence of his boys at the table. The men rolled a joint and were busy passing it, content and completely oblivious. He let out a deep, exasperated gasp and dropped his chair back to the ground. He closed his eyes and began humming, while shaking his hair wildly. Finally, he stood up and began violently beating his chest like an angry gorilla.

Everyone around the table stopped what they were doing to watch.

"Who was it? Who fucked with my boy?" He asked as he continued to bang on his chest. "Say the name, Jay, say the name."

His obnoxious display straightened the backs at the table. They were interested, awake, and engaged. Their focus seemed to sway, between my bloody face and Mickey's monstrous stance. The weight of my decision pushed my shoulders down and I was now slouching in my chair as I watched the fuse I just lit burn toward an explosive outcome. Mickey continued to beat his chest. The inquisitive glances grew wider. My blood was in the water and they were circling.

"Who fucked with my boy?" He asked again.

"Some jocks at the park."

"Cranberry Park?"

"Yes."

"Mother...Fucker..." He yelled as he pounded on his chest even harder.

"In my fucking park, this shit just got personal."

Mickey took a glance around at the hungry parasites intently focused on him. They were drooling, ready to feed, and eager to hear what was on the menu. They continued to shift their focus. A confused enthusiasm radiated as they waited for more information. This had been Mickey's aim and now that he had everyone's attention he dropped backward into his seat.

"Where are they? Still at the park?"

"The Tar Pits, probably."

"What the fuck's a tar pit?"

"It's basically a parking lot."

The Tar Pits was the name for a large, secluded gravel parking lot on the outskirts of my town. For decades, lit had been the chosen destination for the town's most prominent jocks from the wealthiest families. On weekend nights, the area resembled a frat party without the house or established frat. They would light a bonfire in the middle, drink cheap beer, play loud music, and have sex in their cars. The town police knew this, but they turned a blind eye to the deserted rocky square.

"That's where they'll be?" Mickey asked.

"Probably."

"So we can crack a skull and fuck a cheerleader? Is what you are saying?"

"I guess so," I answered, even though that wasn't at all what I was saying.

"How many punks are we thinking?"

"Three kids jumped me. There might be a few more down there, but it's late so, I wouldn't say more than five."

Mickey looked at the men around the table, "Anyone feel like cracking some skulls and fucking some cheerleaders up in Wilton?"

The men stood up knocking their chairs to the ground. I looked at them, realizing that Mickey and his mod squad were for real. I grabbed one of the bottles that appeared to have a little rum left in it. This was crazy. I just offered a contract with an obscene amount of variables. I tilted the bottle toward the sky and sucked the remaining liquid out. I sobered up instantaneously, and the thought of taking Mickey and his boys down to the Pits, elicited scenes from the Thanksgiving Day massacre. Real laws had been put into place since then. My father understood drug-addiction to an extent, but mug shots, black fingertips, and a conspiracy-to-commit murder charges in the local newspaper was something he would be less forgiving about. I grabbed a second bottle and sucked that one dry as well. "What's the problem?" Mickey asked.

"I'm just really sober all of a sudden."

"Relax dude, you'll have a bat. No need for liquid courage when you're holding a piece of steel."

This information did not relax me like it was intended to. My whole body tightened, my chest pressed hard against my lungs, and I struggled to breathe. Eight eyes were focused on me and I felt like a crack-whore during her first porn shoot. This was no time for a panic attack. I was getting what I signed up for and needed to bend over and take it like a pro.

"Get up," Mickey demanded as he kicked my seat.

"I don't think we need bats. Just a good old-fashioned beat down."

"You don't need to tell us our business. "Johnny angrily responded.

These were the first words he had spoken all night. His voice was deep and full of rage. .His eye seethed with anger and the scowl on his face explained my options. Someone's head was going to be smashed. It could be mine, it could be someone else's, and he didn't appear to have a preference, so I stood up.

"I was just saying that these arc dumb, Wilton jocks. Are bats really necessary?" I asked.

"Bats are always necessary." Johnny answered.

"That's a universal rule?" I stupidly asked. It was a rhetorical question that I hoped would lighten the mood, but I realized that neither my sarcasm nor my vocabulary was going to be understood.

"Jocks play baseball, don't they?" one of the men asked. It was a simple question with a surprising amount of validity.

"So, seriously, how many are there going to be?" Mickey asked.

I knew this was an irrelevant question. The mere presence of Mickey and these men would be enough to scare the entire football team. This wasn't going to be a battlefield. These men were savages invading a village full of women and children. They could rape and pillage as they pleased. I resisted the urge to try and stress this point again.

"We are only talking about five, maybe six, and they will be drunk; there won't be much fight to them, really, they're a bunch of bitches."

"Bitches have claws sometimes." Mickey informed me, but I didn't fully understand what he meant.

"You know what I'm saying though, these kids aren't fighters."

"Is that right? Maybe you should tell that to your face." Johnny instructed me. "What's up with your boy, Mickey? This feels like he's trying to set us up."

"Look at the mother-fucker. He has brain damage, he isn't thinking right." Mickey responded. "You never have been much of a fighter. You are more of a lover, aren't you, Jay? But sometimes, love isn't all you need, right?"

These were rhetorical questions, posed with purpose. He wanted to shame me. The men standing around the table now knew I was a pussy. More importantly, he was reminding me that I asked for his help, he was the devil and he owned my soul.

"Let's get the fuck out of here and go have some fun." Mickey exclaimed as he wrapped his arm around me and led me to a gate at the end of the alley." We can go out this way. I don't think my Jamaican friend wants to see you for a while and that's one head I can't crack for you. Never, ever, fuck with those Jamaicans, they will put a voodoo curse on your ass and shrink your dick up like a pea."

"Mickey, you know what I'm saying; you and your boys don't need to get too crazy. "I whispered.

"Yo, you need to shut your mouth with that bullshit. Johnny ain't right…he has some paranoid personality situation happening."

"Great."

The secret gate at the end of the alley opened up into a small parking lot, resembling an uptown, automobile dealership. Each car in the lot was shiny, relatively new, and probably cost more than the average house in the area. I assumed they were all stolen as well. A triple beep sounded, then the lights of a black Escalade blinked twice.

"Where you at son?" Mickey asked.

"What is this back here?"

"Yo man, you know better than to ask questions like that. You need to stop acting like you're from that bitch-ass town of yours. You're in my ghetto now, don't get me shot for helping your dumb ass. "He warned me, as he smacked me in the back of the head. "Where's your ride?"

"It's on the street, the Cutlass."

"Lenny's piece of shit?"

"I stole it."

"Great, two stolen cars." He informed me as he winked. He then looked at Johnny. "Yo Johnny, ride with this fool."

"Mickey." I objected.

"Fuck that, my fat ass can't fit in no Cutlass. Plus, my rep." Johnny agreed with my objection, but for different reasons.

"You just got out of jail, mother-fucker, that's your rep."

"He's right, Mickey, it's not the biggest car."

"No, it's a fucking boat, it's not even a car. Who you trying to kid?" Mickey laughed and then looked at the other two men. "I'm guessing neither of you want to ride in the Cutlass with Jay?"

Both men shook their heads no, and I exhaled. I couldn't imagine that conversation going well. I hadn't shot or stabbed anyone recently, or ever. I doubted that my earlier home invasion, the tale of the Marshall house would entertain. Even if I turned that cat into a vicious panther, which she was, and made it third story window that I leaped from, I was still looking like the asshole.

"Fine, Jay, you ride with us."

"Mickey, I can't, I don't want to leave Lenny's car here."

"No one is stealing that piece of shit, not even down here."

"I stole that piece of shit, and I'd like to keep it. There are cops everywhere down here."

"Fine, whatever, go to your car. We will meet you there."

I walked away from Mickey and past the Escalade on my way to the street. The gang was already at the rear of the car, preparing. Two of the men held aluminum bats. One had on a ski mask and was twirling a crowbar. All three resembled pleased children on Christmas morning admiring their new gifts. When I hit the street I considered walking right past Lenny's car and disappearing into the night. Unfortunately, this really was Mickey's ghetto and he had eyes everywhere.

I sat in the car waiting. Mickey pulled up seconds later and rolled down the window. A ski mask covered his face but his eyes were bulging out through the slits. I could imagine his menacing smile, stretching from ear to ear. Johnny was next to him in the passenger seat, lightly stroking his crowbar while gazing romantically at it. The sight was too much. I swam too far out into this ocean of insanity, my legs and arms were exhausted, and the current was pulling me toward a sandy grave.

"You ready to do this sucker?"

"As ready as I'll ever be."

"We will follow you, I don't know where this pit of tar is."

"Ok"

"Stop a few blocks away and jump in with us, we can creep up together."

I nodded and put the car in drive. I pulled out and got in front of Mickey's vehicle. I drove slowly down the main street, hoping that some cop might happen to be in the right place to notice a man in a ski mask driving a stolen car, with a parolee next to him, stroking a crowbar like a pubescent boy with a nudie rag and jar of lotion. I had no such luck, but Mickey had taken exception to my lack of speed. He began flashing his lights and waving his arm out of his window.

I hit the gas and sped up the ramp onto the interstate. I planned on driving slow and taking the long way, hoping that the Pits would clear out and I could shrug my shoulders and apologize, but changed my mind. I pressed the pedal to the ground and accelerated down the highway, weaving my way in and out of traffic. Mickey stayed close on my tail, his high beams flashed on and off. His horn voiced a loud continuous complaint regarding my speed. I ignored it. I flew down the exit ramp and took a sharp left through a red light. Two tires lifted off the ground for a moment, then fell. The car bounced, but I continued to hold the metal against the floor as I headed deep into our town and the curvy, poorly lit streets. I was asking for simple revenge, not a sea of blood-red gravel with bodies scattered on top; young girls screaming louder than the sirens, while blue and red flashed everywhere.

I cut corners, left tire marks in the middle of lawns, and transformed flowerbeds into piles of dirt. A quick left, followed by a quick right, jerked my head back and worth, but my foot remained heavy. Mickey's lights were close enough to send a bright beam through my car. They weren't giving up, but I was assured that the person designated for the beat down had changed. This left me with one feasible option: a small, unmarked, dirt road that connected two main streets. If I could hit this road with enough distance between us, I could disappear and they wouldn't know where I had gone.

I hit Cedar Street and took a tight right turn mowing down some rose bushes in the process. They hit my hood, bouncing up and over the car. I cut the wheel hard onto Carriage Drive; the

Cutlass slid but straightened. I jammed on the gas and soared over a small lawn to save some time. I could see Mickey's headlights through the sparse woods that separated the streets. I took another quick right and another victim, this time a mailbox became airborne and crashed into the windshield, shattering a large portion of it. I hit Crowfoot Lane and gunned it. At the end of this street there were two options: turn right, or continue straight onto an unmarked dirt road that appeared to be a driveway.

I reached the road going almost fifty miles an hour. There was a pothole large enough to bury an elephant that I couldn't avoid. The wheels dipped. The car shot into the air, soared over a slight curve, into the street and landed in the middle of a lawn. I hit the brakes and turned the wheel hard, but the car slid uncontrollably. A large oak appeared. In slow motion, I watched as the car continued to skid and collide with the tree. All four windows shattered. Smoke poured into the car from the engine. My adrenaline kicked in seconds later and pushed me out of my seat. Fearing the possibility of an explosion, I climbed through the passenger side window, cutting my entire body in the process.

I stood in the middle of the lawn for a moment. The lights of the neighboring homes flashed. I could see the Escalade roaring down the street. I turned and began to run. I ran through the woods like a fox being chased by a pack of hounds. Vines tore at my flesh, branches pierced and scratched my body as I roared my way to safety. I stopped a good distance from the crash and waited. The Escalade stopped, but this was now a crime scene, so they didn't stay long.

I remained on the ground for several moments staring up into the sky. The stars were bright and highlighted by a small sliver of moon. The wind was soft, slightly rustling what was left of the leaves on the tree. I could hear sirens in the distance and I sat up; Lenny's car was surely reported stolen by now and if I didn't move there was a good chance that police dogs would chase me.

Pajama Pants and Slippers

I stood still on the porch, staring through the sliding glass doors into the kitchen. My mother was busy cleaning a sink full of dishes. I grabbed the handle but my courage ended there. If I crossed through this doorway, my white flag was in the air. My mother looked up from what she was doing. My presence startled her and she dropped the dish she was working on, letting out a little scream. Then my appearance smacked her in the face and she let out a shrill gasp that rattled my nerves from outside. Both hands covered her nose and mouth as her eyes widened. I slid the door open and stumbled into the dining area. Her feet remained cemented in the ground while her face continued to sadden upon inspection. I limped toward her seeking refuge in her embrace. She recognized my struggle and met me halfway. She wrapped her arms around me and pulled me tight.

"Darling, what happened to you?"

I didn't know where to start, so I remained silent, hoping she wouldn't release her grasp and demand an explanation. Over her shoulder, I could see thick clouds of smoke pouring out from inside the living room. Loud voices and booming laughter explained why my mother was still awake.

There was a pot of coffee brewing and a group of men were sitting around the coffee table playing cards.I would be discovered, and these men weren't going to be satisfied with a hug and silence.I needed this moment to last as long as possible.

"We need to get you fixed up. Are you cut anywhere badly?" She asked, as she tried to move away.

"No just stay," I told her as I pulled hard on her waist.

An argument erupted in the living room, followed by the sound of cards hitting the table then the floor. Two men then appeared, cutting through the dense haze of smoke, with coffee mugs in hand. One, of course, was Smitty; I knew I'd be seeing him. The other was a large Italian man that I knew fairly well. His given name was Vito, but the men lovingly referred to him as the Big Guinea. This nickname should have been considered an insult, but he saw things a little differently. My father had been the only life preserver in the sea of whiskey in which he drown, so as far as Vito was concerned, my father was allowed to call him whatever he pleased. Besides, there wasn't a more accurate way to describe him. Vito stood six-foot four and weighed about three hundred pounds. He had olive skin, a large pointy nose, and dark curly hair. He even had the stereotypical New York accent.

The men stopped at the edge of the kitchen and peered in. Smitty was bug-eyed. He appreciated any incident that would disrupt the endless string of monotony he referred to as life. The Big Guinea just kept looking at his coffee mug and then the coffee pot, debating. My instincts were screaming, begging me to manufacture an adequate lie, or to run, instead I continued to stand still, surrendering to the safety of my mother's arms.

"What's happening in here?" Smitty asked.

My mother pushed away from me, keeping her hands on my shoulders, and turning me so Smitty could see what I had done to myself. Neither of the men looked shocked. They shrugged their shoulders and nodded as if they had been anticipating this scene for some time. My father's long rants about his drug-addict son had obviously convinced them that I was one of their tribe and tonight appeared to be my baptism.

"What happened? Did you go dumpster diving and run into a raccoon?" Smitty asked.

The attempt at humor was meant to minimize the situation and relax my mother. It failed. The thought of her son being thrashed in a trashcan by a wild animal was more than she could handle. She turned me back around and started examining my face.

"Mom, relax, it's not that bad. I'm fine" I told her. She ignored me and moved her evaluation to my arms and legs.

Vito took advantage of the opportunity and made his way to the coffee pot, filling his mug. He remained in the kitchen sipping loudly and waiting, affording the moment an appropriate amount of time to mask his disinterest. My focus remained mostly on my feet, but occasionally, I would look up at Smitty. He was formulating a sales pitch; he'd be pulling out the big guns and pushing the hard sell.

"Go get Jack." Smitty ordered.

Vito happily turned and made his way back to the living room. I couldn't hear what was being said, but the light from the room cast Vito's large shadow. He was animated in his attempt to convince my father. The loud clank of the lazy boy collapsing signaled my father's submission. This was followed by heavy footsteps. I straightened, not knowing what to expect. My father stopped a few feet from me, seething with what seemed to be disgust. His focus shifted from me to my mother.

"Lil, get him cleaned up, and make sure he isn't bleeding too badly from any of those cuts."

"Dad, I'm sorry."

My father didn't acknowledge my apology. I wasn't exactly sure what I was apologizing for anyway, I just wanted some form of consideration. The voice inside of my head begged for him to yell at me if need be. Tell me what a piece of shit I am. Let me know that you're embarrassed of what I have become. Wrap your arms around me and assure me that everything is going to be okay. Let me know that you still love me. I needed him to do anything other than treat me like a wounded farm animal that could be put down with little remorse if fixing became too expensive.

"Go take a shower. You smell disgusting. Get that blood off of you so your mother can see what's what and we can figure out what needs to be done," my father ordered, failing to alleviate the feeling that I was no more than a diseased pig.

I put my head down and pushed past both of the men without saying a word. I could feel their judgmental scorn. My dream of a loving and compassionate 'father and son' moment shattered. The need for my father's love crumbled under my feet as I climbed the steps toward the bathroom. These cuts that he just caused were deeper than any I had endured over the past days.

I closed the bathroom door behind me, locking it. I turned the shower nozzle half way to hot, then sat down on the toilet seat. A glimpse of myself in the mirror made me flinch. I was grotesque;

deep, dark rings surrounded my dilated, black eyes. My pale skin highlighted the heavy purple bruises on the sides of my head. Thin red slits traveled in every direction. I stood and began peeling off my shirt. Dried blood clung to the clothes and I winced in pain as my wounds reopened. I examined my ribs, they reminded me of a dark sky before a thunderstorm. I took my pants off…more cuts and bruises. Two feet landed in the shower, and I again felt like a farm animal, only this time I was being branded by bright, orange steel.

"Fuck!" I screamed as warm pellets of water stabbed my body.

I reached for the soap, and began washing only the most pungent areas. Regardless of my effort to be stingy, the lather washed down my body and stung to such a degree that I searched the tub to make sure there was no electrical appliance malfunctioning at my feet. Still, despite the pain, the removal of stink made me feel like a new man. The bloody chains of regret and remorse seemed to funnel their way down the drain, while a yearning to preserve my way of life crept to the front of my mind. I began formulating feasible explanations, and by the end of the shower, my father's window of opportunity was barely letting in a slight breeze.

I grabbed the first shirt and pair of shorts I found in my closet, put them on and climbed into bed. It felt good to lie down. I was clean, but my head was throbbing. My face hurt. My entire body ached. I wanted to go to sleep and forget about this world for a moment. I closed my eyes tight, but all I could see was Nikki's bloody hand holding up a fist full of hair. I saw Marshall standing in his window, and a lifelong friendship dissolving as I drove away; the expression on Lenny's face as he waved his final good-bye to me. Mickey was angrily circling the neighborhood the taste of my blood was in his mouth and he desired more. Finally, there was Alex. She was sitting on the fence watching as young men stomped on me repeatedly like it was a spectator sport. My eyes swelled and my throat went dry. I began to choke on my memories and realized that I wasn't welcome anywhere but wanted everywhere.

"Jay, can I come in, hun?" my mother whispered.

I opened my eyes. My mother was peering in. A small sliver of light hit the bed. I tried to answer. My mouth dropped open, but rivers of tears flowing steady down both sides of my face would be my only response. My mother's gentle voice pulled the final plug in the dam that was holding my emotions back. I began sobbing, choking, gasping to breathe. Snot trickled down from both nostrils onto my lip. Despite my best efforts, the salted gelatin found its way into my mouth and I gagged. My mother swung the door all the way open, but remained standing, shocked by the volcano that just erupted. My body began to tremble and my mother had seen enough. She moved to the side of my bed and wrapped her arms around me. She held me tight and waited until I stopped shaking and relaxed.

"Honey, what happened to you today?"

"I don't know."

"Where did all these cuts come from?"

"I crashed Lenny's car."

"You crashed Lenny's car? Where is Lenny? Is he alright?"

302

"I fell out of a window."

"Of the car?"

"No of the house."

"Whose house?"

"Some guys beat me up; Nikki and Lenny are gone. Marshall hates me, Mom."

I could feel my eyes starting to fill again, but this time I was grateful. I lost control over both my emotions and my mouth. Crying would elicit sympathy, but if I kept talking it would arouse even more suspicion. I wasn't confident in my answers, so I bit my tongue and again allowed my tears to overflow and pour. We didn't say anything for the next several minutes. I remained in her arms allowing her to be the mother she hadn't been in years. It felt good. I felt safe. I began to drift. I was almost asleep when the sound of loud, heavy footsteps echoing down the hall grabbed my eyelids and yanked. I looked up at my mother, silently begging her to stop a fate that had already been signed, sealed, and was about to be delivered.

"So, what the fuck? Are you ready to get this fixed, Jay?" My father asked. He was now hovering in the doorway, watching my mother comfort me.

"There's no fixing me, I'm broken ."

"That may be true, but I suppose it wouldn't hurt to try. The worst thing that can happen is you stay broke," he told me as he made his way into the room and took a knee next to my mother. Then he reached out and placed his hand atop my head." Besides, at least then we will know whether or not we are going to keep you or throw you out."

It was a stupid joke, but it forced a surprising laugh from both my mother and me. My father, in return, smiled and I saw the compassion that I had been hoping for down in the kitchen. He was genuine in his desire to clean my slate and see if I could be the son my mother and he always wanted. This idea, however vague, filled me with hope. I suddenly understood that Lenny's seemingly childish wave was a nonverbal surrender.

"What do you want me to do?"

"Just trust me. If you can do that, then I'll take care of the rest. I promise."

"Trusting people isn't my strong suit. Can you give me a little idea of what I'm in for?"

"Pack a bag, you'll be in a safe place for a couple of weeks."

"How big of a bag?"

"Not big. I will be up to see you and I can bring you anything you might need."

"I can do that."

"I just want to see you happy and healthy."

It was a simple statement, but the sentiment hadn't been offered in years. A dense fog, thick with disappointment, resonated from my father when our paths crossed. He barely acknowledged me anymore, and if he did, it was only to bark an order or make a demand. I was a pebble in his shoe, easy to ignore, but preferably gone. That's the way I saw myself in his eyes, but not tonight. Tonight I felt like that little kid in the pickup truck that loved his Dad and his Dad loved him.

"Let your mother fix that raggedy face of yours. Once she's done with that, get up and pack a bag with just necessities in it.

Smitty, Vito, and I will drive you. Your mom and I will figure out the rest later this week."

"So what's the Big Guinea sticking around for? Just in case I decide to run?"

"Do you really think that fat bastard could catch you?" he asked, which made me laugh " Let your mother look at that face. We can't take you anywhere with a mug like that. You'll scare people."

My mother didn't wait for me to accept or even acknowledge my father's demands. She sprung to her feet and made her way out of the room, trampling down the hallway and into the bathroom. The medicine cabinet squeaked as it opened, banging against the wall. Items fell to the ground and bounced. It had been a long time since she had fulfilled a parental duty and she was overly excited. She returned to the room with enough supplies to fix up an entire platoon after an airstrike. She wasn't the best when it came to dealing with emotional trauma, but she was going to make sure that my cuts were clean and covered.

"Jesus, babe," my father exclaimed.

She didn't bother responding to him. She was ready to play nurse. She flipped the bedroom light on, which was unusually bright, and took a knee next to the bed. She grabbed my left foot, and pulled my leg straight. It was badly cut, mostly from climbing out of the car window, I assumed. She soaked her cotton swab with more than enough alcohol, then rubbed me down. I wanted to scream. It was like each cut was getting stabbed with tiny needles. Then she wrapped me up with an obscene amount of bandaging.

"Mom, seriously, I'm going to look like a mummy if you do it like that."

"Shush."

She continued onto my right leg. My father remained in the doorway, even though he was supposed to be downstairs finalizing a plan. Some people take pictures at the Grand Canyon. Other people record the whales jumping at Sea World, but for us, this was a family moment worth noting.

My dad was tight faced and trying not to laugh; I mimicked him, but I wasn't sure if the amusement was derived from my mother's effort or my pain.

Either way, this was the first memorable experience we shared in years.

"You really did a number on yourself, kid," my father told me.

"I had a lot of help."

"I bet you did."

The walls began to shake, interrupting my father's mocking smirk. His head turned toward the hallway, his eyes rolled as the sound of heavy footsteps and panting perked his ears. I had to smile. Neither of us needed to look, we both knew the Big Guinea was gasping his way up the stairs.

"Just stop right there before you hurt yourself," my father yelled.

"What do you need?"

"Smitty needs you, insurance or something."

"Alright, I'm coming." My father took a final look at us. My mother was almost done with the second leg." He looks like a goddamn burn victim," he told us as he shook his head and left the room.

My mom looked me over and shrugged her shoulders. I knew most of the bandages were going to be ripped off and tossed out of the car window during the ride, but I would allow her the moment. She deserved it. She endured years of torture at the hands of my father's alcoholism and just as she had gotten him somewhat under control I decided to jump into the deep end of my own addiction. People would label my father a fighter, and I considered myself a survivor, but my mother was the true champion. She loved two flawed men unconditionally, without fail.

"He can fix it, you know that right?"

"I know he is going to try."

"Do you want to talk about it?" she asked.

"You did a great job wrapping me up. Thank you. "

She was happy with herself and encouraged by my willingness to place my fate in my father's hands. I decided to skip the brutal truth, knowing that honesty would ruin her moment. There would be a time and place for me to be forthright. I wasn't sure where I was going or what was going to happen when I got there. I was sure, however, that at some point the three of us would be sitting in a small room discussing our issues while a man in a cheap suit and glasses too small for his face took useless notes.

"You can tell me anything."

"I think this is more of a Dad situation right now, but I appreciate the offer."

"I was afraid you were like him, that you had gotten that gene. This isn't your fault…you know that, right? It wasn't his fault either. You are not broken you just have the sickness. It's important that you know the difference. Sick people get well."

"You really think that?"

"I believe it with all of my heart. Your father has turned into a great man. He has helped a lot of people. He's even a decent husband," she told me, as she took a minute to laugh and reflect." We both know what a piece of shit he was. I didn't trust your father for a long time, but I think we can both trust him now, especially when it comes to you. He loves you, Jay.

He isn't very good at it, I know, but he is learning all the time."

"I know, mom."

"I love you too, do you know that?"

"Mom please, don't make me cry."

"I'll stop, I need to go gather your toiletries anyway," she told me as she hopped to her feet with enthusiasm.

"Thank you, mom."

My mother smiled as she skipped toward the door. I could hear her bouncing down the hall as I glanced around the room. When I got back home, I would paint the walls and begin a new chapter. Life would be different, and for the moment I would pretend it could include Nikki, even though this lie caused me to chuckle. There was no way to make what happened right. Lenny was gone and Nikki would never hold my hand and walk with me through this new adventure, but I wasn't ready to accept the fact that I would never see her again.

I stood up and walked to my closet. I grabbed a few shirts, a couple pairs of jeans, socks and underwear. Everything was black, so there wasn't much of a choice. When I got home I would buy myself a favorite shirt, maybe even some denim or corduroy pants to go with it.

"You're not going to need that much stuff," Smitty told me.

His voice made me jump. He snuck up behind me and was standing just inside the doorway. The look on his face was one I didn't recognize. There was no judgment or pity in his eyes. There was a sense of understanding that dropped my shoulders just slightly. It seemed as though he knew exactly what I was going through at this particular moment and he empathized with me. He took another step into my room and looked into my closet.

"You go to a lot of funerals, do you, kid?"

"Be honest Smitty...how fucked am I?"

"I don't know you that well, I just know what your father tells me."

"What does my father say?"

"He says you're fucked," Smitty told me. It wasn't a funny statement but for some reason we both chuckled at it." But he's a good old-fashioned drunk, and he doesn't know shit. You tell me honestly what you've been into and I'll tell you how fucked up I honestly think you are."

"Pretty much everything."

"Heroin?"

"No, never"

"Pills? Xanax, Percs, Valium?"

"Not really, every once in a while, but mostly just to help me come down."

"And you aren't much of a drinker."

"Not really, I mostly stuck with the uppers and hallucinogens."

He smiled at me and then put his hands on my shoulders, "You'll eat, you'll sleep, you'll get fat, you'll be bored, but you're going to be just fine."

"Really?"

"Don't tell your dad that though."

"Don't tell him what?"

"This is my last piece of advice, for now, of course. Lie. Tell your pops that you aren't feeling well, and you think you might throw up. We will see if we can get him to stop and get you a bottle for the ride up. It'll help your nerves, trust me."

"Really?"

"That's what I would do."

This was a strange moment. Smitty and I were bonding, but I was somewhat leery of his intentions. It was as if I were the younger brother and my sibling was goading me into a decision that would inevitably land me in hot water.

"Go ahead and do it. Mom and Dad won't mind," he seemed to be saying to me. The sight of my father coming down the hall interrupted my assessment of his intent. Smitty gave me a final wink of encouragement as my father neared.

"How's it going up here?" My father asked as he stopped just short of the room.

"He'll be dressed like he is going to his own funeral ."Smitty told my father as he placed his hand on my back and gently pushed me.

"Hey Dad, what are the chances we could stop and get a pint for the ride. I'm not feeling very well, I think I might throw up ."

My father looked at Smitty who couldn't help but smirk. "Really? That's your contribution tonight." My father continued to stare and I couldn't tell if he was mad or not. "Don't teach him things like that, not yet at least."

"The kid is sick, I don't what him puking on me in the car." "No, we wouldn't want that would we? Jesus, Smitty." "You didn't sell that very well, kid," Smitty jokingly told me.

My father smiled then, which surprised me. I thought he was going to smack Smitty in the back of the head and start yelling at me, instead he was nodding and almost laughing. There seemed to be unwritten rules about this situation that I wasn't privy to. For some reason, this filled me with confidence.

"Get that bag packed and meet me downstairs," he ordered, then he turned to Smitty. "Stop putting this shit in his head, please."

My father turned and walked away. I grabbed a small bag out of my closet, which Smitty took from me and held open. I placed a few sets of clothing in it and then he zipped it up. Together we walked down the hallway like two kids about to go for a ride with their dad.

My mother, father, and the Big Guinea were waiting in the kitchen. My mother was holding a small bag full of toiletries and handed it to me. I stuffed it into my bag and smiled. I was starting to feel a bit nervous. I didn't want to speak. I was afraid of what might come out. Strangely enough, everyone in the room seemed to understand. My father put his hand on the back of my head and began to guide me through the kitchen toward the side door. My mother stopped him as we passed. She wrapped her arms around me and squeezed tight. I cringed, but tried my best not to show discomfort. Tears again filled her eyes. She opened her mouth to speak, but nothing came out.

"I'll be alright mom."

"I love you." She finally whispered as she let go.

The four of us made our way to the Big Guinea's car. I stared into the woods, searching for my deer. I glance across the street, again questioning what my grandparents had been doing in the neighbor's garden. I wondered if they would have been disappointed or proud of me at this moment. I turned around before getting into the car and found my mother standing in the doorway, watching. I sent her a little wave, hoping that it would comfort her. I took a quick peek upward into the sky. I said a prayer to that god I didn't believe in and climbed into the backseat of the car.

We stopped at the first liquor store that we passed. Smitty hopped out of the car and ran into the shop like someone owed him money in there. He returned moments later with two bottles. Ironically, he had chosen whiskey and vodka, which made me smile. He handed them to me and I nodded appreciatively. I opened the whiskey immediately. As I tipped it toward the roof I noticed a shake in my hand. Smitty was right, my nerves needed this. I took a big gulp and swallowed it like that country boy I thought I was meant to become. I didn't even notice the burn as it traveled down my throat and warmed my belly. I leaned back into my seat and relaxed.

"Two bottles?" My father exclaimed.

"I got excited, I don't get to buy booze often. Besides, I don't know what the kid drinks."

"I guess you aren't worried about being thrown up on anymore."

My father rolled his eyes and motioned for Vito to drive. The men talked, laughed, and smoked as we traveled. I drank. I didn't have anything to add to the conversation and they didn't make an effort to include me. Their intention was to keep me calm and they felt acting nonchalant about the ordeal would do that. I didn't mind, the lack of interaction allowed me to focus on my liquor. I was drunk by the end of the whiskey, but moved on to the vodka anyway. Smitty watched me open it and nodded like a proud brother. I somewhat enjoyed affording him the opportunity to live vicariously through me. My eyes shut half way through the second bottle. The last thing I remembered was my head hitting the window. The cool glass soothed my broken face, darkness surrounded me and I slept soundly, comforted by the notion that this was my father's show and there were no more decisions to make.

My eyes opened early the next morning. I looked around. A worn-out comforter with a nauseating pattern covered me. The room was painted in muted colors. There was a set of cheap desks pushed tight against opposing walls and a second bed several feet to the right of me. The door swung open and a tall, slender man took a few steps into the room. He had a goofy face, dark black-rimmed glasses, curly brown hair and a smile that this situation didn't warrant.

"You are awake."

"Where am I?"

"This is Third Chance."

"There's been a mistake, this is only my second chance."

The man laughed politely, but it was obvious he wasn't amused. "My name is Charles, I'll be your guide, and I'm also your roommate."

"Fuck me." I accidently blurted out, but I wasn't happy about this situation for a variety of different reasons.

Charles took a moment to absorb the insult. He faked an empathetic smile, "Welcome to phase one."

"Wait, I thought this was Second Chance?" I asked.

"Third Chance," he quickly corrected me.

"Third chance of the first phase? I'm confused, there's a lot of numbers going on here." I told him, even though I wasn't confused and I was clearly trying to aggravate him. I wasn't even sure why I was being difficult. It just seemed to happen naturally.

"This is Third Chance, and you are in the first phase of it. I apologize for not being clear about that."

"So what's step one of the first phase at second chance?"

He glared at me for a moment, but decided to forego correcting me again, "You get dressed."

He pointed to the chair at the end of the bed. There was a pair of green fuzzy slippers, blue hospital-issued pants, and a shirt neatly folded on top of it. My father had kept this bit of information a secret for obvious reasons. I turned and sat up. I was in my underwear, which was odd. I didn't remember my clothes being taken off. I stood, walked over, and grabbed the clothing. I began getting dressed as Charles watched me like a creepy old pedophile at a children's birthday party. I decided I would sleep with one eye open around this fool.

"What's with the duds?"

"That's the phase one uniform. You have to earn your clothing."

"Jesus, okay, what's next?"

"Breakfast, when you are ready. It's to the right at the end of the hall. Everything you need is to the right at the end of the hall actually. After breakfast, your counselor will find you and you can start putting together a recovery plan."

"Can't wait."

"You ready to eat, cause I'm starving."

"I think I need a minute."

"Okay, I'm going to head down, but you can look for me in the mess hall. I'll introduce you to the community. There are some people that are serious about their new life and some people that are here just wasting time. I'll make sure you find the right people."

"Sounds amazing."

"Alright then, I'll see you down there." Charles told me as he turned and left the room.

I hated Charles. I didn't want to be introduced to my new community by a gay, pothead nerd. I gave him a few minutes to make his way to the mess hall and get settled. I exited the room and walked down the hall, passing several doors in the process. My father placed me in a drug-addict, ant colony. I shuttered when I considered how many people were going to be at breakfast sitting around tables in their green slippers eating powder eggs, but I continued anyway.

A nurse with a kind smile and large breasts was sitting behind an oversized desk just outside the mess hall. I vaguely remembered this area from the night before. I slowed my pace to a crawl so I could get a better look. As I passed by I caught a glimpse of something that stopped me in my tracks. My father was sleeping just outside of the two large glass doors in the lobby. I looked at the nurse to confirm that I wasn't hallucinating and she nodded.

"He's been here all night, he never left."

"Really?"

"We don't normally let people sleep out there, but he wasn't taking 'no' for an answer. Your father is a good man, he has helped a lot of people from here so we let it slide."

I smiled and walked over to the glass door. My father was slouched awkwardly in a chair, asleep. I stared at him for a moment, then tapped on the window. He awoke and stood. A buzzer sounded and the doors slid open. He stepped through the entranceway and grabbed me without saying a word. He held me tight and I buried my head in his chest. Moments later, I felt his body tighten and begin to shake just slightly. His breaths became shallow and I could feel him struggling for air.

I looked up and watched as a tear ran down his face and landed on my cheek.

About the Author

Jason Douglas Smith, was born on January 11, 1977, in Norwalk CT. He was the first of three children born to his loving parents, David and Lillian Smith. From the moment Jason could crawl he demanded constant supervision or else he was bound to end up somewhere he didn't belong. He was a free spirit that rejected conformity even before he understood the notion. His mother would dress him in a suit and tie for Sunday school and if not watched, he would jump on his bike and find the deepest, muddiest puddle to ride through.

His work is inspired by authors such as, J.D. Salinger, Jack Kerouac and Hunter S. Thompson, authors who lived their lives freely and wrote about it. Jason spends his time writing everything from short stories to poetry, including screenplays.

Jason currently resides in Connecticut; his next work germinating within the soil of his brilliant and boundless mind.

More from Cactus Moon

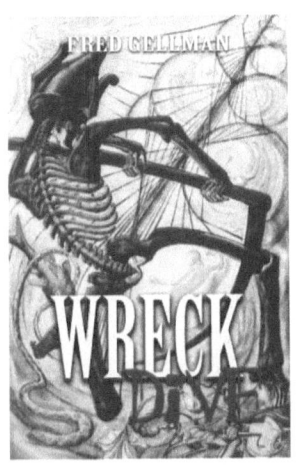

Rob Prager's passion is wreck diving, delving into the history of old shipwrecks right up close - no better way to satisfy the curiosity. One dive in Lake Michigan triggers more than just his curiosity-it feels more familiar. A slide show of images run through his mind like memories. . .but whose? In his visions, he is Captain McKay who longs to free the spirits of his crew. After investigation, Rob discovers photographs and other documents suggesting foul play in the ship's sinking. Is this a former lifetime? Or did Rob's passion draw Captain McKay to enlist his help from beyond?